'Kinnings honed his flair for cynical, treacle-black comedy with his first hit novel, *Hitman*, and here he's fashioned a disturbingly topical satire on celebrity culture and moral relativism. Imagine *Natural Born Killers* with a nod to *Ab Fab*, and you'll be on the right lines'

Heat

'There is real humour running through [*The Fixer*], and it's fascinatingly off the wall – a bit like Guy Ritchie meets Benny Hill . . . the beauty of it is that [Kinnings] has managed to write a novel on the subject of fame that is just as frivolous as the reality TV it trashes . . . [A] funny and stylish thriller'

Mirror

'A chilling satire'

Daily Mail

'Max Kinnings uses his syrupy thick style . . . as an illumination of media culture. It's trashy, insightful and frustratingly addictive'

Jockey Slut

'This shocking take on what might happen to our obsession with reality culture if it were taken to its furthest logical conclusion is a twisted, gasp-a-minute page turner for our times'

Hello

Also by Max Kinnings

Hitman

The Fixer

Max Kinnings

FLAME
Hodder & Stoughton

copyright © 2001 by Max Kinnings

First published in Great Britain in 2001
by Hodder and Stoughton
A division of Hodder Headline

The right of Max Kinnings to be identified as the
Author of the Work has been asserted by him in accordance
with the Copyright, Designs and Patents Act 1988.

A Flame paperback

2 4 6 8 10 9 7 5 3 1

A CIP catalogue record for this title
is available from the British Library.

ISBN 0 340 76632 8

Printed and bound in Great Britain by
Mackays of Chatham plc, Chatham, Kent

Hodder and Stoughton
A division of Hodder Headline
338 Euston Road
London NW1 3BH

For my parents

Thanks to Annette Green, Jon Wood,
Helen Garnons-Williams, Nicola Milsom,
Giles Cooper, Ed Mackintosh, Guy and Becs,
and, for everything, Ange.

WELCOME TO THE SHIT FACTORY

He was picking his nose at the time of the car crash. The impact drove his forefinger up his nostril to just below the second knuckle. This has given his face a lopsided appearance. One nostril is of a pencil-sized diameter and the other looks as though it could accommodate a King Edward cigar, and a fat one at that.

'Now listen, Simeon,' I'd like to say to him, 'let's not put anyone's nose out of joint here.' Or perhaps I could say something about winning by a nose. Instead, as he turns his damaged face towards mine awaiting a reply to his question regarding the fortunes of the new musical he's producing, I say, 'Who knows.'

'You've lost me,' he says, the offending orifice puckering in deference to the furrows creasing his brow.

'Well, I've saved far worse shows than this in the past.'

'But we've got a star problem,' he says. 'Now, we could ditch Sonny and go with Rutger. We'd probably only get him for six months, max, but we could go for the fast buck

1

and pray that when he leaves, audience figures don't fall off a cliff. Alternatively, we could keep Sonny, go big on marketing and just hope that we can weather the slack over the autumn. Then again, we could just close the show and piss off home. Now I've looked at this from upside down and inside out and I just can't seem to make my mind up. So that's why I'm here. I want you to tell me.'

My name is Tobe Darling. I was christened Tobias but people call me Tobe. Not Toby. Call me Toby and I'll tell you where to go. It's Tobe. As in Toad. It *was* Toby for a while, of course. It was what my parents wanted, but God how I hated that name. Sadly, being a kid at the time, and faced with the tyranny of parenthood, changing it wasn't a viable option. When I complained about it to my parents, as I invariably did, they told me it was unusual and I should be thankful for it. And as for the Darling bit, well, never was a name more inappropriate. But then who said names had to be appropriate? If they were, mine'd be a string of profanities.

My parents were sixties swingers, or at least tried to be, so they probably thought Tobias was a cool name at the time. Thankfully, in 1974, I found an escape from the nightmare of my Christian name. In that year, *The Texas Chainsaw Massacre* was released. My interest in the film had nothing to do with its subject matter or its subsequent censorship. I was only eight at the time so I couldn't have gone to see it, censored or not. My attention was drawn to the name of the director, Tobe Hooper. I was reading the showbiz news even at that age. Of course, I subsequently discovered that his Tobe was, in fact, pronounced Toby, but by then it was too late, the deed was done. I informed my parents of my new name – 'like lobe or robe,' I told them, but despite my protestations to the contrary, they continued to call me Toby. The fuckwits. A couple of years later, however, I changed schools, and from day one answered only to Tobe. Even so much as a hint of an 'ee'-sound on the end and I wouldn't respond. Tobe I became and have remained to this day.

I'm a showbiz fixer by trade. Part image consultant, part personal management guru. Armed with an almost pathologically intuitive understanding of the media and the entertainment industries, I can predict the seismic shifts in the tastes of the public with an accuracy that borders on the telepathic. A movie with an identity crisis, a boy band with an embarrassing secret, a stand-up comedian who can't stand up, a tricky in-through-the-backdoor career relaunch – you name it, I'll fix it. And if I can't fix it then it can't be fixed. The entertainment companies nowadays – even the mega-corporations with all the millions they spend on market research – don't know which way the shit's flying any more. Not on their own. It's just too confusing. So, they need people like me to tell them. And for this service, they pay big. The clueless tossers.

Take this bloke I'm with now, for example. Simeon Cruikshank. He's a right bastard. But being one of London's leading theatre producers, he's also a real big spender. He's only had a couple of turkeys as far as I can remember, the most memorable being *Shockwave!*, the musical about the Los Angeles earthquakes. His shows are certainly not the most artistically challenging but they do, as a rule, get the requisite arses on Dralon. His current show, and the one he's here to discuss with me today, is *Popstar!* As you'd expect, the lead is some latter-day Cliff Richard type and not the snotty council estate kid with a guitar and a hair-gel habit which might have made it at least interesting, if not profitable. Cruikshank should commission a musical about a sweaty, middle-aged theatre producer with a second arsehole on the end of his nose. He could call it *Wanker!* It'd tell the tale of a man who spends his life uniting swarms of jabbering American tourists with coach loads of old age pensioners smelling of piss, all just so they can witness a stage full of luvvies who'd rather be doing film or TV if truth be told but can't get the work.

'There is another way, Simeon,' I tell him, contriving a thoughtful expression. He leans forward in his seat as though he can't bear to wait the few millionths of a second more it will take the sound to travel the extra distance.

'You've got two stars to choose between here, one A-list and one B-list. Your A-list star costs ten grand a week and will only stick around for six months, while your B-list star costs five grand a week and would chew his arm off to stay with the show for as long as it runs. So, here's the magic wand. What do you do with it?'

I take a long pause and look him straight in the eye. I listen to myself at times like this and wonder how much I'm earning per word. I reckon if I'm particularly succinct, it probably works out at about a fiver a go. Not bad work if you can get it.

'OK, Tobe, let's hear it,' says Cruikshank.

'It's simple,' I tell him. 'You sign up your B-list guy for the long haul, get it all in black and white, and then you turn him into an A-list star.'

'How?' he snaps back at me as I'm just about to tell him.

'You make sure he does something extraordinary.'

'Like what?'

'Well, any number of things. It's not what he does necessarily so much as how the media cover it. You have to remember you're dealing with a mass-market audience here. You don't want to do anything distasteful. Nothing that could backfire. There's always a certain element of risk with these sorts of things, but I can't foresee any major problems. I know, maybe we could have him save someone's life. That'd be a good one. We could build a warming human story around it. Make him look as though he's totally selfless and publicity-shy. Plenty of oh-no-it-was-really-nothing quotes. Maybe a couple of months down the line we could back up all the press activity by having him release a number from the show as a single. Give the proceeds to charity and Bob, as they say, is very much your mum's-oblique-dad's brother.'

He eases himself back in his chair. When he speaks, his voice is hushed and conspiratorial.

'Call me naïve if you want, Tobe, but surely, for all this to work, Sonny actually has to save someone's life?'

'You're naïve, Simeon,' I tell him. 'Sonny *will* save someone's life. I'll take care of it.' This is certainly not the greatest advice I've ever given to a client, but since Scarlet left me I've begun to feel like one of those people who suffers from that condition which compels you to shout out swear-words at the most inappropriate times. Only with me, it isn't bad language, it's bad advice. How the hell I'm going to get Sonny Page to save someone's life is anyone's guess, but I'll worry about that some other time.

The phone goes. I told Sadie to ring through after fifteen

minutes with a bogus caller so that I could extricate myself from the meeting – I need another five minutes with Simeon Cruikshank like I need a second arse – but it turns out the call's genuine. It's Bill on the line from New York.

Bill Barlow is my business partner and co-founder of Barlow & Darling, Soho's finest. Bill's and my business arrangements are as follows: he gets the business and I do the business. He's got the global network of music and showbiz connections, and I've got the nous. He's the front man, and I'm the back man. As is only right and proper, I suppose, under the circumstances, he's six feet one, tanned and good-looking, and I'm not. Most certainly not.

'How's it going, Bill?'

'Good, mate. Listen, I've just had lunch with Rudi Schneider. He tells me he's got a problem with that Britflick he's producing, *Hoxton Square*.'

'The one where they auditioned all those gay actors for the lead?'

'That's the one. Well, Peter Dugdale got the gig in the end. It's due to open in the States in a few weeks' time and what does Dugdale go and do but get arrested for cottaging on Brighton seafront.'

'Was he set up?'

'No, just unlucky. Schneider's shitting it and I don't blame him.'

'Bill, I'm sorry, I don't get it. What's the problem? He was caught soliciting in the gents'. He's gay. So what?'

'That's just it. He wasn't in the gents'. He was in the ladies'.'

'What the fuck was he doing in there?'

'He says he was drunk and got confused. Now normally

this wouldn't be a problem. If anything, it'd be good for the movie, give it plenty of publicity. But the trouble is, *Hoxton Square* was meant to be cutting-edge. It was meant to be dark and urban with plenty of gritty realism. All that crap. The way Schneider tells it, the papers are going to go big on the laughter factor. They want to make out that Dugdale's a closet heterosexual. Schneider's worried it'll damage the movie. He thinks it'll just become famous for Peter Dugdale getting his collar felt in the ladies'. He's got a point, Tobe.'

'Mmm, maybe.'

'Just remember that, money-wise, Schneider's going to take it like a bastard if we can get him out of this one. He's already giving us points on the movie for helping him find backing, so can you have a little think about it?'

'Yup.'

'Sorry to break up your meeting, Tobe. Who're you with?'

'Simeon.'

'Tell him he's a cunt.'

'Sure thing.'

I replace the receiver and, giving Simeon a big smile, tell him, 'Bill sends his best.'

'Hey, Tobe, listen to this,' he says, ignoring me, his face buried in the *Evening Standard*, and he starts to read the review for *Ho Ho Ho!*, a new musical at the Gielgud. It's clear from the relish in his voice that it's been given a serious panning. But I'm not listening any more. My attention is focused on the headline that reads, SECOND HOTEL MURDER. It's difficult to read much more as

Cruikshank keeps moving the paper, relishing the unfavourable sentiments expounded by the critic. I manage: *Scotland Yard have confirmed that the murder of an American tourist at the Park House Hotel last night bears unmistakable similarities to the murder of an American tourist at the Langtree Hotel last month and is almost certainly the work of the same person.* Looks like we've got a serial killer on our hands and, judging by his modus operandi last time at the Langtree, which involved, among other things, decapitation, disembowelment and amputation of all four limbs, this is a class act. Seriously deranged on the one hand, yet also endowed with a mind of acute focus and almost obsessive efficiency on the other. The police were incredulous to discover after the Langtree murder that the killer had left not one scrap of evidence at the scene of the crime. Not a fibre of clothing, not so much as a hair. One moment a deranged monster, the next an expert thwarter of all things forensic. It gets better as well. A couple of days later, he sent a video of him chopping up the victim to the police. They reckon he must have had a camcorder strapped to his head or mounted on a helmet like a miner's lamp.

'I'm sorry, Simeon,' I tell him while he's still reading the review to me. 'It's time I wasn't here. I've got to be at a meeting across town.' I haven't really but the sight of him sniggering over his snide review is more than I can bear. 'I've got the *Popstar!* angle covered. I'll chew it over and get back to you in a couple of days.'

I call Sadie and within seconds she's at the meeting-room door to usher Cruikshank to the lift that will deliver him to the ground floor and out of my life.

'As always, Tobe, it's been a pleasure,' he says, his sweaty hand grabbing hold of mine.

'Likewise, Simeon, and don't worry, *Popstar!*'s going to be a smash.' Smash my arse.

'I know you're right, Tobe, it's just the lead is so important and *Popstar!* has got to be massive. It deserves to be massive.' Like many of my clients, if he were allowed Simeon would conduct half of every meeting while saying his goodbyes, as though I won't charge him for this bit.

'And although Sonny's marvellous in many ways, Tobe, he just doesn't have Rutger's pull.'

'Not at the moment, Simeon, but trust me, I'll fix it.'

With that, I usher him out of my space and into Sadie's. Sadie locks on to him, and once Sadie decides you're leaving, you're gone. Sometimes I feel as though she and I are involved in some sort of psychic dancing. We can move people around in rooms.

Sadie's been here for a couple of years, and in that time she's taken over the entire administrative side of the company. Our lives, Bill's and mine, are organised with military efficiency. She gets us from one meeting to the next, providing us with all relevant information, paperwork, figures – you name it. She never fails. As far as Bill's concerned, I sometimes think she could tell me when he's taking a shit. But Bill's and Sadie's relationship and mine and Sadie's relationship are very different. Mine and Sadie's relationship is complex. It's not your normal employer/employee thing. You see, Sadie beats me up and I like it.

With Cruikshank gone, I snatch up the *Evening Standard* and start reading about the killer. This guy's certainly earning himself the column inches. The front page and page three are devoted entirely to him. There's a piece on page four concerning the history of serial killers in London from Jack the Ripper onwards, and another piece on the impact the killings will have on American tourism in the capital now the second killing has established a pattern. The Yanks'll shit themselves, that's for sure. The killer couldn't have chosen a demographic to concentrate on that would have given him more exposure within the world's media. And how easily the American eagle is humbled by a dose of paranoia. They wouldn't come here a few years ago because they were scared of getting blown up by Middle Eastern terrorists; now, by the time the American media machine has finished with this little lot, there'll be a latter-day Jack the Ripper on every street corner. The Americans will stay away; the hotels, especially the ones that've hosted a killing, will earn themselves a glut of bad publicity and have to spend a fortune on security; the London tourism industry will take a nosedive; and every day the killer remains at large the dear old boys in blue will get more and more beaten up by the press and public alike. The only winners in all of this are the people who like to learn about this sort of thing, the likes of you and me. And the media, of course. You, me and the media. We just can't get enough of it.

When I've finished reading, I walk back along the corridor to my office, where Sadie's waiting for me. She stands by my desk as poised and erect as an on-duty guardsman. I sidle past her and go to switch off my computer.

'I'm off now, Sadie,' I tell her.

'I know,' she says, her Polish accent more pronounced

than usual, as it always is before one of our confrontations. 'Don't be late in the morning, you have a nine-thirty meeting with Eric Massey concerning his boy band project.'

'OK,' I tell her, catching her ice-cold stare. 'Have a good evening.'

I manage to make the doorway before she calls me back.

I spin around to face her.

'Come here,' she snaps.

'What is it, Sadie?' My voice is piss-weak and tremulous.

'Come here,' she repeats, but hisses it this time. I stand in front of her. She undoes my zip fly and puts her hand into my jeans. Her slender fingers close around my balls. She raises her chin and stares down her nose at me. As the first stirrings of arousal start to tingle in my loins, she makes a fist. My scream is pathetic. Hollow and high-pitched. She opens her hand and I drop to my knees. I sob a little. I'm not sure why. I'm not sad or anything. I'm in pain, sure, lots of pain, but I like it.

SCARLET AND RALPH

My balls are still aching when I step out into Soho Square. It's a warm evening for the time of year and people crowd the pavements, chatting and laughing. I push my way between them, catching scraps of conversation as I go, random words making tiny contributions to the soundtrack of my life.

I cross over Dean Street, turn right into St Annes Court, and then my heart sinks. Standing in the middle of the passageway is a figure dressed in a suit so filthy and old it looks as though it's only the encrusted foodstuffs and bodily excreta on it that are holding it together. He has shoulder-length grey hair matted into brittle tresses like apprentice dreadlocks. Meet Ralph.

Ralph has been knocking around Soho for years. The story goes he was a roadie for numerous bands in the sixties, including the Who and the Yardbirds. He wasn't up to much as a roadie but never found himself out of work on account of his excellent drug contacts. He ended up scoring for all the bands he worked for and a fair few he didn't. One night, he went out on a mission to fetch some acid for a Jimi Hendrix after-show party. No one knows exactly what happened to him other than he ended up taking a huge amount of the stuff himself. One theory is he was the target of a set-up by some bent coppers who wanted to muscle in on his lucrative sideline and, to teach him a lesson, they made him eat an entire sheet of the stuff. The long and short of it is Ralph went up so high that night he's never coming down.

He's got his back to me and he's showing a card trick to a couple of somewhat frightened American tourists who would run a mile if this happened to them back home in the States but are desperately trying to tolerate it and appreciate it here because they're on vacation and they think this might be a precious moment they should endure as part of their London experience.

I don't have a problem with Ralph because he's a sand-wich short; my wariness of him stems from the fact that he's developed a fixation on me. It started about five years ago. I'd been to my club, the Belljar, after work and was more than a little the worse for wear. At the time, our offices in Soho Square were being kitted out in readiness for the newly established Barlow & Darling operation to move in. Finding myself bursting for a slash in Soho Square, I decided I'd pop into the office and go there before grabbing a cab home. The electricity had been switched off during the refurbishment so the whole place was in darkness. Fortunately, the streetlamp outside cast enough light through the windows for me to pick my way between the timber and bags of cement. As I was shaking myself dry in the toilet I heard a series of coughs emanating from somewhere in the office. Sobered a little by fear, I investigated their source, which turned out to be a mound of old carpet that had been pulled up and slung in the corner of what is now the meeting room. I pulled back a length of the carpet and there was Ralph, fast asleep. I nudged him in the ribs with my shoe and he came to, muttering. After he'd rubbed his eyes and let out a prolonged fart, he peered up at me and asked, 'Kelly?' There was no way he could see me clearly as I had my back to the window and was framed in the light from the streetlamp outside, so, just for the hell of it, because I presumed Kelly was a fellow bum I'd been mistaken for, I said, 'Yes.' This response sent him into a blue fit and he started cowering and shaking as though I were about to kill him.

'Get out,' I told him, enjoying the fear his erroneous identification of me had instilled in him, and he did, stumbling out of the room and down the fire escape stairs.

The next time I saw him, I was convinced he wouldn't recognise me. After all, the only time he'd seen me before, he was suffering from delirium tremens and had thought I was someone else. But recognise me he did, although owing to some crossed wire in his head, he still thought I was the Kelly character from before.

I have no idea who this Kelly is that he's mistaken me for, but Ralph becomes highly agitated whenever he sees me. Sometimes he skulks away muttering to himself – that's the best-case scenario; other times he starts shouting and trying to explain something to me, the crux of which I never manage to grasp.

He's so absorbed in his card trick that, hopefully, he won't see me. Keeping my head down, I walk as fast as I can. Just when I think I've made it, I'm rugby-tackled around the legs and sent sprawling.

'Kelly,' he gasps at me with his arms around my legs.

'For Christ's sake, I'm not Kelly. Now get your filthy hands off me.' I can't abide being involved in any form of public incident, anything that will draw attention to myself, so wrestling on the ground with this old git is purgatory. Managing to get one of my feet free, I boot him on the side of the head and he lets go of me. I jump to my feet and hurry off. As I do so, I think I can hear one of the Americans taking a picture of me – I heard a shutter click – like I'm some sort of fucking interesting local character. If I weren't so concerned with making a hasty exit, I'd give him a demonstration of some good old London charm and tell him where to go. Sadly, Ralph hasn't finished with me yet and slopes along behind shouting unintelligible phrases.

At the end of St Annes Court, where it intersects with Wardour Street, there's a black cab relinquishing its load of suited-up businessmen on to the pavement. I make a dash for it. The driver is still sorting out the receipt for one of the suits when I dive in and slam the door. Ralph is close behind and slaps his filthy hands against the glass. The driver tells him to piss off and sets off up Wardour Street.

'Desford Gardens, off Ladbroke Grove,' I tell the cabby, and turn to watch Ralph as he's absorbed into the Soho backdrop.

'See that serial killer's struck again,' says the cabby. I turn back to see him watching me in the rear-view mirror.

Despite his rather lowly position in the media food chain I can tell he's bursting to tell me all his halfwit theories about the case. I know I'll regret it but I do it anyway and acknowledge his comment with a desultory 'Yeah'. Reassured that he now has a captive audience, he starts banging on about the killings. If only he'd let me, I could tell him what he's going to say before he even says it.

'It's some sort of sick bastard does that.' Yeah, yeah. 'I mean, what sort of person could do that to another human being? I ask you. He obviously done it just for the fun of it.' Yeah, Yeah. 'When they get hold of him, they should string him up.' Yeah, right. As he's talking, I've moved forward on to the very edge of the seat as though in a bid to hear him better. Every so often, he looks at me in the rear-view mirror and I nod as though I'm genuinely interested in the drivel he's coming out with. Fortunately, I've got a zip fly today – buttons are tricky for this sort of manoeuvre – and I ease my Johnson out and piss on the floor of the cab, nodding all the while. If only more people would do this then our simple salt-of-the-earth London cabbies might get the hint and realise that if they bore people with their crappy opinions then their cabs will end up smelling of piss and, in time, so will they. He drops me off in Desford Gardens and, despite the fact that I wait for my exact change, gives me a 'Cheers, mate' and drives off, unaware of the half-pint of steaming sewage I've left in the back of his cab.

Home. Calamity Towers. When Scarlet lived here, I used to stick the key in the lock and feel a thrill of expectation. Now I feel hollow. I open the door. It's stuffy. The heating's on. I don't mess around with timers and thermostats; I switched the heating on in September and I'll turn it off again in May. It's not like I have to worry about fuel bills any more. In fact, if I'm honest with myself, I reckon I could probably stop working tomorrow and, what with this place and all the money I've got salted away in various bank accounts, I could have a pretty good standard of living for the rest of my natural born. So long as it's not a very long time. But then it won't be. It can't be. Not with things the way they are.

I shut the door and stand motionless in the hallway, listening. There's a distant rumble of traffic but, in here, not a sound. It wasn't always like this. Scarlet was a media junkie. We both were, but Scarlet especially. She'd have the radio on and the TV, sometimes two TVs tuned to different channels, and in the few brief pauses in transmitted sound I could often make out the clicking of her fingers on the computer keyboard as she wrote her articles for *Zone* and, later, *International Profiles*.

When Scarlet lived here, everything was spotless, almost clinically so. Conscious, no doubt, of my propensity to be a domestic disaster area, she employed a cleaner to come in every other day. My kitchen is testament to four months without Scarlet and the cleaner. It's a celebration of the inverted Midas touch I bring to my home. My domestic life is confusing and frightening, but with work, everything's instinctive. My business partner, Bill, once referred to me as a 'showbiz weathervane' and, crass comment though it undoubtedly is, he's got a point. I've always been like that, ever since the day I read my first music paper and showbiz column. It could be the same style puff piece about two virtually indistinguishable acts but I can always tell the swans from the turkeys. It's as though someone's feeding me inside info. But here in Calamity Towers, I have no such intuition. There's just so much to think about, so much to obsess about. This is not a small house. It is multi-layered. Someone could get lost in here. If I allowed anyone in, that is, but I don't. Not since Scarlet left. Hence the state of the place.

The centrepiece of my kitchen nightmare is on the draining board, where there's a tall, precariously balanced stack of plates from between which mould cultures have spewed forth in a variety of colours and textures. An intricate weave of turquoise and magenta fur leads from the plates into the sink, in which an oily brown liquid has developed a scab-like crust.

I pull the kitchen door to in a futile attempt to keep the stench confined and climb the stairs past a row of X-hooks where a series of original Bernard Sorell newspaper cartoons once hung. They were Scarlet's and now they're long gone, of course, stripped from the house along with everything else. When we were together, this house was the sum of our two parts, not an equal sum on both sides by any means, but a sum none the less and, when she left, the mathematics fell apart. Now I'm left with an unbalanced equation, nothing more than a series of random numbers leading nowhere.

The trail of clothes begins on the first-floor landing. I buy them on the Internet and, because I've given up on laundry altogether, I have to buy in bulk. They're piling up – mounds a couple of feet deep in places – but I can't let anyone in here to take them away or wash them. I can't let anyone see me living like this. So I'm doomed to make extravagant donations to the coffers of the mail order clothing industry. Behaving like this does offer one consolation, though – I never have to put up with the horrors of the modern retail experience.

It's all good stuff I buy. Nothing particularly fashionable but, if you look like me, it's not advisable to wear clothes that are too daring. You need to melt into the crowd, not stand out from it. My clothing philosophy focuses on a desire to achieve a sort of visual anonymity at all times. If I could make myself invisible, I think I would. I'm a naturally scruffy person, but being scruffy makes you stand out from the pack, as does being overly well dressed, or fashionably dressed, or, God forbid, colourfully dressed. They used to call the writer William Burroughs *El Hombre Invisible* because of his ability to blend into the crowd and attract no attention. Well, that's what I want, zero attention. Sometimes I'd like to disappear altogether.

If I put my mind to it, I could probably work out how many T-shirts and pairs of discarded jeans, socks and boxer shorts there are lying around here. As a rule, I eke out about a week's worth of use from each pair of jeans, bar disasters (which are becoming more frequent), when a splatter of food or something worse renders their lifespan at an end. Shirts I am more particular about. I try to manage a new one every day, although it doesn't always work out like that. Because of this behaviour, I have become something of an expert at sniffing articles of clothing in order to gauge their potential wearability. I sniff the armpits of shirts, socks as well, but I draw the line at boxer shorts. No one should have to stick their nose against one of my gussets, not even me.

There are fewer discarded clothes up here on the second landing. It's altogether cleaner and tidier up here. As I always do before I enter Scarlet's room, I stand outside for a moment composing myself before I turn the handle and open the door.

Scarlet and I met eight years ago. I was working for Ripstop & Carnage, a press agency dealing exclusively with record companies that came to us as a last resort to try to salvage acts which their in-house press charlies had failed to shift. At the time I was talking up a young R'n'B teen queen who went by the name of Sherry Baby. She had a great voice, great songs – if you like that sort of thing – but you just couldn't get away from the fact that her ultimate aim of global pop stardom was always going to be hampered by her obesity. She was a fat lass, and fat lasses don't sell. Not in that market. It was owing to my on-going quest for exposure for Sherry Baby that I called *Zone*'s number that day. *Zone* was one of those early nineties style magazines that was so trendy and up its own arse it was doomed to fail from the start, having as it did a readership of no more than a couple of thousand Soho vampires who didn't buy it anyway as they were all on the mailing list, man. The thought of Sherry Baby in a bible of hip like *Zone* was laughable, but I thought I'd give it a go, mostly as an excuse to speak to the editor, Scarlet Hunter, who was developing a reputation as one of the toughest people in the business. The rumour was she was only biding her time at *Zone* until an editorship at one of the top lady mags became vacant.

When I started giving Scarlet the Sherry Baby spiel, she was receptive at first. Taciturn to a degree, but civil at least.

There I was giving it loads about Sherry Baby's new single, 'Sweet Lovin" and we were sharing a joke – or so I thought – about the naffness of the title when it was almost as though someone else had pulled the receiver from her and hissed into it in the most menacing tone you ever heard, 'Listen, you useless little prick, you've clearly got about as much to offer as the talentless piece of shit you're trying to promote, namely, fuck all. Why don't you do us all a favour and die.' As the line went dead, I knew I was hooked. She was, no doubt about it, the rudest person I had ever spoken to. It wasn't just what she said as much as how she said it. Her manner displayed a genuine hostility towards me, as though if I didn't fuck off as she suggested, I would be in genuine danger. In my world of twisted values and broken logic, she had transformed herself from Scarlet Hunter, brusque magazine editor, into Scarlet Hunter, goddess. I think I loved her from that moment on.

I bided my time. I knew I had to speak to her again. I knew I had to hear that voice and be subjected to another tirade of abuse. What I needed was a really hot story I could offer her as an exclusive, something that would really make her sit up and take notice. Thankfully, I didn't have to wait long. Chad McRae of the US grunge band Crash'n'Burn had started a relationship with Melanie Hopkirk, presenter of kids' TV programme *The Big Red Bus* and all-round media whore. This scoop had come my way courtesy of Micky Beaumont, a concert promoter friend of mine who had seen them swapping spit backstage at a Crash'n'Burn gig. What made the story all the more juicy was our Melanie was only a fortnight away from a high-profile celebrity wedding to Jonathan Tindle, her co-presenter on *The Big*

Red Bus. Exclusive coverage of the wedding had been sold to a leading snap mag and the whole event was shaping up to be the year's top media beanfeast. The fact that Melanie Hopkirk should be snogging with Chad McRae – a man possessing all the grace and charm of a dung-beetle – so soon before her squeaky-clean nuptials was a scoop the showbiz editors of the tabloids would eat shit to get hold of, and there I was prepared to hand it to Scarlet on a plate. Our second conversation would be a whole lot different from our first, of that I felt assured.

'Lunch?' she said when we next spoke, as though this were the most absurd suggestion she had ever heard.

'Yes, lunch. How about tomorrow?'

'You've lost me. We've got a well-known kids' TV presenter getting moist with a big-name American rock star, a story that could, I'll admit, be of interest to my readers, and from nowhere Mr No-dick wants to meet me for lunch. Why on earth would I want to do that?'

'Well, I thought if we were to do some business together, we might as well meet and put a face to it.'

'Look, if that's all you want, I can send you a photograph. Don't waste my fucking time.'

'Give me an hour and you'll get the full story, names and all.'

'God, OK, one o'clock tomorrow at the Shrubbery. I can't promise how long I'll hang around. One whiff of bullshit and I'm out the door.'

With that she hung up. I don't think I ever heard her say goodbye to anyone on the telephone. Scarlet always hung up when she deemed the conversation to be at an end.

In the early nineties, even more so than these days, the

Shrubbery was at the epicentre of London's media and showbiz shit factory, playing host to the very cream of the crop. On any given day, you would find the cluster of white starched tablecloths crowded by supermodels, pop stars, actors, comedians, producers, directors, magazine editors, ad types, PR types, publishing types and assorted Soho cheeses.

'You're late,' she told me as I sat down opposite her. It was reassuring to find she made no compromise to courtesy even face to face. And what a face it was. I knew what she looked like, having seen her byline photo in *Zone* and a couple of shots of her at book launches and publishing do's in the trade press, but these didn't do justice to the extremities of expression of which she was capable. The look of disdain on her face as she watched me make my apologies was of such intensity it signalled a desire to inflict physical pain.

'So, how are you?' I enquired in an attempt to instigate small talk.

'Gorgeous. Now, who was she kissing?'

I decided to front it out and said, 'What's in it for me?'

She smiled and shook her head.

'You're quite an ugly little man, aren't you? Quite fat and misshapen.' She was right, of course, and I laughed nervously. 'I should imagine you don't get much, other than the occasional sweaty fumble you are forced to pay for.' Again she was right and again I laughed nervously.

'So, here's the deal. If you tell me the names of the happy couple, I'll come to a hotel room with you this afternoon. How does that sound?'

I couldn't believe what I was hearing. The first woman

I'd found attractive in years and here she was offering to hand it to me on a plate. What the hell did it mean? She couldn't be that desperate for the story, could she? Did she find me attractive despite her words to the contrary? Highly unlikely, I grant you, but maybe ugly little men were right up her alley.

'It's a deal,' I told her, the words falling over themselves to get out. 'Do you have somewhere in mind?'

'Just leave that to me. Now, who was she kissing?'

'Chad McRae from Crash'n'Burn.'

'And this is watertight. We have witnesses, I take it?'

'Absolutely. It's as safe as houses and it's all yours.'

'Good. Now, for the rest of the meal I would appreciate it if you didn't speak to me.'

I didn't say a word lest she change her mind. Unlike the salad-and-mineral-water brigade all around us, Scarlet tucked into her food with gusto and devoured all three courses before rounding things off with a hearty, unselfconscious belch.

The Gardens Hotel is tucked away in a Covent Garden side street and is, as you would expect of London's premier location for the illicit liaisons of the rich and famous, almost totally anonymous. No signs, not even a plaque, just a black door set into a Georgian terrace. I've heard a rumour there's a secret entrance via a tunnel under the street which is accessed through a bogus dry cleaner's opposite. But on that day I wouldn't have cared if the massed ranks of the world's paparazzi had snapped me, such was my excitement at the thought of a mid-afternoon game of hide-the-sausage with Scarlet Hunter, editor of London's hippest magazine. The checking-in procedure at the Gardens Hotel is unusual in that the clerk on reception only takes your real name if you offer it and is quite happy to be given a false one. We were Mr and Mrs Somebody – I can't remember the exact name Scarlet gave – but it was double-barrelled, which seemed kind of pointless.

We were shown to a room by a distinguished-looking middle-aged man who asked me surreptitiously if we had any 'special requirements'. It turned out he could procure us any sex aid we might want from a condom to another person. I told him no, I was quite happy with the situation just as it was, thanks.

Once in the room, Scarlet threw her bag on the bed and turned to face me. She was smiling but there was something cruel about her smile. It was the smile of a spiteful child who is about to pull the wings off a fly. She began to undress and I followed her example. Her slender, well-toned body accentuated my physical shortcomings, and my lustful intentions were tempered by more than a little incredulity that this whole situation should be unfolding with me as the male lead. The scene was far too reminiscent of the porn I used to watch for me to accept that my involvement in it should extend far beyond my watching it on a video, Johnson in hand. Not that I'd have wanted me as the male lead if I had been watching it on a video, of course. No, when a man watches porn, he wants the projected version of himself to be a good-looking, muscular bloke with a dick like a French loaf. What he doesn't want is a short, fat bloke hung like a chicken.

I moved towards her, my stomach sucked in and an expression on my face I hoped would convey an air of nonchalance and experience, as though this sort of thing happened to me all the time. I was convinced I was only moments away from an energetic coupling with the most attractive and intriguing woman I had ever met. Which made what she did next all the more of a surprise. She punched me in the face.

It was no spur-of-the-moment flail but a well-judged blow. She stepped forward and leaned into the punch, putting all her weight behind it. Her fist caught me on the side of the jaw and sent me tumbling over backwards. Barely had my flabby arse made contact with the carpet than she was pulling me to my feet for no other reason than to knock me down again. She helped me up once more, only this time she jabbed a fist into my stomach which doubled me over. Before I had time to contemplate the seeming inability of my lungs to inflate themselves, she hit me with an uppercut to the chin which lifted me off my feet and sent me sprawling across the bed, where I must have lost consciousness.

When I came to, I found myself in bed and Scarlet gone. Despite the pain in my jaw, all I could concentrate on was the image of her standing in front of me, naked, drawing her arm back to administer a punch. That she'd chosen to be naked while beating me up was a point that sent my brain into hours of deliberation. What did it mean? Was it, despite the aggression apparent in her actions, a sexual act? I decided it most certainly was and congratulated myself accordingly, nursing my wounds – a hairline fracture of the jaw and a broken tooth – as though they were trophies sustained in the heat of passion. What's more, having beaten me up, she was good enough to settle the bill for the room.

Following Scarlet's exclusive in *Zone*, the Melanie Hopkirk/Chad McRae story was splashed across all the tabloids. This attention put La Hopkirk at the centre of a major shit storm. Jonathan Tindle, her intended, gave her the elbow, which inadvertently pushed the ratings of *The Big Red Bus* through the roof as the world and his wife tuned in to see them presenting the show complete with cheesy grins and feigned good humour when it was patently obvious they would rather be tearing each other apart than discussing where the eponymous vehicle had found itself this week in the twilight world of kids' TV.

In the end, Melanie played the only hand she could under the circumstances and made out that her infidelity was all part of a bigger picture of too-much-too-young celebrity burn-out involving cocaine, bulimia and all-round depression. It was a highly effective countermeasure – the tabloids churned out the little-girl-lost stories and the snap mag that had the rights to the wedding was amply rewarded for swallowing its lack of wedding coverage with an 'at home' piece featuring our Melanie spilling the beans on her tortured life.

Tindle himself had struck pretty much the same deal with a bloke mag, only his angle was his 'heartbreak over Melanie'. And Chad McRae quite clearly didn't give a shit as the situation gave him some much-needed coverage for Crash'n'Burn's much-maligned new album *Blow-hole*. As for me, I was far more interested in engineering another meeting with Scarlet than with the fall-out from my little bit of gossip. Thankfully, I didn't have to wait long. Just as I was busy trying to think up an excuse that would allow me to call her, she called me to thank me for the scoop. Scarlet thank me? This was an eventuality I hadn't anticipated. I suggested we meet for dinner and, when we did, she even allowed me to speak to her. Afterwards, we came back here to Calamity Towers, although any thoughts I might have had that we were establishing a more traditional relationship were soon put out of my mind when she kicked me in the balls before I'd even closed the front door. She blacked my eye and split my lip but, this time, I managed to remain conscious and she ended up staying the night.

These explosive beginnings set the tone for our on-going relationship, and what I soon came to understand was that Scarlet enjoyed administering the violence as much as I enjoyed receiving it. Scarlet and I traded in extremes. The violence was an extension of the emotional intensity we aroused in each other. When she moved in with me, this house became the stage upon which we fought our battles. It became our theatre of war. But there was one thing she insisted on having, and that was her own room which was to be strictly out of bounds to me. Even in war there have to be rules, and the main one for us – if not the only one – was that I was never to set foot in Scarlet's room. On numerous occasions, I stood outside the door, willing myself to have the courage to enter. But I never did. She would have found out. I couldn't have kept it from her. Scarlet possessed an almost psychic ability to know when I was lying. My curiosity was understandably intense. There's nothing like a closed door to ignite the imagination.

At first I fooled myself that our relationship wasn't so unusual. There'd been the occasional gentle slap – either given or received – with the more playful of my few and infrequent sexual partners, so I convinced myself there must have been an underlying current of sadomasochism in me that Scarlet had brought to the surface. From time to time, I found myself needing reassurance that there were other people out there like me. On one occasion I persuaded Scarlet to come to an S&M party. It was more of a festival, really, and was held inauspiciously at a conference centre in Croydon. The most scary thing about the place was not the half-hearted thrashings and bloodied arse-cheeks but the people who got off on it all. There's always been that assumption – I'd always thought it was an urban myth – that the people at these sorts of events largely comprise respectable bank manager types with their shrewish wives who turn up looking like a picture of normality and then emerge from the changing rooms transformed into these rubber- and leather-clad fetishists. The thing is, it's true. A hell of a lot of them are. The remainder are made up of people who look like they've got into it through the death metal scene and an inappropriate fondness for body piercing. My lasting memory of the evening was a fat woman in black PVC standing next to a wooden construction that looked like a Punch & Judy stall complete with miniature curtains and spotlights. When she pulled the curtains back, instead of a stage there was just a man's skinny arse. I presume the arse belonged to her husband or boyfriend, and you could spank it if you wanted to for a fiver a go. Surprisingly, she had a lot of takers. This place wasn't our scene at all, and I came to realise just how much it wasn't our scene when we returned home and, as foreplay, Scarlet pushed me down the stairs.

Although we didn't acknowledge the rituals and symbolism associated with the S&M scene, there was one practice I tried to encourage Scarlet to adopt. This was the introduction of a 'safeword' which either of us could use at moments of extreme violence in order to halt the proceedings and avoid injury or even worse. I suggested it should be for both of us to use, even though the only pain Scarlet usually felt was as a consequence of administering pain to me. I really tried to sell the idea to her, but the few times I tried it, as an experiment, she either greeted its inclusion in my symphony of screams and groans with the utmost indifference or, alarmingly, it actually spurred her on to hurt me even more. I clung to the fragile belief that should my life appear to be genuinely in danger, or if I stood to be mutilated beyond a few scars – of which she gave me plenty – the 'safeword' might just make her pull back from the brink. I clung to the hope that perhaps she had ignored it or hurt me more when I'd said it because she knew I was testing her, and I wasn't really asking her to stop. As with every aspect of our relationship, she was in control. She was pursuing a chain of thought and I was left trying to figure it out, confused and always just one step behind her. In time, I came to realise that in the strange sexual contract Scarlet and I had entered into, there were no get-out clauses. And the 'safeword' or rather words? 'Cor blimey'. Derived from the old English expression, 'God blind me'. Don't ask why.

About four months ago – it was a Saturday morning, for what it's worth – Scarlet told me to come to her room with her. It'd be ridiculous to say we'd not been getting on well prior to that day, as what went on between us was based almost entirely on our not getting on well. Not getting on well was a positive thing. A blazing row in which we both tried to say the most damaging and hurtful things possible was, for us, an affirmation of our union. Let's just say that, in our twisted world, things had not been as they should have been. Our flashpoints had become less frequent. By flashpoints, I mean those moments when we'd pushed each other so far that the only release from the unbearable tension would be an act of physical violence. And the few times when we had achieved the requisite emotional impetus for a flashpoint to occur, she had diffused it, which from my point of view was strictly against the rules. It was a cop-out. You didn't just walk away from that sort of situation. Life couldn't get any more real for me than at the precise moment when I knew neither of us would back down. When we were locked on course for a collision.

I didn't want to go to her room. I panicked. This was a reward I had to earn through a surfeit of emotional intensity and turmoil. It wasn't something that should be just handed to me on a plate. She flung the door open wide and dragged me in. Part of me craved the truth about what lay behind the door and part of me recoiled from the knowledge that whatever was there might not live up to my fantasies. I was desperate for verification of Scarlet's sadism. I wanted a dungeon. I wanted some perverse operating theatre where, with blunt instruments and no anaesthetic, she would carry out operations on my very soul. I wanted anything other than what I got. Scarlet's room was normal. Curtains, bedspread, chest of drawers.

'It's all over, Tobe,' she told me. 'Cor blimey and all that. I'm sorry.' She had never apologised to me in all the years

I'd known her and it sounded strange. It was as though she had dropped an act and this was the real her.

She sent a lorry for the rest of her stuff a couple of days later. She'd given strict instructions to the removals company about what was to go and what was to stay, and everything in this room was to stay. It was as though she wanted it left as a shrine to our separation. When I'm being optimistic, which isn't very often, I think that perhaps leaving me was all part of the game. That maybe the ultimate pain she could inflict on me was the pain of losing her.

Sadie's behaviour in the office helps a little sometimes, but it doesn't mean anything, and I have to face up to the very real possibility that unless Scarlet comes back soon, I might have to kill someone, and that someone might have to be me.

TORTURE

Eric Massey started his career managing a punk band called the Fuckin' 'Orrible Bastards. Faced with the insurmountable problem of their name and the fact that because of it he couldn't get them a single gig throughout the country, he suggested they change it, or at least shorten it. As the 'Orrible Bastards – as opposed to the Fuckin' Bastards, which the band themselves, in a typically uncompromising mood, had suggested – they went on to have a number 47 'hit' with a song called 'Gimme Gimme (Some), You ****'. Through a craftily worded contract which he had drawn up between himself and his protégés, Massey managed to keep nearly all the royalties from the single and subsequent album, *Weeping Bum Sore*. The money didn't amount to much but it was enough for a deposit on an office in Denmark Street, and there Stigmata Management was born. After the demise of the 'Orrible Bastards in the early eighties, Massey focused his attentions on the new romantic end of the market. The walls of his office at

Stigmata were covered with photographs of serious-looking men and women, their faces thick with make-up and their hair every which way but the way God intended. Perhaps his best-known act was Berlin Under Siege, which was in fact just one po-faced youth from Doncaster called Kelvin Devereux (né Winterbottom). Berlin Under Siege's stage show consisted of Kelvin standing behind a bank of synthesiser keyboards which he would prod occasionally with a nicotine-stained finger. As clouds of dry ice billowed around him he would croon his incomprehensible lyrics in a deep monotone voice. Although Berlin Under Siege only achieved marginal success in the UK, in Europe he/they were massive. Fair play to Massey, though – when Berlin Under Siege started raking it in for him, he didn't let it go to his head. He maintained the same ruthlessness he had shown with the 'Orrible Bastards a couple of years before, and he screwed Kelvin for every penny. By the time Massey had finished with him, Berlin Under Siege front man – only man – Kelvin Devereux was back with his parents in their two-up-two-down in Doncaster. Eventually, Kelvin had to retire from the music business altogether, because he literally couldn't afford to continue. Carried away with the first flushes of stardom, he had signed a contract stipulating that all the overheads, the production, marketing and distribution costs, the concert promotion and travel, in fact every cost expended in his career as a jobbing pop star, would be met by him and him alone, and all the profit thereafter would be shared with Massey. The fact that it was Massey who decided exactly how the sharing should work explains why, when Berlin Under Siege had run its course, Massey was living in a six-bedroom house in Holland Park while Kelvin Devereux, the poor dumb bastard, was back home under his Rupert the Bear quilt cover.

Massey used the money he had made from Berlin Under Siege to finance his next venture – the promotion of raves around the home counties. He developed a series of events under the name of Ubiquity. A couple of them were closed down in high-profile police raids, and Massey's Ubiquity events ended up being championed by the Freedom to Party movement – the best marketing he could ever have hoped for. When he moved over into legal dance parties in the early nineties, Ubiquity was established as one of the leading series of events in the dance calendar, and regularly pulled in crowds in excess of ten thousand a time. The money started to pour in once again for Massey, but his involvement with the Ubiquity organisation came to an abrupt halt one day when the company who dealt with all the security at the events, Headlock Security, decided to renegotiate their fee structure so that they would take a percentage of the door profits. A hundred per cent, to be precise. Massey was holding the shit-end of the stick for a change. Headlock allowed him all the revenue from the merchandising and all of the bar takings, but as they were the people who manned the merchandise stalls and the bar, this didn't look too attractive a deal. Massey's options were few. He could tell Headlock to go fuck themselves, hire a new security company – part of whose remit would be to keep him out of the local orthopaedic ward – or he could bend over and take a shafting. Massey bottled it and walked away, leaving Headlock with sole control of the organisation – not that it did them much good. Their attempts at promoting major dance events were shambolic, to say the least, and within six months the Ubiquity events moved from huge warehouses and arenas to the back room of a pub in Catford. Having been force-fed a spoonful of his own medicine, however, Massey now set his sights on an altogether different sector of the music business.

'They're called the Lifeboys,' he tells me as he presses the Play button on the CD player and eases his ample arse-cheeks into the black leather upholstery of the seat opposite me.

'They're five good-looking lads from Devon. Not a GCSE between them but the girls can't get enough. We've got Albright & Talon doing the press and they've got us blanket coverage in the pre-pube girlie mags; we've got a hefty chunk of advertising all booked and ready to go and the lads have got promotional appearances back to back until the single comes out. This is it. It's called "Honeygun".'

A half-baked attempt at British pop mixed with a dash of soulless American R'n'B issues forth from the speakers. It's crap.

'If all goes according to plan, we'll have *Top of the Pops*, *The National Lottery Live* and all the kids' Saturday morning programmes falling over themselves to get hold of them. Everything's in place, or as in place as it can be at this stage, but I have to admit to you, Tobe, I'm scared. I'm haemorrhaging money and, as you know, this is a crowded market. I'm wondering if there's anything we can do to guarantee the Lifeboys go all the way. Maybe there's an angle I've missed. Any ideas?'

I'm like a psychiatrist to people like Eric Massey. They come in here and expect me to cure them of their paranoias and phobias. 'Everything's fine, Eric' – that's what he wants to hear – 'the Lifeboys will be huge and you'll make a fortune.' The truth of the matter is their chances of making it are somewhere less than awful. For starters, they're just not good looking enough, and the single stinks:

> *You can't hide and you can't run,*
> *I'm gonna find you, gonna love you,*
> *Gonna shoot you with my honey gun.*

I've got to tell him the truth. That's my job. I must give serious consideration to the Lifeboys' careers. The advice I give will have far-reaching implications, not just for Eric Massey himself, but for the individual and collective destinies of these five simple lads from Devon, not to mention their families and all the people who will be involved in their careers. But it's not as though I have to spend long thinking about it. It's patently obvious that the only way the Lifeboys will make any ripple on the surface of the pop pond is if they can be embraced by that peculiar strain of British pop irony which dictates that some entertainers are so bad, so laughably awful, 'you just have to love them'. In that case, they'll have a flurry of media celebrity then people'll get bored and they'll eke out a living for a few years on the chicken'n'chips-in-a-basket circuit. Maybe one of them will become an alcoholic and die, or maybe one of them will be exposed as a child molester and the others'll try and sell their story to a tabloid – 'I always thought there was something wrong with Bobby', that sort of thing. So, all things considered, it doesn't look rosy for the Lifeboys. But as for Massey, I could save him if I told him to bail out now before he's in too deep.

I look at him sitting there in his flash designer suit with that expectant look on his face they all wear. That 'come on, Tobe, tell me I'm being stupid' face, that 'tell me I don't really need you' face.

I grin at him and the corners of his mouth dimple as they rise to match mine.

'Eric, the Lifeboys are going to be massive.'

'Really?'

'Really.'

'You don't think they're maybe too ordinary?'

'Not at all.'

I look down at the press shot of the five Lifeboys on the table between us. Massey follows my gaze and jabs a fat finger at the Lifeboy on the far right, a tall, skinny character wearing shades.

'You don't think Darren maybe looks a bit too old?'

Now he's pointed it out to me, Darren looks like someone's dad.

'How old is he?'

'Twenty-eight, just.'

Twenty-eight is fine if you're in a band, a real band if you like, where there's some creative integrity going on, but if you're in a boy band you're well past it. It's laughable that Massey should even attempt to get away with this. At the end of a boy band's career, when they all want to go solo and try to become George Michael or Robbie Williams, it's just about OK to be the wrong side of twenty-five. But twenty-eight? At the start? I should laugh in his face.

'There are no rules, Eric. You know that. You've got

a bloody strong product here. You could make the fact that Darren's twenty-eight into a feature of the band. He could be the elder statesman. How old are the rest of the them?'

He runs his finger along the line. 'Next to Darren, we've got Rory. He's the youngest, he's twenty-two, then Marky and TJ are both twenty-five and Christian's twenty-six.'

Eric Massey. You have lost the plot to life.

'They're all handsome young guys,' I tell him, 'and the single is fabulous. "Gonna shoot you with my honey gun"? They're gonna shoot to the top of the charts, that's for sure. Look, Eric, you're bound to feel apprehensive. You've been here before with Berlin Under Siege. But you know the score. You've just got to keep in the saddle and ride with it. Who sings the lead on "Honeygun"?' He points at Christian, twenty-six. 'He could get into movies. He's got star written all over him.' He can't sing, he's overweight, he's too old, and with his target audience of pre-teen females he'll be about as popular as a turd in a bouncy castle.

Massey's giving me a big stupid grin that says, 'You're right, I am being silly, they are going to be huge,' and I could almost pity him.

'Eric, you know what? I'm not even going to bill you for this. You've wasted my time and you've wasted your time. So leave me a copy of the single and get the hell out of here.'

'Tobe, what can I say? You're a one-off.'

This is good work. So I've managed to lose myself a few grand. So what? I've also managed to get this wanker in and out in under fifteen minutes. If he tries to give me any comeback about this later on when the Lifeboys have gone down like a cup of cold sick, I'll tell him, 'I'm sorry, Eric, I was being *ironic*.'

When he's gone, I go to my office and sit at my desk with the morning papers. Looks like our serial killer's been keeping himself busy. Not content with killing just the one American tourist yesterday at the Langtree Hotel, it now looks as though he popped around the corner not long afterwards and bagged himself a second at the Lancing. This really ups the ante for him. Not only is he earning himself plenty of attention for the sheer brutality and daring of his murders, but in one fell swoop he's put himself on the serial killer A-list. A methodical serial killer who picks off his victims one by one is all well and good and it scares the shit out of people, but there's nothing like doing two in one night to really make a splash. And the murderer has even been good enough to provide the media with a nickname. The boys in blue have confirmed that at each of the crime scenes, 'The Piper' was written on the wall in the blood of the butchered victim. And by the sound of things, it won't be long before we hear from him again. They reckon these two killings are even more gruesome than the first one last month. It seems increasingly obvious that whatever lusts and cravings the killer is subject to they're becoming more intense, and just the one act of carnage is not enough to satisfy them.

'*The body of Winifred Parnell, a retired teacher from Tallahassee, was left in the most appalling state I have ever seen during my twenty years on the force,*' says Chief Inspector Brian Woolcot in the *Mail*. Thanks for that, Bry. Other policemen too were said to be in a state of shock by what they had found in the two hotel rooms. *'I'll never forget what I've seen here today. The sight of what's been done to these poor people will haunt me for the rest of my life.'* All good, earnest stuff. I feel as sorry for the victims and their families as anyone, of course I do, but I also feel admiration for the killer. These are tough times for serial killers. It's becoming a crowded market. The Americans, and more recently the Russians as well, are churning them out nineteen to the dozen, and with modern forensics what they are, even an ambitious serial killer doesn't have long to develop a career and notch up a decent body count. This Piper fellow looks as though he's ambitious, like he really wants to build himself a legend.

London is a great choice of setting, as well – the site of the first truly great serial killer, Jack the Ripper, who almost single-handedly invented the genre. And although there've been some really twisted, fucked-up bastards since Jack, many of them with considerably higher body counts, no one will ever, to my mind, conjure up the intrigue and fascination that Jack the Ripper's legend is imbued with. For me, it's the ultimate murder mystery, and not only was the Ripper a man who could carve 'em up with the best of them, he also knew a thing or two about managing his own publicity. When he chose to taunt the police, he didn't send his letters directly to them, he sent them to the Central News Agency, thereby guaranteeing that his message would be broadcast far and wide via the burgeoning mass media of the day. Either Jack had secured himself some canny personal management, which I doubt somehow, or he had a first-rate understanding of the rules of celebrity, one of the most fundamental being: give the public what it wants, but only up to a point. Always keep something back. In the Ripper's case he managed to hold back his entire identity, the most tantalising and integral aspect of the story and the one that would guarantee him immortality. If they had managed to catch him, he would still have been a big star. For a short time, perhaps even a bigger star. Fuelled by a rejoicing media, the public would have gone into a feeding frenzy and gorged themselves on every minute detail of the man until there was nothing left of him. Despite his obvious psychopathy, the bloodlust of the great British public would have carried him to the gallows for a high-profile hanging. He would have had a few books devoted to him and attained a certain evil notoriety among the pantheon of great British murderers, but he wouldn't be remembered as Jack the Ripper. Rather, he would be known as Bert Snodgrass, aka Jack the Ripper, which is a different concept altogether. His legend would have been diminished to the level of people like Crippen and Christie. There'd probably be a waxwork dummy of him in Madame Tussauds. As it is, his legend is assured, and for a modern-day serial killer with ambition to be the best it's a hell of a tough act to follow.

The phone goes, which snaps me back from the foggy Whitechapel alleyways of 1888.

'It's Paul Devonshire from Poison Arrow Productions for you,' says Sadie.

'What does he want?'

'Do you want me to find out?' Sadie's tone suggests she will find out if I *really* want her to but she won't be happy about it.

'No, it's fine. Put him through. Hello?'

'Hi. Toby?'

'It's Tobe.'

'Oh, I beg your pardon. It's Paul Devonshire from Poison Arrow. We produce *The Church of Q&A*. You may have heard of us?' I can tell from the off this guy's your typical TV executive with his singsong voice and steadfast belief in his shitty product.

'No, I can't say I have, I'm afraid.'

'It's like a kind of *Question Time* for teenagers, but instead of politicians on the panel we have celebrities from the music, show business and fashion industries, the sort of people a young demographic can relate to. It's lively and irreverent and goes out on Friday nights at eleven o'clock on UK Today. Ring any bells?'

'UK Today. Satellite isn't it?'

'It is, yes.'

'No, I can assure you I've never heard of it.'

'Well, Tobe, we want you on the show.'

'What the hell for?'

'You see, we don't just want celebrities on the show. We also want to meet the people behind the headlines. People like you, Tobe. The people who oil the cogs of the show business machine, if you like. We feel you are perfectly positioned within the entertainment industry to offer some intriguing insights into the true nature of celebrity and why society feels the need to create celebrities.'

And then it hits me. This guy's done his homework on me. I've been researched.

'What do you know about me?' I blurt out as panic stabs me in the guts.

'Just what I read in your biog.' The knife twists.

'What the hell do you mean, my biog? I don't have a biog.'

'It wasn't a biog exactly, it was just some notes your PA faxed me.'

'Sadie?'

'Yes, on behalf of your partner.'

'Bill Barlow?'

'Yes, Bill, that's right.'

My palms have moistened. There's not a spot of saliva in my entire head and it feels as though someone's pushing a needle into the base of my skull. I've been betrayed by my own partner, Bill Judas-I-fucking-scariot Barlow.

'So, what does it say, this biog?'

'I'm sorry?'

'Read it to me.'

'Bill's letter?'

'Yes.'

'Dear Paul, thanks for the fax. Here are some brief details regarding Tobe's career thus far. In 1987 Tobe dropped out of college in order to take up full-time management of the alternative cabaret act Steel & Merryweather, who went on to win a Golden Bagel at the New York Festival of Comedy. In 1988, Tobe expanded his roster of artistes to include the comedian Steve Jennings (*One in the Eye*, *Hurry Up Harry*, *Listen Here Mister!*) before his appointment in 1991 as Head of Operations for Ripstop & Carnage, a leading PR specialist to the entertainment industry. In 1996, Tobe was recruited by the prestigious William Travis Agency to head up their international pop music division, where he managed, among others, the career of the Belgian international pop sensation Tan-ya, whose album *(Say Hello to) the New Groove* sold twenty-five million copies worldwide. The following year, Tobe was promoted to Head of Artiste Development, consolidating his position as one of the UK's leading breakers of new acts, not just in the world of pop music but also theatre, comedy and film. In 1998, Tobe co-founded Barlow & Darling, a consultancy which undertakes a variety of high-profile special projects on behalf of the world's leading entertainment companies. Tobe has been described as a "media terrorist" (the *Guardian*, 9 January 1998), "one of a new breed of image brokers" (*Variety*, 14 July 1999) and "a show business genius" (*Sunday Times*, 5 November 2000). And that's about it.'

'No it isn't. The letter doesn't just stop there, does it?'

'Erm, no. It says: "I am sure Tobe is the man you are looking for. If you require any further information, please call me or, better still, speak to the man himself. Yours sincerely, Bill Barlow."'

I don't know what to say. I've spent my adult life reducing people's careers and achievements to a few choice sentences, and now it seems it's my turn.

'So, you want me to appear on the show, right?'

'We'd love you to, yes. Would you like to hear who else is on the panel?'

'Not really. In fact, Paul, me old china plate, you can take your *Church of Q&A* and you can take your fax from my wanker of a partner and you can roll them up into a ball and you can shove them up your arse.'

Slam. Straight into the cradle. Inch perfect. I'm good at throwing the phone down. I can hit the mark across ten feet of office. But it doesn't stay down for long. I snatch it up and call Sadie.

'Sadie, when's Bill back?'

'He is on his way in from Heathrow but you will not be able to call him.'

'Why the hell not?'

'He turns his phone off now when he is in the car. He says using his phone makes the car like a microwave oven and it will cook his brain.'

At another time, this might even be funny.

'I'll do more than cook his fucking brain when I get hold of him.' The line goes dead and within seconds she's at the door with that look on her face.

'What did you say?' she asks me in that schoolmistressly way like she knows exactly what I said but she's daring me to say it again, to make the situation a whole lot worse. I could do without a run-in with Sadie at this precise moment, but to back down would be a terribly wasted opportunity.

'I said: I'll do more than cook his fucking brain when I get hold of him.'

She goes to say something but stops herself and strides towards me. She takes hold of my ear and pulls me out of my seat by it, forcing me into a kneeling position. I hear myself squeal and it's not a pretty sound. She raises her right foot and holds the sole of her shoe against my face.

'Lick it,' she hisses.

This is a new development. On other such occasions – and there have been other such occasions, I'm not sorry to tell – she has made me lick the upper side. What this new development means I will have to ponder on later. I presume there's something of an ideological leap from making someone lick the top of your shoe to making someone lick the bottom.

There's a small raised area on the sole of Sadie's shoe about the size of a ten-pence piece. Now, there are a number of possibilities as to what this object might be and I'll plump for the most likely: a masticated piece of chewing gum with a myriad of pavement minutiae trapped within its sticky grasp. Then again, it may be an encrusted pat of dog shit that's grown hard and will only rehydrate and yield up its foul contents after contact with liquid. Saliva perhaps. Thankfully, after about thirty seconds of trying to avoid the object with my tongue, Sadie deems my punishment to be at an end and I'm left with a combination of tastes in my mouth, the most active components of which I would guess are oil, rubber, cigarette ash and something I can't place but I presume belongs to the mystery object. Sadie gives my ear a final twist which she accompanies with an 'Ugh!', as though the disgust she feels for me is beyond words and can only be expressed with the most base of sounds.

I pull myself back on to the chair as Sadie turns on her heels and marches out of the office. Next to the pile of newspapers, there's a pile of music and style magazines. Bibles for the followers of hip. I flick open the first one while rubbing my ear and scan the contents page for anything of interest. It's full of the usual creatively challenged chumps doing the press rounds. New book, new film, new LP. Deals struck, meals eaten, cracks filled. The whole sticky bolus of celebrity chewed up, swallowed and squeezed along through the intestines of the media until it's shat out into the face of the great British public. I scan through a few articles as a means of killing time until Bill's arrival, when I can let rip.

Bill Barlow was born thirty-five years ago to loving, supportive parents, schoolteachers, in an English market town. The Barlows are educated middle-class. No family secrets, no skeletons in cupboards. At school, Bill was a star pupil. Good at sport, good exam results, popular. Even his acts of self-destructive teenage rebellion proved to be successful. With his band, the Crayons, he released an album in his gap year and earned a support slot on a tour with XTC. But recognising his limitations, and realising pop stardom didn't beckon, he attended Sussex University, where be became the Student Union Entertainments Secretary. He completed his degree (something scientific) before being snapped up by Seamus Darvel, an agent and concert promoter whose business fortunes were in decline until Bill managed to turn them around. Realising Darvel was getting an easy ride on his successes, Bill moved and set up Bill Barlow Entertainments, which after a shaky start went on to become a highly successful – if maybe a little small-time – show business agency. Bill's only problem was that, although excellent at all the schmoozing, he always seemed to miss the boat when it came to securing the big clients. That is why Barlow & Darling has been a business marriage made in heaven. Until now, that is.

He'll give me some bullshit as to why he supplied that Devonshire bloke with the information about me and our conversation will follow a pattern. Although I know I'm in the right and he's the bastard who's let me down, I know I'll be the one that'll end up feeling as though I'm being unreasonable. It is this knowledge which makes me feel even more antagonism towards him as he steps out of the lift and says good morning to Sadie. Sadly, he's not alone.

He's got some tall, long-blond-haired rock bloke with him in a leather jacket and cowboy boots. Who the hell he is I neither know nor care, and if he's going to hear what I've got to say then so be it.

'Ah, Bill, you're back.'

He gives me that big, warm, everything's-coming-up-roses smile, like he always does.

'Hi, Tobe, how goes it?'

He doesn't give me time to respond before turning to the guy with the hair and saying, 'Tobe, this is Dougie-Ray Christiansen.'

It's an unspoken rule between us that even if we've never heard of the person the other one is introducing us to, we will always make out we have. I should be saying, 'Oh yeah, Dougie-Ray, how you doing?' as though I'm his number-one fan, but unable to keep my anger at bay any longer, I stand up and, ignoring Dougie-Ray's hand extended towards me, I say, 'I don't give a fuck who he is.' The hand is retracted sharpish. 'What I do give a fuck about is my partner giving out confidential information about me to some little shit from a TV station.'

'Oh, that. Tobe, I'm sorry . . .'

'Don't even bother.'

'Tobe, can we talk about this later? Dougie-Ray's only in town for a few hours.'

'How dare you?'

'Look, you're going to have to excuse us, Tobe.' He's chewing his lip and throwing me a look that says 'shut up now', but when he realises this isn't going to work, he says, 'Look, Tobe, I just gave the bloke some general details regarding your career. Nothing you wouldn't want anyone to know.'

'It's not what you told him, Bill, it's the fact you told him anything. You know what I'm like. I don't like being discussed. I hate any form of exposure.'

'Oh, come on, Tobe.'

'Yeah, come on, Tobe.' This is the guy with the hair. He's got one of those drawly Californian voices. He obviously thinks this is a bit of a joke. I transfer my withering gaze from Bill to him. I can just about make out his eyes behind his sunglasses.

'And who the fuck do you think you are, you poodle-haired cunt?'

'Whoa,' he says, and holds his hands up.

'I thought you lot had all finally wised up to what dickheads you look like and cropped your hair and grown goatees. I didn't think people like you still existed.'

'Tobe, for God's sake, let's talk about this later,' shouts Bill, looking as agitated as I think I've ever seen him.

'No, and I would prefer it if this streak of piss would keep his nose out.'

'Cool it, man,' says Dougie-Ray.

'Listen, why don't you just fuck off back to whatever seventies time-warp shithole you crawled out of, *man*.'

'I'm sorry about this,' Bill says to him.

'What are you apologising to him for?' I shout.

'Can you excuse us for a moment?' Bill says to him in a calm, measured voice, his composure returned. Dougie-Ray nods and Bill puts his arms around me and picks me up.

'What the hell do you think you're doing?' I shout. I was

ready for any eventuality, or so I thought, but not this. I struggle, but he's a strong bastard.

Bill carries me into the meeting room, puts me down and shuts the door.

'Get your fucking hands off me,' I tell him.

'I had to do that, Tobe, I'm sorry. I couldn't have you behave like that in front of Dougie-Ray. Now, I know you've been having a hard time since Scarlet left.'

'Scarlet's got nothing to do with this. What has Scarlet got to do with you betraying me?'

'I didn't betray you, Tobe. You've got this all out of proportion. An old friend of mine, Richard Agnew, phoned me up and asked me to appear on a programme he's producing. *The Church of Q&A* I think it's called. I was quite happy to do it but I actually thought, and still think, you'd be a much better guest than me. Besides, it sounds like a good show. All I did was give him some brief details about your career and suggest he had one of his researchers contact you.'

'You know I never put my head above the parapet. I've always avoided any form of publicity or media attention like the plague. I'm not cut out for it. So what do you go and do? You give some little tosser my life story.'

'Tobe, I'm worried about you. You're overreacting wildly. You've been working too hard. Do you think your behaviour back there was rational? Was it?'

'I don't care. I was pissed off.'

'Look, Dougie-Ray Christiansen is a big guy. He's important. I don't want him telling everyone who'll listen that Tobe Darling is having a nervous breakdown because, if I'm being brutally honest, Tobe, that's how it looks.'

'That's how it looks, does it? Like I'm losing the plot.'

'Tobe, you're becoming a hermit. I can't remember the last time I saw you outside work. I can't remember the last function I saw you out at.'

'So? It's not my job to go out schmoozing. Among all the many and varied aspects of this industry I find abhorrent, hanging around with vacuous dullards talking shop comes about top of the list.'

'I'm not criticising, Tobe. Let's face it, you've probably forgotten more about this industry than I'll ever know. It's just, as your partner and friend, I think I have every right to be concerned. You're just not the Tobe we all know and love.'

'OK, Bill, I'll admit it, I'm having a tough time at the moment, but I would appreciate it if you would cut me some slack and not go behind my back and try to manoeuvre me on to some godawful TV programme which I could do with like a second arse.'

'I've been cutting you some slack for months now and I don't think you're getting any better. If anything you're getting worse. So I think it's time to change the treatment and bring you out of yourself. Help you get stuck in again.'

'And you really think that's going to make me feel better about life, do you? That's going to take away the feelings of despair I have gnawing away at my insides and the loathing I feel for every over-ambitious, socially challenged piece of shit that walks through these doors?'

'I want you to do the show.'

'That's going to bring me out of myself, is it? Some piss-poor satellite programme watched by a handful of sweaty teenagers who've finished their daily quota of spot-picking and masturbation and have got nothing better to do.'

'I think it'd be a good start. Like you say, no one watches it so who cares if you fuck up? It doesn't matter.'

'That's not the point, Bill. It's not *me*. I can't believe you even think I could do it.'

Bill sits at the table and slaps his hands down on the smoked-glass top. This is one of his symbolic gestures. This is his my-barriers-have-come-down gesture. I sit down opposite him and he leans forward with big compassionate eyes and I can tell I'm in for a speech. I slump back in my chair. This too is a symbolic gesture which says to him, 'Go on, then, if you must.'

'In case you hadn't noticed, Tobe, despite your personal problems and the fact you despise everyone we deal with, you're doing very well at the moment. We're both doing well, but you're doing especially well. Let's face it, it's you that does the work. You're the ideas man. You're the man they pay the frankly ludicrous amounts of money for. Without you, I'm nothing. I just sell you, in effect, and I'm thankful you let me. You've let me lead the life I've always wanted and I don't want to lose this life. I'm too selfish for that. I can't let you destroy yourself. I won't let you destroy yourself. You need to start living again. You need to get out there and feel hungry for it again. You need to feel the buzz again. You need to start enjoying yourself again. We're nearly there. Don't blow it now. Do this show. Do *The Church of Q&A*. I know it might seem crass but I think it'll do you some good. Richard Agnew is a decent bloke. He'll make sure you're looked after. It'll make you focus on something other than yourself. Do it for me, Tobe.'

Bill's not very good at this. He tries to arouse a sense of brotherhood in me as though he and I were locked together in some sort of crusade. As though we were involved in something worthy, something other than packaging shit and feeding it to the masses. It doesn't work.

'When I was a kid, Bill, I dreamed of being a rock star, of walking out on stage in front of thousands of people who were going berserk. That was my dream. But as I grew up I came to realise the downside of the dream. There're only so many times a rock star can walk out in front of thousands of people and they go berserk. After a while, they don't go berserk. They clap and they cheer but there's something missing. It's over and, after that, life is never the same again. It becomes a never-ending anticlimax. As it is, I don't have to worry about that – I can access my berserk crowds vicariously through my clients, and I can keep getting my berserk crowds all my life. I don't have to worry about being washed up. I'm not sticking my ego up there. Nobody's pinning their hopes on me. I've not got one fan. And that's exactly how I like it. All I want is the exact opposite of every wannabe pop star, actor, model, comedian or celebrity. I want nothing.' I want to say, 'I want pain,' but I can't. Bill's not to know about the pain. I don't think he'd understand. He's nodding his head and looking sincere. 'You've already told this mate of yours, this Agnew bloke, that I'll do the show, haven't you?'

'Not exactly.'

'And you'll feel a dickhead if I don't do it, won't you?'

'I'll admit it'd be a little embarrassing if you didn't, yes.'

'OK, I'll do it' – his face lights up – 'as a favour to you.

Not because you think it'll do me good or any of that. I'll do it so you'll piss off and leave me alone. This will be my first and only TV appearance. Now, when is it?'

'It's tonight. They'll send a car for you about five.'

'Bloody marvellous.'

We walk back through to my office, where Dougie-Ray's sitting at my desk reading a music paper. It's difficult to make polite chitchat with someone after you've called them a poodle-haired cunt, but I try. And fair play to the guy, he doesn't treat me with anything other than the most thinly disguised disdain. None of that 'shucks, we all have bad days' brainless bonhomie so prevalent among Americans.

My decision to appear on *The Church of Q&A* is beyond stupid. I can't even work out exactly why I said I'd do it. It's not so much out of a sense of duty to Bill as an unspoken acknowledgment on both our parts that I owe him. I owe him big, if truth be told. Mind you, I could still pull out even now. So Bill would look like a bit of a twat in front of his mate, the producer. So what? I can live with that. It's this thought that comforts me as I nod and smile at our dear curly-permed American friend as he drones on about his new project – a supergroup comprising a load of old guys who played in West Coast progressive rock bands in the early seventies. It's probably better not to ask why, if they're a supergroup, I've never heard of a single one of them, nor any of the bands they hail from. But I'll give him a break after my earlier outburst. He's lounging back in his seat now, and every inch of him says rock'n'roll. But it isn't the cool end of the rock spectrum. This guy's more Def Leppard than Hendrix, and he's got the uniform to prove it. The biker's leather, the flannel shirt open to the third button down and tucked into his jeans, the chain around his neck, the rings on his fingers, the cowboy boots and the aviator sunglasses. Sociological historians in the future will probably study the likes of this guy and his accompanying subculture and piss themselves laughing.

As he's droning on about his ghastly supergroup, I imagine how he would stand up to a spot of torture. We could strip him completely naked and peg him out spread-eagled on the ground. We could take off all his rings, bracelets and necklaces. We could yank out all the junk he's wearing in his piercings, shave off all of his golden locks of flowing rock hair and paint over his tattoos with flesh-coloured paint. We could denude him of all his subcultural baggage and make him totally anonymous, restored to his postnatal form. This would be plenty painful enough for him in itself, but we'd discover more about him if we utilised a little torture to probe his psyche. I reckon he'd be OK at first, before the true horror of his situation had sunk in. There'd be some swearing, but he'd still be in character. He'd still be Mr poodle-haired American rock dude, even with a burning cigarette end pushed against his skin. So, we'd need to probe deeper, cut through the gristle of his personality and ego and get right to the very primeval grey matter of the man. What we'd need is to put something really tasty into the mix, like a chainsaw, its petrol engine whining and spluttering, and, crude though this undoubtedly is, it'd really scare the shit out of him. Then we could tell him we're going to castrate him with the chainsaw and, by now, we'd really have his undivided attention. There'd be tears by now, maybe an uncontrolled bowel movement if we're lucky. My imagination is my saviour at times like this. I can watch a split screen. There's reality on one side and my alternative reality on the other. On the one side: confident, relaxed Dougie-Ray, rock dude, running a desultory hand through his golden barnet; on the other, a screaming long pig shitting himself with fear as the faint breeze from the chainsaw's snarling teeth blows cool across his recoiling testicles.

'OK, Bill, it's been great, but I gotta go.' He's on his feet and shaking Bill's hand. He shakes my hand but our eyes don't meet. Bastard even has the cheek to tell me to 'cheer up, pal'.

'See you later, Dougie-Ray,' I tell him. He blanks me and heads off down the corridor. Elsewhere in my head, I'm standing in a drizzle of warm blood as the chainsaw tears through his scrotum and my eardrums ache from his hopeless screams.

THE GERM

I've always had a thing about rats. As far as I'm concerned, they're an aberration of nature. Mice are OK. We need mice. I can't think what for but I'm sure we must do. Same goes for hamsters and guinea-pigs. I'm not a fan by any means, but I can live with them. Rats, on the other hand, are a breakdown of everything that's human. Just thinking of them causes me acute psychological pain. So, when I open my eyes and find one staring straight back at me, I'm frozen with dread.

For a moment, my entire world consists of just the rat and me. But as the focus of my perception widens, I can see that the rat is just the centrepiece of an entire tableau of horror. I'm lying in the bath. I've got my shirt and socks on. Nothing else. The bath is full, but it's what it's full of that concerns me because, instead of water, I appear to be engulfed in a freezing cold slurry as though my body has evacuated every single waste product of which it is capable. Suspended in a thick scum on the surface are feathery flecks of vomit, some in varying shades of orange and brown and others like gristly morsels of pink sausage meat.

The rat breaks my stare to lean forward and sniff at something floating near by, the touch of its nose sending the offending object bobbing. Then I realise what it is. It's a big brown turd, and I can feel another one stuck half in and half out of my arse. A spasm of acute nausea jolts my body rigid and I wretch and gag, which yields nothing more than a dribble of phlegm that slithers snakelike down my cold blood- and vomit-splattered shirt. This movement causes the contents of the bath to splash around me, and I don't know whether the turd rising up on a wave of displaced liquid has unseated it or whether it's just lost its balance but the rat's in with me now, paddling hard towards my genitals. I scream as it clambers up the nearest available solid surface, which happens to be my shrivelled member, hops on to the side of the bath and scarpers, out through the bathroom door to claw and bristle and squeak its way through this suppurating wound of a house.

My screams develop into a series of convulsive sobs which I manage to bring under control more out of necessity than anything as each one puts another split in my agonised skull and the tears that stream down my face represent moisture my dehydrated body can ill afford to be without. Why I'm weeping like this I have no idea at present. It can't just be on account of the rat and the bath full of sewage. There must be something else, and all I can assume is my subconscious knows what it is and is feeding me the requisite emotion before revealing the facts.

This is the second crying fit I've had in the past couple of days. I don't know what's wrong with me. I'm not the crying type. I'm not one of those people who likes to show their emotions. I don't subscribe to the let's-let-it-all-hang-out school of self-therapy. I can't abide people who attempt to rationalise the human condition and provide answers to questions that are impossible to fathom. However you want to live this life, whatever your dreams and whatever the actuality of your circumstances, it all boils down to the fact that, rich or poor, celebrity or unknown, fixer or fixed, we are all just frightened rabbits trembling in the headlights of our own mortality. We scramble around trying to fill our lives with something, anything, so that we can avoid facing up to the futility of our own fragile existence. And as for the religious types, they can shove it up their arses. None of it is convincing. None of the theories stand up. My own theory is it's all just one big cosmic joke, but who the joker is and who the joked I have no idea. Maybe the human race, you and me – maybe we're the punch line. Well, ha, bloody ha. I challenge any psychologist, New Age fuckwit, philosopher, holy man or mystic to tell me why I'm lying in a bath full of piss, shit, bile, vomit and tears. Welcome to my life.

I squeeze the second half of the turd out of my arse and, once it has disengaged and floated away, I pull myself to my feet and step out of the bath. I pull on the plug chain and the vile fluid starts gurgling down the plughole. Unfortunately, anything larger than a pea will be strained out by the grille in the hole and leave me with a disgusting mound of marinated excrement. I'll worry about it later.

I trudge through the piles of clothes left strewn along the landing, take the stairs to the second floor and Bathroom Number Two. This was Scarlet's bathroom and is in pristine condition owing to my not having been in here since she left. There's a spider in the bath which I carefully remove with a piece of tissue paper and set down on the window ledge. I turn on the shower full bore and lie down on the bottom of the bath, letting the water hammer down on me, blasting away the remains of the sewage clinging to my body.

Now I suppose I must turn my attention to the loathsome task of attempting to establish exactly how I ended up in this state. My first deduction is somewhat obvious to say the least – namely that last night and possibly this morning, or some of it at least, I was totally and utterly shitfaced drunk. Another clue is provided by my nose, which feels as though someone's taken a lump hammer to it. But it's no good, my physical condition won't supply the necessary triggers to activate my alcohol-ravaged memory banks. Guess I'm going to have to start at the beginning and take it from there.

The car dropped me at Metropolis Studios near Southwark Bridge, where I was met by Paul Devonshire from Poison Arrow. He was an over-enthusiastic college leaver who'd clearly banged up a couple of lines of charlie in the misguided belief it'd make him more confident and interesting conversationally. He didn't seem to bear a grudge about my belligerent attitude of earlier and was all smiles and handshakes as he took me through to the green room. I was the first guest to arrive. Devonshire told me to help myself to the drinks, to the beers and wines and, more worryingly, my favourite, a bottle of tequila. It was a good twenty minutes and three tequilas later before he returned, grinning and obsequious with the first of my fellow guests.

Tamsin Murray is a twenty-one-year-old glamour model whose existence I am aware of only because an old mate of mine, a ne'er-do-well called Muff Barclay, has started managing her in an attempt to hoist her career from being wank fodder in the tabloids and bloke mags to being wank fodder on the telly. Cheap, crap telly, of course. Devonshire introduced us to each other, referring to me as a show business image consultant and to Tamsin as a TV presenter.

'It's a bit premature, isn't it?' I asked her once Devonshire had smarmed his way back out of the door.

'I'm sorry?' she said, all spangly lip gloss and expensive dental work.

'Well, what TV presenting are you doing at the moment, Tamsin?'

She was on the defensive straight away. It was cruel of me – she was only a kid – but I couldn't resist it.

'My agent is in negotiations with a major satellite channel over the format of a new adventure game show we've developed.'

Old Muff's really been talking the bollocks with this one, I thought to myself. I couldn't even be bothered to ask her which woefully inadequate channel Muff was in negotiations with, or even if there was a channel at all, which I doubted, and as for the adventure game show, I imagined it to be a series of none-too-subtle televisual contrivances, their sole purpose being to display Tamsin's tits in as many revealing tops as possible. The one question I did want to ask her would, under normal circumstances, have remained unasked, but with four glasses of tequila slopping around my inner tube and a fifth on the way, I thought, fuck it, and went for it.

'So, Tamsin, has Muff tried to shag you yet?'

Before Tamsin could formulate the words to express her indignation, Devonshire was back with the next guest, some dweeb who's developed an interactive computer game that's made him something of a netheads' celebrity. His name was Calvin Too, or maybe it was Calvin 2, like the name of his most famous creation, Liberator 2. I didn't get to find out. He was tiny, quite the smallest man I think I have ever seen. He wasn't a dwarf, and didn't appear to have anything congenitally wrong with him, he was just a miniature man, maybe four feet five at the most. You'd have thought that at that height he'd just accept it and get on with being a tiny bloke, but he's obviously decided he's going to give it the hard-man number and he swaggered into the room and shook my hand as though he wanted to crush my fingers. The tequila made me want to ask him what he was hoping to achieve with this laughable façade but the sound of his voice rendered me speechless. He hoisted himself up on his chair, cleared his throat, and to some question Devonshire asked him about the new game he was developing, came out with a totally incomprehensible, impossibly high-pitched Glaswegian warble at which I laughed as though I'd just been told a killer punch line. It takes a lot to make me laugh but, when I do, I find my laughter difficult to control. When Devonshire tried to rectify matters and turned to Calvin 2 and said, 'I'm sorry, I didn't quite catch what you said,' I nearly pissed myself. Thankfully, before Calvin 2 could reply, thereby rendering me helpless, some bloke with headphones around his neck whispered in Devonshire's ear and he went off to usher in guest number four, and blow me if it wasn't Malcolm Copestick, the disgraced former Tory MP.

There's something rather fishlike about Copestick, especially around the eyes, which bulge out of his head as though his voyeuristic tendencies have started to manifest themselves physically. Copestick was the guy, you may remember, from a few years back who was discovered by the local constabulary to have a telescope and cameras with telephoto lenses through which he spied on his neighbours and recorded their most intimate and compromising moments. Copestick chose to fight the charges, claiming all his equipment was purchased in order to pursue a burning fascination with astronomy. He even produced photographs of distant constellations he claimed to have taken. What neither he nor his defence team had bargained on was that one of his neighbours had turned the tables on him and had a photograph of him completely naked holding an incriminating object in each hand. In one hand his telescope, and in the other his erection. Copestick was bang to rights. As it was a first offence and only minor, he was let off with a caution and a fine, but his parliamentary career was in ruins. The tabloids lapped it up and, after much cheque-book-waving, managed to get hold of the incriminating photograph which they splashed across their front pages with a deliberately tiny patch covering the hapless MP's organ so as to cause maximum humiliation.

I was still giggling about Calvin 2's voice when Copestick was introduced to me. Before I could say anything childish to him like 'eye-eye' or something equally crass, all vestiges of mirth were wiped from my face as the next and final guest walked through the door. I downed my fifth tequila in one.

Despite the deluge of hot water from the shower, my skin feels rubbery and cold, not unlike a corpse's, I shouldn't wonder. I stand up and, as I do so, crack my head against the shower head. The pain is such I wish I could die. In the mistaken belief that lightning doesn't strike twice, I step out of the bath without, perhaps, paying as much attention to the dangers of slippage on the wet enamel as I should have done. One foot goes one way and the other goes the other and I end up straddling the side of the bath, the chrome handle on it bisecting my scrotum so that one testicle goes one side and the other goes the other. If a new language is required to express how I feel then now's the time to invent it. Profanity, blasphemy, excessive usage of F and C word just won't do. I feel almost as wretched as I did last night when I saw Hugo Blain striding into the green room of *The Church of Q&A*.

My schooldays were the happiest days of my life. Were they fuck. At their best, they came within spitting distance of being bearable; at their worst they were a seemingly futureless frogmarch through labyrinthine corridors of fear, insecurity and humiliation. Some kids, kids like me, shouldn't mix with other kids. It doesn't encourage them to develop the social skills required in adulthood or any of the other bogus assertions made by the guardians of our educational establishments. It just gives them a thirteen-year lesson in alienation. And just to make matters worse for me, to compound my loathing of school, what did my parents do – my sensitive, understanding, *modern* parents? They sent me to boarding school at the age of seven. It was called St Luke's. At first it wasn't too bad. Although poor at sport, I excelled in the classroom and, while not extrovert by any means, I was quick-witted and good with a funny put-down. I learned how to tap into the mechanisms of childhood humour so they worked for me rather than against me. I was cruel, I suppose. It was my only way of surviving. Always do it to him before he does it to you. That was the motto I lived by.

By the age of eleven, I had managed to carve myself a niche within the school. I was almost always top of my class and though nowhere approaching what you would term popular, then at least respected for my ability to issue a good tongue-lashing if required. The other kids left me alone. I managed to achieve a sort of anonymity, invincibility even. I was allowed to go it alone. Until Hugo Blain arrived, that is.

His parents lived in the Far East. I saw them a few times at school events. Hugo's father was tall with a disproportionately plump head in comparison to his body, which was gangly and thin. I remember how he smelled more than anything. He was one of those people who give off a really strong smell. He smelled of expensive toiletries and the leather interior of his Daimler. He also smelled of whisky, and it was that which killed him in the end. Hugo's mother was a slim muscular woman, and it was her physique and looks Hugo inherited. She was an attractive woman and the object of many a schoolboy crush, I'm sure. She was certainly the object of mine. It was her calf muscles which really stand out in my mind. I loved watching her walk. She'd been a model, I think, and she strode around elegantly as if she owned the place, and her calf muscles used to flex and bulge. I wanted to lick them. She wore this slightly haughty expression on her face as though she would demand satisfaction in her sexual encounters. I'm pretty sure she must have been into S&M. She had that look about her.

In appearance, Hugo was more than the product of his parents' gene pool. It was as though there was a little bit of angel in him, and one day he actually shone, I kid you not.

It was our last sports day, just a few days before me and my contemporaries were due to leave St Luke's and go our separate ways to our various public schools and, in my case, five more years of purgatory. Hugo had won virtually everything in the track and field events. His parents and a group of their friends, a bunch of overpaid, over-tanned bores, had followed him around all day, cheering him on. At the awards ceremony later, whenever Hugo went up to collect one of his seemingly endless stream of medals and cups, his parents and their entourage clapped and cheered increasingly loudly. The top prize at St Luke's sports day every year was the Arthur Hearst cup given in remembrance of some former headmaster. It was presented to the boy who was the top sportsman and all-round good egg. Our headmaster, the Reverend Eric Ward, known to his pupils as the Old Cunt, stepped forward to announce the winner of the 1978 Arthur Hearst Cup. As he did so, someone among the Blain entourage started chanting, 'Hu-go, Hu-go, Hu-go.' Owing to a mixture of end-of-term good humour and sheer affection for the winner, it was rapidly picked up by the other parents, the teachers and the boys, so within moments everyone on the sun-drenched lawn was chanting 'Hu-go, Hu-go, Hu-go'. Everyone, that is, except me. The Old Cunt even encouraged these horrendous proceedings by hamming it up and saying, 'Oh, I wonder who it could be,' which set off peals of competitive laughter.

'The 1978 Arthur Hearst Cup goes to Hugo Blain.'

Hu-go, Hu-go, Hu-go.

He walked forward, picked up the cup and turned to receive his adulation. Just as he did so, the sun went behind a cloud, casting a shadow across the land. But it was as though the cloud had a hole, through which a shaft of sunlight like a cosmic super-trooper struck Hugo and inflamed his entire being, so that light poured out of him, enveloping us all in its warm glow. The only still pair of hands and silent mouth in the entire crowd belonged to yours truly, and as Hugo looked out across the massed ranks of his adoring fans, I wasn't surprised when he sought me out in the crowd. He couldn't resist it. This was his ultimate moment of superiority over me. There he was, shining like an angel for all to see, basking in his heavenly glory, but it was to me he turned to receive the ultimate praise. Our hatred for each other was more important to him than all this spontaneous outpouring of love and admiration.

We had been friends, of course. All the greatest enemies start off as friends. That's just the way it goes. When Hugo came to St Luke's, he actively sought out my company and I was flattered, if not a little surprised that the golden boy would want to hang out with the introverted fat kid. It was as though he could see something in me others couldn't. Despite there being numerous other boys in the class who were a hell of a lot more fun to be with than I was, Hugo was determined I should become his friend. He saw my solitary, introspective nature as a challenge, and as time went on I came to realise his attempts to bring me out of my shell were not born of altruism but of a desire to create of me another success story to add to his ever-expanding library of them. His interest in me was akin to some pompous rock star getting his picture taken with starving Third World children. It made him feel good. It gave him a cause. The only problem was I didn't want to be rehabilitated into school society and wasn't prepared to become the emotional plaything of some thirteen-year-old Narcissus. But the more blatant my disinterest in his attempts to achieve his goal, the harder he tried until, when it finally sank in that I wasn't going to play ball, he took it as a personal affront. He couldn't comprehend that I didn't share in his vision for me, and that's when it turned ugly. Like a spurned lover, he set out to exact his revenge.

It was subtle. There was no confrontation. He started taunting me about being a weirdo. At first I managed to cope with it, but as he became increasingly malicious and incited others to behave similarly, I felt support for me ebb away as the tide came flowing in on his shore. Boys who only months before wouldn't have dreamed of crossing me joined in his spiteful jibes and seemingly developed a collective immunity to my increasingly desperate retorts. Hugo had clearly decided that if he couldn't drag me out into the light through friendly encouragement then he'd achieve his goal through public ridicule.

In a boarding school of a little over a hundred pupils, it's impossible to avoid someone. My life became intolerable as my lovingly nurtured invisibility faded under the scrutiny and derision of my peers. I had a habit of saying 'erm' a lot when I spoke and, as is always the way with these things, the more conscious I became of saying it, the more I said it. Within a few weeks of Hugo calling me Erm, all my classmates had joined in. There was even a master, Shitpipe Palmer, so called because the smoke from his pipe tobacco was vaguely redolent of fecal matter, who joined in too. Then some bright spark chose to amend it to Germ, and subsequently I became the Germ to one and all. Erm, erm, here comes the Germ.

As my popularity rating plummeted, Hugo's soared. In our last year at St Luke's, he was appointed head boy. In an uncharacteristic use of the democratic process, the Old Cunt allowed the boys to vote for who they wanted as head boy. Ward gave a lecture on the day of the vote on the virtues of democracy, and then we all stuck our voting slips in the ballot box. Hugo won by the widest margin in the history of the school, receiving the endorsements of almost three-quarters of the boys. I, of course, received not one vote. During the ballot, however, someone had defaced their voting slip. Instead of writing down the name of their preferred choice of head boy on the blank piece of paper, they'd written 'Hugo Blain is a wanker'. The Old Cunt was furious and told us he would keep us waiting – the newly elected head boy and all – until the culprit owned up. He didn't tell us what the defacement said, just that there had been one. I only know what it said because I found out later. We'd been sitting there for about ten minutes when Hugo stuck his hand up.

'Yes, Blain,' croaked the Old Cunt, and all eyes settled on Hugo's cherubic face.

'Sir, I think I know who did it,' he said.

'Well, I hope you can support your accusation with hard evidence.'

'I can, sir. I saw the boy in question do it, sir. I've been sitting here wrestling with my conscience. I don't want to be thought of as an informer but then it's not fair everyone should have to suffer because of one boy's cowardice.'

Hugo had won the hearts and minds of his audience, and all he needed now was a fall-guy. I must confess to being as excited as everyone else. It was always fun to watch some other kid's humiliation. Just so long as it *was* some other kid's.

'It was Toby Darling, sir.'

Every pair of eyes in the assembly hall burned into me. The first thing that dawned on me was a sense of crushing inevitability. This was his trump card. There was no way I could hide away from this.

'Well, Darling, what have you got to say for yourself?'

It felt as though the entire world had stopped in anticipation of my response. But there was no response. I was paralysed by fear. My capacity for reasoned argument had shut down entirely. Subsequently, I have spent countless hours obsessing over responses I could have given, cleverly worded salvos that would have pointed the finger squarely at the true culprit. As it was, robbed of all rational thought and succumbing to the basest and most immediate of my primeval instincts, I ran for it. What I thought I could achieve by doing this, or even where I thought I was going, I have no idea. I just knew I had to try to escape. Not the most co-ordinated of athletes, and starting out from within the very centre of the assembly hall, I managed to collide with a number of boys as I made for the door and, as I did so, I could make out the sound of footsteps behind me. They were approaching at speed. There was no way they could belong to the Old Cunt. He'd never move that fast. They could only belong to one person, the same person who had engineered this entire scenario. Not content with his role as false accuser and architect of my downfall, he now wanted to play the role of gallant captor. I ran as fast as I could but I was no match for Hugo's athleticism. He caught up with me before I could reach the door and rugby-tackled me. As we writhed around on the floor, I managed to get a couple of kicks in but these were little consolation for the ultimate humiliation which awaited me when I sat up.

There were probably no more than about a hundred and twenty faces turned towards mine at that moment, but it might as well have been a million, and their expressions spoke to me, saying, 'You deserve this, you're a loser, we despise you, Toby Darling.'

The Old Cunt put the defaced voting slip on his desk so I could look at it while he bent me over and gave me six of the best. I suppose he must have thought there was a poignancy to this, as though I might receive some benefit from pondering the evidence of my crime while receiving the punishment for it. I didn't bother even trying to explain to him it wasn't me who had defaced the voting slip, that in fact, in an attempt to be ironic, I'd voted for a kid called Bates, who was completely inept and smelled of bacon. There were no handwriting experts to call on to support my story, just Hugo Blain's handwriting staring up at me:

HUGO BLAIN IS A WANKER, beaten into me so that I'd never forget.

He looked good, I'll give him that. The years had been kinder to him than to me. But I took it as a bad omen. No good could ever come of Blain and I becoming re-acquainted.

'Tobias Darling, I knew it was only a matter of time before we bumped into each other.'

He was right. It's only been a pathological hatred of going to any social functions on my part which has prevented our meeting up until now. Bill has met Hugo many times and, despite my protestations to the contrary, actually quite likes him.

'Hi, Hugo.' He held out a smooth, dry, carefully mani-cured hand into which I slid my clammy nail-bitten fingers.

'Quite the maverick these days, I'm told, Tobe. It is Tobe nowadays, isn't it?'

'Yeah, it is.'

I suppose in comparison with Hugo's work, what I do is somewhat independent, free-spirited even, but that's because Hugo's a big corporate cheese at the moment in his role as MD of Big Noize Inc., purveyors of Big Noize TV, a relatively new digital music channel going head to head with MTV and having enough clout to make or break careers with its choice of playlist.

Careless of Paul Devonshire's proximity, I couldn't resist asking Hugo, 'What the hell are you doing on a poxy show like this?' Hugo threw his head back and laughed with all the sincerity of a TV evangelist.

'You haven't been reading your trade press, have you?'

'Not if I can avoid it.'

'Well, if you had you'd have seen that Big Noize bought out Poison Arrow a couple of weeks ago. Just thought I'd come along tonight and get involved with the new product. *The Church of Q&A* is going places, Tobe, you mark my words.'

It's reassuring to know that Hugo Blain has developed into just the sort of loathsome bastard for which he showed so much potential as a child.

Before I could think of anything derogatory to say, Paul Devonshire had rounded us all up and we were off to meet Petina Durrant, *The Church of Q&A*'s presenter and all-round media bunny.

I'm out of the bathroom now, testicles in hand, just in case, and I walk through to my room and lie down on the tangled mess of sheets I call my bed. Owing to my laundry problems, I have a rolling order of bed-linen with a catalogue company, and when each set of linen is grubby I cover it with some of the new stuff and sleep on that, one sheet nearer the ceiling each time.

Petina Durrant is one of those growing breed of TV presenters you see when you switch on the telly in any country in the world. You know the type – they're good-looking in a cardboard, non-sexual way, and so efficient and dependable they achieve a sort of transparency. You never hear of them outside of their regular spots unless they own up to a drug addiction, do shedloads for charity, or die.

Petina and a serious bloke in a yellow sweater whose name I forget chatted with us about the questions the studio audience might ask. The bloke in the yellow sweater gave a title to each of us. Tamsin Murray was 'the pin-up

TV presenter', Calvin 2 became the 'the computer games wizard', Malcolm Copestick appeared to take no offence at being called 'the disgraced MP', and with a flagrant display of sycophancy to his new employer, he referred to Hugo Blain as 'the media mogul'. He called me 'the image man', which didn't bother me unduly, but what did bother me was the way he said it, like he was calling me a child molester or something. It felt as though, in *The Church of Q&A*'s exploration of celebrity, he wanted to set me up as the bad guy. Not the airhead tit flasher nor the peeping-tom MP, not the techno-dwarf nor Mr Golden-Balls Blain, so, for whatever reason, it looked as though it was going to be me. Maybe it was a paranoid delusion but, if it was, why did Petina treat my fellow guests with the utmost deference and me as though I'd trodden dog shit into her living-room carpet?

As we were taken off to have some make-up applied, I found myself thinking of Bill Barlow, the scheming fucker. Not only had he coerced me into appearing on the telly when he knows I have a terror of attracting any attention whatsoever, but he'd managed to coerce me on to a programme on which I was to be fed to the audience like a sacrificial lamb, and to top it all, he'd managed to throw me together with a man whose very existence causes me acute psychological discomfort, a man who I had hoped to avoid for the rest of my life. I should have just walked away there and then, but there was something that made me stay, something that made me want to prove myself. Added to which, five large glasses of tequila is, for a man of my build and mental disposition, enough to cause radical perception problems. While my outward demeanour is to all intents and purposes unchanged, my inner being is stumbling around the dance-floor of some shithole Birmingham disco in the early eighties.

'Slap it on, love,' I told the make-up girl. 'Once I'm under those lights, I'll be sweating like a vicar in an orphanage.'

They stuck me in the middle of the table between Calvin 2 and Blain. Tamsin Murray and Malcolm Copestick were at either end. The guy with the yellow sweater told us to chat to one another as Petina introduced the show. I wasn't paying much attention to what Hugo was saying to me until the mention of the word Scarlet snapped me out of my malevolent reverie.

'I hope you don't mind.'

'Mind what?'

'Mind me taking her out. What with my divorce and me being so busy recently, I haven't seen anyone for ages.'

'You're seeing Scarlet?'

'We've been out a couple of times.'

'Scarlet Hunter?'

'Yes. I met her when she came to interview me for *International Profiles*. She mentioned you and she were together for a time.'

'Let me get this straight. You are going out with Scarlet Hunter?'

'Welcome to *The Church of Q&A*,' said Petina to camera. 'On tonight's programme we will be discussing the nature of celebrity. What is a celebrity? What do you have to do to become a celebrity? Why do some people spend their entire lives seeking celebrity and never finding it while others find it overnight and spend the rest of their lives trying to avoid it? Why are we so obsessed by the lives of celebrities? On our panel tonight, to answer these and other questions, we have five people who are either celebrities themselves or are directly involved with the creation and management of celebrities.'

I was in a blind tequila-fuelled panic. The crumbling of my universe was about to be broadcast. I couldn't think what to do. My mind was racing between the external world and the internal, between Petina, who was busy introducing Tamsin Murray and Calvin 2 to the studio audience, and Scarlet, my Scarlet, going at it hammer and tongs with Hugo Blain and, just to make my torture complete, loving every second of it.

'To some, he's a manipulator of minds, to others a show business genius whose Midas touch has launched a thousand careers on the rocky road to superstardom. Ladies and gentlemen, Tobe Darling.' Was it me or was the applause I received hollow, derisory even? Petina introduced Blain as 'one of a handful of executive prime movers who are shaping the future of British broadcasting', and his applause was more enthusiastic and lasted a whole lot longer than mine. It took all my strength of will to stop me picking up one of the Biros they'd left on the table for us and stabbing it into his face. Even Copestick did better than me on the applause front after Petina had made out he was some harmless old eccentric rather than the seedy little pervert we all know him to be.

The first question came from a Melvin or a Kelvin or something, a lab technician from Willesden, who wanted to know of Blain – thank Christ it wasn't me – what sort of qualities he was looking for in a potential star. Hugo went into a long diatribe about what made someone a star, that elusive something known as star quality. While he was speaking, my hands began to shake and I could feel the make-up lose its grip on my skin and, carried aloft on a moving glacier of sweat, move down my face like a slipped mask. I felt nauseous, saliva flooded my mouth. Hugo was concluding a brilliant exposition on the nature of celebrity and I wanted to throw up. Another question was in the pipeline, this time from some woman chiropodist from Surbiton.

'I would like to ask the panel why they feel in modern Western society we appear to be more interested in the private lives of the rich and famous than we are in serious political issues and the plight of people both in this country and abroad whose standard of living is well below the poverty line. It seems to me we've got our priorities all wrong.'

Petina steered this towards Copestick, who came across as all hard done by and, completely ignoring the crux of the question, started on about how the media had ignored all his political policies for twenty years, preferring instead to poke fun and snigger at his downfall. Hugo and Scarlet were still going at it like rabbits in my head and causing me an overload of pain. But it wasn't good pain. It wasn't pain I could use.

I started hyperventilating, and my heart felt as though it would explode at any moment. I am not prone to fits. I've never actually had a fit. What I am prone to is their symptoms. Whenever I end up feeling like this, I think perhaps all the symptoms I've ever been subject to over the years that haven't developed fully are saving themselves up for one big seizure that'll mean curtains for me. Steve, a hospital porter from Hackney, asked the third question.

'I'd like to ask Tobe Darling . . .' No, I wanted to say to him, please, not me, ask someone else, ask Tamsin or Calvin 2; better still, why not ask the bloke in the yellow sweater? But no, my time had come. People wanted to know the opinions of the fat, sweaty image consultant. '. . . in the light of the recent murders in the West End of London, what he thinks about the salacious way the media cover such tragic events so a cult of celebrity grows up around the murderer.'

'I take it,' said Petina, 'you are referring to what have become known as the Piper murders?'

'That's correct.'

All eyes were on me, some of them peering at me through TV cameras, recording every move and sound I made so that more, thousands more, could scrutinise every pixellated fraction of my entire being.

'Well, it's bound to happen.' Any relief I might have felt for having broken my silence was countered by the reali-sation that this one phrase was not enough. They wanted more, much more. 'We love murder, we're obsessed by it. The murderer has become the single most important character in popular entertainment, and of all murderers, the serial killer has become the most celebrated. But what this does for the real-life serial killer is that it raises peo-ple's expectations and, contrary to what the writers and film-makers would have you believe, most real-life serial killers are nobodies, misfits, losers. So, for a serial killer to become a global success, he's got to have that special something, that star quality we heard of from Mr Blain here. There's no surprise any more in finding out that this year's serial killer is a kindly-looking Mr Chips type who was so nice with the kids. For a serial killer to capture the public imagination, he's got to have the same essential ingredients a top celebrity has. He's got to have a good image, a good name, he's got to do something unusual, and he's got to be seen to have talent. When a killer like this comes along, the public never tires of all the gruesome minutiae of his crimes and with its hunger for information ends up resembling a junkie awaiting his fix, and the media – if you want to take the analogy still farther – are the drug dealers. They become complicit in the crimes themselves. We've all seen *Natural Born Killers*. Now this Piper character looks like he's all set to become a big star. In fact, if he continues on his current course of action and remains at large, there's no reason why he couldn't transcend his serial killer status and become a bona fide legend.'

This was too much for the hospital porter from Hackney, and he came out with a comment only a bleeding-heart po-faced liberal twat like him could come out with: 'What about the victims and their families?'

The audience wanted compassion. They wanted 'Of course, the victims and their families, how awful', etc. But what they got was something quite different altogether. It wasn't so much a knee-jerk reaction to the question as an expression of disgust at the whole situation, at my appearance on the show, at Bill Barlow and his conniving stupidity, and at Scarlet and Blain, who were still going at it hell for leather in my head. What I said to the question regarding the victims and their families was, 'Fuck 'em,' and the whole place erupted. Steve, the hospital porter, was up on his feet and shouting at me. Petina set about trying to calm him down while the rest of the studio audience hurled abuse at me. Calvin 2 decided to join in with words and phrases of such a high pitch I had difficulty hearing them, let alone working out what it was he was trying to say.

'Well, Toby,' said Blain – he got it wrong deliberately, I'm sure – 'I think you'd better explain yourself seeing as you've touched on such a thorny issue. I, for one, would like to hear why anyone should behave with anything but the utmost compassion towards the victims of these hideous crimes.'

The fact that it should be Blain having a go at me made it all the worse. His question was greeted by a round of 'hear hears' from the studio audience. Of course I didn't mean what I'd said. It had just popped out. But it was too late for sorry and, besides, I was feeling victimised. I had Mr Hospital Porter almost foaming at the mouth with East End righteous indignation, Petina was looking at me in her schoolmistressly you've-got-some-explaining-to-do manner, Calvin 2 was wittering away in some new language only audible to dogs, and Hugo Blain was twisting the knife I'd stabbed myself with. They expected – no, they demanded – a retraction and an apology. But they weren't going to get them. Not from me, and especially not in the mood I was in.

'Look, make no mistake here, the Piper is bringing a lot of happiness to a lot of people.' This set them off again but I wasn't going to be shouted down. 'Show me one person here who isn't fascinated by this case and I'll show you a liar. The people get what the people want and if you want my opinion, and let's face it, I wouldn't be here if you didn't, then I think the Piper is every bit as relevant and worthy of respect as some actor or pop star or comedian with some new piece of product to flog. No, I take that back, he's more worthy. And as far as the killing of innocent people is concerned, what's the difference between one of "our boys" shooting the shit out of some Iraqis for which they're applauded and a cunning, media-hungry psychopath slicing up tourists and recording it for posterity? I'll tell you what – the psychopath is a damned sight more entertaining.'

The hospital porter from Hackney was on his feet hurling abuse at me once more, Calvin 2's voice had gone one tone higher, if such a thing were possible, and Hugo was chuckling the most derisory chuckle you ever heard.

'Look, I'm sorry if I've offended anyone. You wanted me to talk about celebrity so that's what I've done, and if you don't like it, well, that's your problem. I didn't want to come on this programme in the first place.'

Calvin 2 appeared to have taken everything personally and was shouting, if that's the right word to describe the noise he was making, right in my ear.

'Listen, mate,' I said to him, 'I can't understand a word you're saying so there's no point shouting at me. Why don't you learn to speak properly, and while you're at it, how about growing a few inches as well. I tell you what, why not make that a few feet.'

It was then that he head-butted me. He came out of his chair like a little ginger bullet. The bridge of my nose took the impact. It was inch perfect. He'd clearly done this many times before and knew exactly how to cause the maximum damage. Where once I had a nose, I now had a throbbing canker radiating pain, and although I was the victim of the attack and totally disorientated, Hugo Blain made a big show of pulling me away from Calvin 2 as though I were the aggressor. I must have been slightly concussed because I can't remember much about the next few minutes. What I can remember is that, immediately after Calvin 2 head-butted me, there was applause. They clapped him for twatting me, the bastards, and as I looked up and saw the expressions on their faces, I was transported back to St Luke's assembly hall all those years before, and saw those same expressions on the faces of the schoolboys as they stared at me in disgust.

Back in the green room, someone pressed a towel against my battered nose in an attempt to staunch the flow of blood from it. Paul Devonshire was speaking into a mobile phone and a bloke in a suit who I hadn't seen before was standing at the far end of the room watching me, smoking a cigarette.

'You can tell that little bastard,' I said to no one in particular, 'I'm going to press charges. I'll sue him for every penny he's got.' The bloke in the suit ground out his cigarette in an ashtray and walked towards me.

'Hi, Tobe. My name's Richard Agnew, I'm the executive producer of the show. I'm so sorry for what happened tonight. We can never anticipate exactly how guests will react to the subject under discussion, and clearly Calvin overreacted to what you were saying.'

'I'd say that was a bit of an understatement, pig boy.'

'But what I would ask you to bear in mind before you decide whether to press charges or not is that Calvin's sister-in-law was the victim of a brutal murder in Glasgow a couple of years ago which the police believe to be the work of a serial killer who has never been caught. This can in no way excuse his actions, but I hope you can at least understand his motivation.'

'Why didn't someone tell me that? You must have known there was going to be a question about the Piper?'

Paul Devonshire broke off from his phone conversation as though he'd been listening out for this and had his answer all prepared. 'I was going to tell you on the phone this afternoon,' he said, 'but if you remember rightly, you hung up on me, and when you turned up this evening it just totally slipped my mind.'

'Well, fuck you all, then,' I said, pushing the towel away from my nose, and I made my way to the door. Paul Devonshire followed me, asking whether I felt all right and shouldn't I wait a little while longer before making my way home. I met his questions and suggestions with a string of obscenities. In the reception area, I let him order me a car, as there was no way I could have flagged down a taxi looking like that. As I climbed in, I told him, 'If I were you, Paul, I'd seriously consider suicide.' Then I told the driver to take me to the Belljar Club in Compton Yard.

I pick up the phone on the bedside table and call the Belljar to see if anyone there can fill in the blank I've drawn on any further memories of last night, but it's too early and there's no one up yet. Then I call a number that is etched into my brain owing to my once constant dialling of it.

'Good morning. *International Profiles.*'

'Scarlet Hunter, please.'

'I'm afraid she's in a meeting at the moment.'

'Interrupt the meeting. Tell her Tobe Darling's on the line. It's urgent. She'll take the call.'

Scarlet comes on the line. During the past few months, I've played this moment over and over in my head. I'm now up to about version ten thousand of possible first-conversations-since-break-up. But this isn't one of them. 'Have you fucked, are you fucking or do you intend to fuck Hugo Blain?'

'Tobe, what do you want?' She sounds as though she knew this moment would come and now wants to get it over with as soon as possible.

'I want you to answer the question. Yes or no.'

'I had dinner with him a couple of times. Don't you think you're overreacting?'

'You didn't answer my question. I haven't got long.'

'Knowing you, you probably want me to say yes. All the pain and jealousy will turn you on, so, if that's what you want to hear, then yes, I'm going to fuck Hugo Blain. I'm going to give him the most depraved, savage fucking of his life. How's that feel? Look upon it as a final little favour for old time's sake.'

Whether she managed to hear the 'fuck you' I got in before she put the phone down is anyone's guess. I jump out of bed and wade through dirty laundry to the walk-in wardrobe, the progenitor of my clothing fiasco and home for the spring, summer, autumn and winter collection of the invisible man. I grab a pair of boxer shorts, a pair of socks, a grey shirt and a pair of black 501s. I open a shoe box and take out a pair of black Kit Benson shoes which are like Doc Martens only without the bumper-car sole. It's a relief to cover myself but owing to the exertion of my hurried dressing and the intensity of the hangover, my skin oozes a cold slick, causing freckles of damp to appear on my shirt.

My body never tires of sweating. The most minute amount of exercise will cause it to pour off me. Even taking a shit I'll end up sweating like a bastard. I read somewhere it's possible to have surgery on your sweat glands. Disconnect them or something. I think I might try it.

A BIT OF THE ROUGH STUFF

In the cab, I fiddle with my mobile phone so it looks as though I'm about to make a call. That way, the driver won't talk to me. He's got a photograph of his family stuck to the dashboard. They all look like him, even his wife. They've all got the same fat, pasty faces and can't muster one smile between the lot of them. They're all piled up on a cheap Dralon sofa staring at the camera. With a family like that you'd think he'd want to forget about them rather than keep a constant reminder of them in front of him all day.

In the building in which Barlow & Darling's offices are situated there are seven other companies, all of them media and show business related. I don't pay much attention to any of them, apart from the company on the fourth floor called Ringleader PR, which has an extremely attractive receptionist called Esther. I like to fantasise about her beating the shit out of me. This causes me to blush every time I end up in the lift with her, as I do now. I realise my somewhat pathetic attempts to ingratiate myself with her will always prove fruitless, but they do at least offer me a minute sniff of sexual intrigue in my otherwise barren sex life. She appears to be agitated by my appearance. I think it must be my black eyes and bloody nose. She says, 'Well, you've certainly made a name for yourself, Tobe.'

That Esther from Ringleader PR should even know my name is strange enough – I know hers only because I heard her boss, some skinny bloke with a birthmark on his cheek, call to her down the corridor one day – but that she should be telling me I've made a name for myself is not only bewildering but more than a little frightening too.

'I'm sorry?' She doesn't reply, just pulls out a copy of the *Evening Standard* from under her arm and opens it. On page three, there's a video grab from *The Church of Q&A*. It's taken from about a second or two after Calvin 2 head-butted me. It shows all five of us on the panel. At one end, Tamsin Murray is rising to her feet, watching the events as they unfold next to her. Owing to her momentum, her tits are, as luck would have it, on an upward swing and, I have to say, look fanfuckingtastic. This bit of free publicity will do her the power of good. Next to her is Calvin 2. There's a dribble of blood down his cheek, my blood no doubt, and it looks as though, given the chance, he'd be more than happy to administer another head-butt. Next to him, there's yours truly holding my nose with blood seeping between my fingers. Next to me, seemingly unperturbed by the situation, is Hugo Blain. He looks calm and composed, as though he is fully in charge of the situation and everything is proceeding as planned. And next to Blain, there's Malcolm Copestick, who is not even watching what is going on and stares back at the camera with a quizzical expression.

The headline above the photo reads: TV BUST-UP OVER PIPER KILLINGS. That's all I can manage before the lift doors open on to the third floor and the offices of Barlow & Darling.

'Do you want to keep the paper?' asks Esther from Ringleader PR.

'No thanks,' I tell her, and then, as though I need to offer some explanation, I say, 'It was all just a misunderstanding.'

Sadie looks up from her computer as I enter the office.

'Hi, Sadie.'

'Hello,' she says.

'Are there any messages?'

'There are many messages.'

'May I have them?'

She ignores my question and comes around the desk to stand in front of me and inspect my nose.

'It is broken, yes?'

'I think it probably is but not for the first time. I broke it at school once—' Before I can finish, Sadie has taken my nose between her thumb and forefinger and squeezed it. A knitting needle of pain is stabbed up each nostril and tears stream down my cheeks.

'Jesus Christ,' I shout at her, 'won't you fucking leave me alone? Can't you see I'm not playing this game any more?'

'You make me sick,' she hisses.

'Please, Sadie, this has got to stop. Maybe we can carry on with it some other time, but at the moment I can't cope with it. There's so much going on in my life right now. This is just making it worse. I'm sorry if I've confused you or given you the wrong impression.'

She stares at me and for a moment I think I can see beneath her armour-plated robot exterior. A smile creases her lips and, spurred on by this hint of compassion, I smile back. She takes me into her strong arms and holds me tight. Then, just as I am about to pull away, confident we have reached some sort of understanding, she pulls up the back of my shirt, grabs hold of the elastic on the edge of my boxer shorts and, in one fluid movement, yanks the gusset up hard between the cheeks of my arse, crushing my already bruised testicles. When she lets go, I drop to my knees. She takes a handful of my hair so that I can't move my head then, bending her knees slightly, she pulls her arse back and thrusts her groin forward, hitting me in the face with her hip bone. While I'm trying to decide whether it's my nuts or my nose which hurts more, she takes my list of messages, screws it up and stuffs it into my mouth, which is lolling open mid-groan.

'For God's sake, pull yourself together,' she says as Bill's office door is opened. I jump up, take the piece of paper from my mouth and pull my shirt down over the elastic from my boxer shorts, which is halfway up my back.

'God, you look terrible,' says Bill. 'Don't you think you should be in hospital or something?'

'I'm OK.'

'But your nose is bleeding.'

'Yeah, I know.'

'Look, why don't you come through to my office. I think we need to talk about last night. Can you rustle up a couple of teas, Sadie?'

Owing to Sadie's violent behaviour towards me, my anger towards Bill has diminished. I need to claw some back. I take a seat opposite him and he passes me a tissue from a box in the drawer of his desk.

'You must be *so* pissed off,' he says to me as I dab at the blood dribbling on to my top lip.

'No, Bill, whatever makes you think that? You know how I love appearing on the telly. You know what a keen self-publicist I am. Any excuse to steal the limelight. And getting head-butted by a shrunken imbecile, well, that just comes with the territory.'

'Tobe, I am so sorry. I had no idea—'

'Bill, answer me one question. Did you know Hugo Blain was going to be on the show?'

'I must admit I did.'

'Bill, you're my partner. Fuck it, Bill, you're meant to be my bloody friend. Yet not only do you put me forward for a television programme when you know I have an intense, almost psychotic hatred of appearing in front of people, let alone TV cameras, but then you omit to tell me I'm about to appear on television with my worst fucking enemy. What kind of relationship do we have here, Bill? How am I supposed to trust you?'

'I'm sorry you feel that way, Tobe. I didn't realise Hugo Blain was your worst enemy. I knew you'd fallen out but that was at school. That was twenty-odd years ago. You can't still bear a grudge, surely.'

'I always bear grudges, Bill, always. I nurture my grudges. I feed them with vitriol and malice and then I let them fester.'

'I presume you've seen the *Standard*?'

'Yes, I have had the misfortune.'

'Well, I've been fielding calls all morning. They all want

to run stories about us tomorrow. Now, we can either play ball and give them the stories we would like them to run or they'll just write the stories themselves. I think we need to play this very carefully, put together a general press release and then choose the paper we think will give us the best coverage and talk to them about an exclusive.'

'Fuck that.'

'I'm sorry?'

'Bill, I know how this works. Christ, I'm a fucking expert in it, but that doesn't alter the fact I want no part of this. We're owed shitloads of favours from the papers so now's the time to call them in and tell them we want the story killed stone dead.'

'But this is a golden opportunity.'

'An opportunity for what?'

'To make a name for ourselves, to get some free publicity, to push this company as far as it can go. I've even had a call from a TV producer who's interested in doing a fly-on-the-wall documentary about us.'

'Did I miss something here? Did I miss you having half your brain removed? We make other people's names, not our own. The rest of the world might want to become media stars but I don't. Now, you're very welcome to make a name for yourself if that's what you want, but leave me out of it.'

'Listen, Tobe, we either use the favours we're owed by the press to make them work for us or we let them run whatever they like, and let's face it, Tobe, they're not going to say nice things, are they? People feel very strongly about this Piper character. He's killed three American tourists in the most appalling fashion imaginable, and you go and say he's doing a good job and deserves our support. The papers are going to go one of two ways – they'll either make a story out of the fact you were drunk and said some stupid things or, as is more likely, they'll take the outraged angle and paint you – and me by association – as a ruthless, heartless bastard. The choice is yours.'

'Fuck 'em.'

'Oh, come on, Tobe,' he shouts. 'That's becoming your bloody catch-phrase. I'm trying to help you out. They're going to savage you if you let them. For God's sake, let's go for some damage limitation at least.'

Before I can answer, Sadie comes through with the tea tray and we maintain an awkward silence while milk and sugar are distributed. Despite my behaviour to the contrary, I do think he may have a point. Maybe I should just make some noises of contrition, say I was drunk, that I've been under a lot of pressure recently, that I overreacted and leave it at that. Short-term discomfort in exchange for the long-term benefit of Barlow & Darling. More importantly, that way I get to crawl back under my stone of anonymity. Once Sadie's shut the door after her I say, 'OK, Bill, I give in. Do whatever it is you think we should do but do me one favour – leave me out of it.'

'Yes? Thank God for that.' He's beaming at me. I throw him a half-smile just to show there is some good humour left in me, somewhere.

'I tell you what, Tobe, this could be the making of us. Yesterday's disaster might very well be today's godsend. It could put us on the map. Now, I know you don't want to hear the name but Hugo Blain called earlier to see how you were and to ask that we make some good noises about *The Church of Q&A*. In exchange for that he'll say your drunkenness was partially his fault for having arranged for the bottle of tequila to be left in the green room beforehand.'

'That was his idea, was it?'

'Yeah, he phoned me up and asked what your favourite tipple was.'

I feel as though someone has just injected ice-cold water into the top of my spinal column and it's slowly seeping its way down through my vertebrae. Bill is still too euphoric after my agreement to his damage limitation plan to notice my change of demeanour, and I'll try to keep it that way.

'Yeah, I knew it was a set-up as soon as I saw the bottle.'

'Oh, it wasn't really a set-up, we just thought you'd open up more if you had some of your favourite brew there to lubricate your tongue. We never thought for one moment Calvin what's-his-name would react like he did.'

'We?'

'Yeah, Hugo and me.' He's looking at me now, searching for signs in my face. I'm trying to remain deadpan so he'll dig himself in even farther, but he knows me too well and realises he's said too much. 'It wasn't like – you know – let's stitch Tobe up. Get him on the show, get him drunk and then see what happens. It wasn't like that at all, but seeing as what happened happened then we might as well go all out to capitalise on it, especially as Big Noize Inc. are all set to become one of our clients.'

'Did you know Hugo Blain is seeing Scarlet?'

'Your Scarlet?'

'Who else?'

'I didn't know. I'm sorry.'

'You know what, Bill, I'm not the only one who's been set up. You have too. Only it's worse for you because you still care. You still want all this. You still want to be the big player, don't you? Well, I don't, so go ahead and speak to the papers. Call a press conference if you want and tell them that owing to your naïvety, your stupidity and downright thoughtlessness, Barlow & Darling is no more. It's now just Barlow & No one. Got a nice ring to it, don't you think? Oh, and I bet I know who wants to commission the fly-on-the-wall documentary about us. I'll fucking bet I do. It is, isn't it?'

'Yeah, it is.'

On Bill's wall there are pictures of some of the artistes whose careers we have applied the electrodes to over the years. It's like a roll of honour for Barlow & Darling, testament to who we are and what we've done. I launch my mug of tea at it. The mug smashes against the wall and the tea splashes across the photographs.

'What the hell are you doing?'

'I'm quitting, Bill.'

'Jesus, Tobe, you're just so touchy at the moment.'

This description of my present demeanour lights the fuse, and when he tells me 'You've got to stop letting things get on top of you,' I explode. I stand up and scan the desk for the nearest object to hand, which is a fancy digital telephone. I pick it up, the handset and the base together in one. I can't quite believe I'm going to do this. I am not a violent person but the phone has left my hand by now and there's no turning back. It has already travelled a good quarter of the distance it will need to travel before it hits him. Nothing will stop it – there's plenty of slack cable both on the mains lead and the phone cable, easily enough to allow the entire appliance to travel all the way unimpeded. His only hope is if he can take preventative action to avoid the impact, and that doesn't look very likely as he doesn't appear even to have realised what's happening.

When it comes to men, my life has been relatively violence-free. Not so with women, of course, but I've only rarely been faced with an it's-him-or-me situation and, when I have, I've always employed what I call the Long Game, as I am doing now with the telephone, which is at least halfway to colliding with Barlow's head. The philosophy behind the Long Game is you disable your opponent when he least expects it, *before* you're within hitting distance. For example, once I upset some bloke because I'd been staring at his girlfriend and he gave it the 'outside now' routine. I tried to dissuade him but he was insistent. It was a cellar bar we were in and, on the way up the steps, I couldn't make up my mind between Plan A, which was to apologise profusely, plead for his forgiveness and then kick him in the balls when he was off his guard, or Plan B, run like hell. Then I saw the hanging basket at the top of the steps which I unhooked and dropped on him. After that, he didn't seem so keen on fighting me. In fact, he didn't seen keen on doing anything much apart from lying on his back and staring at the stars. Another time, a skinhead was coming at me fists clenched owing to a misunderstanding over a pint of lager in a pub in Carnaby Street. Once again, I decided to play the Long Game. His posture and demeanour were unequivocal – he wanted to beat the shit out of me. So I picked up the bar stool I was sitting on and threw it at him. As it sailed through the air, I had terrifying visions of him catching it and throwing it back at me or of it bouncing off him and succeeding in nothing more than antagonising him and altering my fate from just a good beating to being maimed for life. But once again, I was lucky. The bar stool knocked him off balance just as he was walking past the stairwell to the gents' and down he went, pure slapstick.

The telephone base and the handset have come apart in midair and are now heading towards Barlow's head on parallel trajectories. But he still doesn't appear to have cottoned on to what is about to happen to him.

They say that pride comes before a fall, and just as I was starting to believe – physical prowess to the contrary – that I was somehow blessed with an uncanny ability to come out victorious in potentially violent situations, my fall came in the shape of Bernie Scarbrow. I knew he was a hard bastard. I'd never seen him in action but his reputation preceded him. You didn't mess with Bernie Scarbrow, that was the general idea. But at the time I fancied myself a bit of a clever bastard and didn't appreciate that I was playing with fire. There was a show being touted around town called *Lift Off*, a musical dealing with the first lunar landings. It had done great business in the States and Bernie Scarbrow, who was a concert promoter by trade, had hooked up with the American producers and assured them it would go down a storm on the Avenue. Despite being new to the theatre industry, I thought I knew it all, and after looking at the more than healthy money it had taken Stateside, I dived straight in as a co-producer, putting up a couple of hundred grand into the bargain. I've always been fairly straight in my business dealings over the years, but when an opportunity for a little scam has become available I've usually weighed up my options and the odds of detection and, if everything looks watertight, I've gone for it. This scam involved ticket allocations. The theatre held 963 seats but, as far as Bernie Scarbrow and the Americans were concerned, it held only 928. This fact remained undetected owing to my old friend Eddie Haymer, the general manager of the theatre, who co-ordinated the fiddle in cahoots with the people in the box office. We made about ten grand a week from the 'invisible' seats. Four grand went to Haymer, four grand went to me, and two grand went to the box office staff. The show did well at first and played to full houses. After a couple of months, however, it began to run out of audience and sales slumped. But even though the house was only half full each night, we still made sure the thirty-five 'invisible' seats were in the full half.

Whether I was grassed up by one of the box office staff who didn't think they were receiving a big enough cut, I don't know, but one day Bernie Scarbrow went to the theatre and walked around the auditorium and counted the seats. He didn't phone me – Bernie didn't do business like that; he preferred the personal touch. His background was South London villainy and getting solicitors involved wasn't his style at all. I knew there was something wrong when he limped into my office. He was limping because he was only wearing one shoe. The other one was in his right hand and it was with this that he beat me. The whole situation was made all the more humiliating by the fact that I was in the middle of a meeting with a couple of people from an advertising agency we were using at the time, and they watched the whole thing. Bernie didn't hold the front of the shoe and hit me with the heel, as you might have expected, but held the heel end like a dagger and hit me with the front of the shoe with a kicking action, only using his hand instead of his foot. He didn't say a word throughout. He didn't even appear to be particularly angry, just went about his work with calm deliberation. When he deemed my punishment to be at an end, he put his shoe back on, apologised to the two people from the advertising agency, and walked out. I was in a terrible state, covered from head to foot in bruises. The advertising agency people offered to act as witnesses if I wanted to prosecute Scarbrow, but I decided it wasn't wise under the circumstances and declined their offer.

Thankfully, not long afterwards, *Lift Off*'s fortunes improved when we secured Tina Martinez, the ex-glamour model, as Neil Armstrong's wife and added an extra scene in which she took all her clothes off. This allowed me to pay back Eddie and the American luvvies all the money I'd embezzled from them, and no sooner had I done so than I walked away from the production and I've been as straight as a die ever since. The whole experience made me realise I'm not cut out for the rough stuff. Nowadays, my somewhat unusual sexual impulses aside, I live with the maxim that you don't dish it out if you can't take it, which makes my throwing the phone at Bill all the more perplexing.

The handset strikes him on the side of the head, the base hits him between the eyes, and down he goes behind his desk, sprawling on the carpet. I turn around and walk out of his office. Alerted by the sound of Bill's subsequent swearing, Sadie's on her feet and, as we pass in the corridor, she stares daggers at me while I smile back at her mock-sweetly. I press the button for the lift. I can hear them speaking in Bill's office and then she appears in the doorway. She pulls the door to so Bill won't be able to see out and strides purposefully towards me. I can hear the lift approaching, then it stops on the floor below. It's not going to reach me before Sadie does. She's got that look on her face she always wears when she's about to inflict pain on me. Before I even consider taking the stairs, an idea formulates in my mind and I find myself warming to it as she raises her hand and goes to hit me. I manage to duck the blow and, as I do so, I decide to put my plan into action immediately. I hit her. It's a transgression of every code of human decency but what the hell, this is self-defence, and she's bigger than me anyway. I don't hit her hard. It's a rabbit punch to the chin, a glancing blow which works with her forward momentum and sends her tumbling to the floor, cursing in Polish. By the time she's pulled herself to her feet, I'm in the lift and the doors are closing.

'Bye, Sadie,' I tell her. 'Pleasant evening.'

By the time the lift reaches the ground floor, I have a fully operational torture chamber constructed in my head in which Bill and Sadie are stretched out screaming while I go to work on them with my extensive arsenal of power tools, soaking myself in their blood as I reduce their respective body masses, limb by limb and chunk by chunk. My imaginings of torture and violent murder have become so much more satisfyingly vivid of late. It's like I can almost hear the chug of the chainsaw's engine, taste the droplets of warm blood on my lips and smell the burning flesh as I write slogans on their bodies with a soldering iron.

CONTACT

In the 1960s, while the Krays were carrying out their nefarious activities in the East End, there was another pair of brothers operating more small-time scams in the West End. Neville and Vernon Healy, or the Healy Boys as they were more widely known, may not have shared the notoriety of the Krays but their criminal intentions were no less ambitious. To say the Healy Boys controlled organised crime in the West End is to do a grave disservice to all the other gangsters and villains who competed for a slice of dodgy pie. Although they'd tell you otherwise, in truth the Healy Boys only controlled about half of the organised crime in an area of no more than a few hundred square yards on the westernmost fringes of Soho and just east of the Charing Cross Road. At the height of their business dealings, they owned or had stakes in fourteen establishments in the Soho area, all of them somewhat less than legitimate. There were three strip clubs, Red Hot Ladies, Live Girls and Girls! Girls! Girls!; two bars, the Soho Tap and the Belljar; three amusement arcades known collectively as Healy's Amusements; two peep-shows, the Gallery and Girls! Girls! Girls! (again); and in addition to these, they administered protection rackets on four sandwich and coffee bars owned by a Greek family by the name of Scopolos who eventually terminated the extortion themselves when they no longer found the Healy Boys scary enough to allow them to get away with it.

You've probably heard the story about the naïve tourists or Soho first-timers who go to a Soho strip club with the earnest belief they will see a strip show. They sit down and order a couple of drinks from the bar and before so much as a nipple has appeared, they are presented with some absurd bill, like fifty quid a drink and a hundred quid service charge. When they say they haven't got enough money they are told to leave all the money they have and get out. With a couple of tasty-looking blokes on the door, it works a treat. Well, it was the Healy Boys who started that whole scam. For a few years, it served them well until they were faced with a staff shortage and couldn't find, and didn't have the resources to pay for, hard enough looking blokes to work the door and do the frightening. When they were down to their last strip club, Girls! Girls! Girls!, the Healy Boys worked the scam themselves with money haemorrhaging left, right and centre. Well over half the punters told Nev and Vern to fuck off and walked out without paying for a thing. It even became known as a place where, if you had enough front, you could drink for free. You see, the problem with the Healy Boys both then and even more so now they're old men is they just don't look hard enough. Them being short, round and almost cherubic of countenance with blond hair and blue eyes, it's always been clear to everyone except the boys themselves they're in the wrong line of work.

When all their other activities had dried up due to ineptitude in business and inability to instil fear in potential extortion victims, the Healy Boys were left with just the Belljar, which, despite various efforts to the contrary, became a perfectly legitimate private members' drinking club in the late seventies. I became a member when I first started working in Soho, and it appeared that the only criterion they based membership on was the potential member's ability to listen to long, rambling stories about the Old Days and the network of small-time operators, failed hoods, petty low life, ex-cons and ponces the boys used to knock around with. I'd like a pound for every time I've heard the story of Neville and Vernon's one and only foray into violent crime. It was a South London post office job and, being unaccustomed to the use of guns, Vernon managed to shoot Neville in the leg before they'd even got through the door. Thankfully, they'd invested in a top-notch getaway driver, the near-legendary Tooting Dick, who managed to get Neville to the local accident and emergency unit in under four minutes.

Sometimes a character from the old days, such as Tooting Dick or the guy who used to cut Jack 'The Hat' McVitie's hair, comes along to the Belljar, and they'll all reminisce for hours about their failed attempts to crack the big time.

The Belljar is, for me, everything a private members'

drinking club should be. It's small, dingy, off the beaten track, completely understanding of its members' often bizarre drinking schedules and, unlike the Groucho and all those other cliquey holes dotted around Soho that are rammed full of industry fuckwits, other than me, the nearest anyone who drinks in the Belljar gets to the media and show business worlds is a copy of the *Racing Post* and a ten-quid hand shandy on the way to the night bus.

Even if I haven't been in for a couple of months, as was the case last night, I'm still assured of a welcome. To them I'm just Toe – 'All right, Toe?' – the bloke with the mysterious job who comes in from time to time to get pissed and talk bollocks. The reason my job is mysterious to them is I make sure I talk about it as little as possible. I go to the Belljar to escape my job, not to analyse it. So when they ask me what exactly it is I do, I tell them management. If they knew the circles I moved in and the money I earned, they might treat me differently, and I don't want that. The Belljar is a shrine to failure and thwarted endeavour, and I want to remain a part of it even if – in my case – it isn't strictly true. These two old men once genuinely believed they would make names for themselves, would achieve power and wealth, and now all that has turned to dust. But though they failed, their failure is a fuck-it-at-least-we-tried sort of failure and I love them for it.

Last night, the Belljar was, as always, being supported by the alcoholism of a handful of regulars who weren't unduly surprised by the sight of me with half a pint of blood down the front of my shirt. Owing to a lifetime spent on the fringes of the criminal underworld, they are always fascinated by violence and pumped me for information.

'I was mugged on TV,' is what I told them, and for once I gave them a few more details about my life than I normally would. Not that it felt like my life, not at all. It felt like I was playing out the part of some sad bastard who has to appear on the telly to validate his existence. I remember the first few glasses of tequila going down, easing the pain in my face and bolstering my desire for revenge. After that I remember absolutely nothing, although I do have a vague recollection of stumbling up the stairs to leave in the wee small hours.

'Jesus, Toe, you're getting to be a fuckin' regular,' says Neville as I come down the stairs, 'and it's not often we get to have a genuine celebrity in here.' He waves a rolled-up copy of the *Evening Standard* at me.

'Oh, it's all bollocks,' I tell him as I sit down on a stool at the bar. 'You know what the papers are like.'

'How's your head?'

'Like a bag of spanners.'

'And your nose?'

'Worse.'

'You were the most pissed I think I've ever seen you,' says Vernon, appearing in the doorway behind the bar. 'Bet you can't remember offering me a thousand quid to keep the bar open, can you?'

'What do you think?'

'It's a good job we're such good, honest, upright citizens,' says Neville. 'Now, what can I get you? Hair of the dog?'

'Go on, then, I'll have a bottle of Bud.'

'Oh,' says Vernon, and points at me as though he's just remembered something he needs to tell me off about, 'you can keep the bloody riff-raff out next time an' all.'

'Meaning?'

'That bloody down-and-out you brought back with you.'

'What are you talking about?'

'Well, you said your goodbyes and you left. It must have been, oh, what, 'bout two o'clock. You were already in pieces by then but not five minutes later you came back with that tramp bloke with the long hair and you carried on drinking for another hour. It was then you offered me the grand to keep the bar open, but grand or no grand, I figured you'd had enough.'

'So, let me get this right, I was in here with the tramp who keeps muttering to himself?'

'Ralph, that's right. I wouldn't have let him in normally, but you were insistent and I was too tired to argue. He stank the place out. I had to get the air freshener out this morning.'

This information regarding Ralph has stimulated some electrical activity in the alcohol-ravaged circuit boards of my grey matter and my brain starts downloading some blurred and shaky images from its memory banks. It was dark. I was outside the Belljar. I'd just left. I was going home. I was drunk but not hopeless. I headed towards Charing Cross Road through Compton Yard and there he was, slumped against a wall. He was clutching a bottle of cooking sherry and as soon as he saw me he started going on and on about Kelly this and Kelly that as always, but for some reason – it must have been the tequila – I found myself wanting to talk to him, wanting to connect. It was as though he were warning me against this Kelly character and calling me Kelly at the same time.

I'm beginning to feel increasingly uncomfortable, as though there's a piece of information locked within a memory of last night that's just out of reach and it's something I know I'm not going to like. Vernon is speaking to me, but none of it's going in. I'm getting flashes of last night after I'd left the Belljar for a second time, stumbling along shiny, rain-drenched London streets with Ralph, pissing in shop doorways, throwing up, shouting at cabbies who wouldn't pick us up. Me and Ralph. The two of us. Together. Going home. But why? Why did I want to take Ralph home? What was my motivation? I feel the blood rush to my cheeks as I finally catch up with last night's dark secret. I took Ralph home with me because I wanted to kill him.

'Sorry, Vern, Nev, I've got to go. I'll explain later.' I take the steps two at a time and sprint down the alleyway on to Charing Cross Road, where I manage to hail a taxi.

'Where to, mate?'

'Ladbroke Grove. It's an emergency. Please go as fast as you can.'

Unfortunately, this isn't very fast. We're caught behind a line of buses. I'm thinking so hard it makes my head ache. I can remember ushering Ralph through the front door of Calamity Towers and feeling an almost sexual rush of nervous excitement in anticipation of what I was going to do to him. I wanted to release the rage and hatred gnawing at my insides, erase my humiliation and build a bridge to a better place. The real Tobe Darling was breaking out of his cocoon. I'd bludgeon Ralph with a hammer – that was it, it's coming back to me now – I'd cave his head in, snuff him out, dead him, whack him, rip him from this mortal coil, then leave his corpse amidst the remains of my former self.

'Can't we take to the back streets?'

'Won't make any difference.'

'But it's an emergency.'

'So you keep saying.'

My memory finally throws in the towel and refuses to yield any more information, and I sit staring at the back of the cabby's head, imagining him telling some future passenger about the murderer he had in the back of his cab the other day. 'You know, the one from Ladbroke Grove who killed that old wino for no apparent reason whatsoever. They should string him up, if you ask me.'

By the time we turn into Desford Gardens I'm sick with fear, and because I don't want to wait for the cabby to sort out the change, I do what would normally be unthinkable and I tell him to keep it. My first-ever tip for a taxi driver. My trembling-jelly fingers fumble with the keys, unlock the front door and I'm in.

This morning, when I left Calamity Towers, there was no sign of him in my bedroom and he wasn't in the living room because I called the cab from there. He wasn't in either of the bathrooms and he wasn't in the kitchen, which leaves three more bedrooms and the dining room.

'Ralph?' My voice trembles and cracks and bounces back at me from the bare walls. 'Ralph?' Louder this time, as though I can muster a reply through sheer force of will. If only it were that easy. Silence. Fear makes me angry and I growl 'Ralph' one last time before stomping up the stairs.

The doorbell rings. I'm two steps short of the landing. Whoever it is will have heard my shouting and will know I'm here. Besides, God willing, it might even be Ralph. I turn around, go back down and pull the door open. It's the bloke from next door. Michael Willoughby. He's an investment banker or something. Shedloads of money. We've never had much to do with each other. He likes to involve himself in local affairs, runs the local residents' association. He has always eyed me with suspicion owing to my refusal to join in with any of his self-important little gatherings.

'Hello, Tobe, how are you?'

'All right.'

'Good.' He makes a move towards the door, assuming I'll ask him in. I don't so he checks himself and takes a step back, making no attempt to disguise the disdain on his face.

'I was wondering if we might have a brief word about the state of your garden.'

'Oh yeah?'

'Obviously, how you choose to maintain your garden, if maintain is the right word, is entirely your own business. However, when your garden is no longer contained within the confines of your own land then I'm afraid it becomes an issue that affects your immediate neighbours. There are four gardens directly adjoining yours. All the residents concerned have voted me as their representative. I have their names here' – he waves a scrap of yellow legal paper at me – 'and I'm here to tell you enough is enough.'

I know he's right. My garden, once a haven of tranquillity in the midst of the urban wasteland, is now a dark, overgrown canker erupting into my neighbours' gardens on every side. I watch it from the upstairs windows sometimes, and it just never stops. Every day it grows wilder, the grass and shrubs and weeds grow higher and cast deeper shadows. I know I'll have to do something about it sooner or later but now is not the time. I have to find out whether I'm a murderer or not.

'Can't we talk about this some other time?'

'I'd much rather come to some sort of arrangement now. You see, I'm away at a conference for the next few days and I really feel we need to resolve this matter as soon as possible.'

Willoughby is one of those upper-middle-class types who feel they have been blessed with the ability to communicate with any person on any level of society. They maintain this false front of amiability which they wrongly assume will conceal their total lack of sincerity.

'Look, Michael, I'm very busy. I'm just on my way out to a very important meeting, so if you'll excuse me . . .' I go to shut the door but the cheeky bastard reaches out to prevent me.

'I'm sorry, Tobe, but you see we've spoken about this before and, if you remember, you did promise you would consider employing a gardener.'

'That's correct, Michael. I have considered a gardener and I've decided I won't bother. I'm quite happy with how things are at the moment.'

He laughs in that haughty you're-being-so-unreasonable way and I consider continuing my new-found trend for violence and lamping him one. The thought of Ralph and what might or might not remain of him stops me.

'Really, Tobe, this won't do.' His hand is still propping open the door.

'Michael, please let go of my door.'

'Tobe, we have to speak about this.' He's getting angry.

'Yes, but not now.'

'When, then?'

'Soon.'

'Come on, Tobe, name a time.' He's really beginning to piss me off and I can't contain my anger any longer.

'Michael, I'm going to shut this door now. What you're involved in at this particular moment in time is trespass. So please, I'm sure you don't want to break the law.'

'I need to know when we can discuss this.'

'Fuck off, Michael.' I manage to get the door closed and, as I do so, he shouts, 'No, you fuck off, Tobe. You really are the most odious little creep I've ever had the misfortune to come across.'

He's right, I probably am, but I find it a personal affront that someone like Willoughby should even exist, let alone try to come into my home, violate my privacy and slag me off. He even fucking swore. The cunt. When someone like me swears it doesn't really mean a lot. When someone like Willoughby swears, its incongruity lends it a certain gravity. Still, I've got better things to worry about than my public image with my neighbours.

I check each of the bedrooms on the first floor bar mine – I know he isn't in there. Nothing. I take the stairs to the second floor. There are two rooms up here, a boxroom and Scarlet's room. I try the boxroom but he's not in there. I throw open the door to Scarlet's room and step inside. There's someone in the bed. I pull the covers back. It's Ralph. He's asleep. I'm not a murderer. An enormous wave of relief breaks over me, marred only by the thought that it was probably just my being so rat-arsed that saved him. I consider waking him but he'll only start rambling on as he always does so I pull the covers back over him. As I do so, the phone rings and I go down to the first-floor landing and wade through the clothes in my bedroom to take the call on the phone on my bedside table.

'Hello.'

'Hello, Mr Tobe Darling.' The voice is distorted by some electronic gizmo and sounds like a metallic Donald Duck.

'Who is this?'

'I'm the man who's bringing a lot of happiness to a lot of people. Your words, I believe.'

'Look, I'm not playing games. Tell me who you are or bugger off.'

'I have many names but the one that appears to be most popular at the moment is the Piper.' I always thought all that stuff about the hairs on the back of your neck standing up was just a fictional device that never really happened in real life but mine're bolt upright and I'm shit scared.

'Bollocks, you're not the Piper. You're just some wanker winding me up because you've seen me in the paper or on the telly.'

'If you want me to prove it to you it can be arranged.'

'OK, then, I'll take you up on that. If you're the Piper I want you to go and find that bloke who was on the show with me last night, Hugo Blain, and when you do, I want you to kill him. Now, piss off and leave me alone.'

R'n'R

She wears satin shorts and a white singlet and prowls around me like a cat. Her name is Oy and we do this every day. I like the routine. I come here at about noon and she gives me a massage. It's painful, she makes sure of that. It's probably a good massage as well, but I'm not particularly interested in whether it's good for me or not. I'm only here for the pain. I moan a bit as she digs her fingers into my clammy flesh, but no one's listening or if they are they don't care. I know the massage is at an end when she cracks me across the bare buttocks with her open hand, a blow of such ferocity it makes the follicles on my head tingle. Then it begins. She pulls me to my feet and loosens me up with a couple of jabs to the solar plexus. While I'm attempting to inflate my lungs, she spins around, the blurred outline of a leg lashing out towards my groin. The precision of her blows never ceases to amaze me. She used to be a professional kick-boxer so you'd expect her to be accurate, but to kick me with such precision that she flicks the end of the meat without touching the veg? It's astonishing. When she did this on the first day I was here, I thought it was a fluke, but now she does it every day. The pain is intense, of course, but causes no lasting damage. That's the great thing about Oy. She's a professional. She causes a lot of superficial pain but apart from the occasional minor bruise, there's not a trace of her handiwork.

I stagger backwards, feeling as though the old chap's been slammed in a car door. This amuses her and she cackles gleefully before spinning around and slamming her foot against my throat. Slaps rain down on my head, none of them particularly hard but of such speed and frequency it feels as though she's got about five pairs of hands. She takes hold of my wrists and pulls me on top of her with her legs bent and feet pressed against my stomach. When she pushes her legs straight, I flip over and land on my back. It's like the wrestling I used to watch on TV when I was a kid. The thing is, all those guys knew how to fall and I don't. It seems as though every time I'm on the point of taking a breath she steals away my prize. Every day, I lie here, as now, wondering whether she's gone too far and today will be the day she kills me.

'You like?' she asks me, but I can't reply – to do so would require air of which I have none. I do nothing except lie here and stare at her. Colourful patterns swim in my peripheral vision and I take these to be the onset of unconsciousness brought on by loss of oxygen. Then she starts to walk upon me, only it isn't walking as much as stamping on me. Despite this onslaught, I somehow manage to get some air into my lungs. Enough to keep me breathing, that is.

If I were capable of screaming I would. It's not so much the impact of her feet against my skin which causes me so much pain, it's the action she makes with her toes. It's as though, in the fraction of a second it takes to stamp on me, she manages to pinch my skin and pull it, as though trying to tear it away from my body. It's like being whipped with barbed wire. It's excruciating. The only sound I can hear during my silent agony is Oy's faint breathing and the action of her feet ripping at my skin. When she's finished, I can see great flashes of white light before my eyes, each flash of light corresponding to a pulse of my orgasm.

I sometimes think that, bearing in mind how much I pay her, she might not laugh at me in quite such a derisory way. It isn't in her brief. Mind you, I suppose it comes with the territory. She gives me a few seconds after the money shot then douses me with iced water. That isn't in the brief either. Well, the ice isn't, only the water. The thing is I genuinely think Oy enjoys her work and likes to see the job done properly. So, I get iced water. It's about ninety in the shade with a hundred per cent humidity so it comes as quite a shock to the system even when you know it's coming. The moment the water touches my clammy skin, my dick retreats into my body like a rat up a drain. She pulls me to my feet and wraps me in a sarong. I stumble out into the sunshine from under the palm-thatched canopy. There is a series of pathways through the woodland. I follow one meandering between ornamental pools in which languid carp are suspended, motionless save for the occasional flick of their gills. Some monkeys playfully chase a monitor lizard into the under-growth. Amidst the chatter of the insects, a bird – I presume it's a bird – makes a whooping noise that rises and falls in tone like someone blowing random notes on a recorder. Dotted among the tall coconut palms and raised up against the cliffs like tree-houses are cream pavilions, home to us guests of the Royal Rayuda Lodge.

Whether or not the management here are aware of my unusual tastes in massage, I don't know, but at five hundred quid a night they don't seem to care. As far as they are concerned, Oy is my private nurse. I procured her services through an agency in Bangkok called Wet Tomato, which specialises in unusual sexual partners. They cater for the connoisseur collector of exotic sexual experiences. While I wouldn't include myself in this group, I do appreciate their attention to detail and broad-minded, no-fuss attitude towards the huge catalogue of sexual urges an individual may fall prey to. They do a great line in chicks with dicks, I'm told.

At the beach, a smiling young Thai bloke in a white starched uniform hands me a couple of fresh towels and escorts me to my sunlounger, where I've left my sunglasses and my book. I order a double Scotch and, as he goes off to fetch it, I sit down and stare out at the beach and the sea breaking on it in white curls. A couple of British backpackers wander past. The only problem I have with Thailand is all the young Western holidaymakers who come here dressed in their Khao San Road sarongs and rip-off Oakley sunglasses clutching Lonely Planet guidebooks and dog-eared copies of *The Beach*. This is the hippie ideal, filtered down through thirty-five years of copping out. When the bloke comes back with the Scotch I'll tell him they're trespassing and see if I can get them evicted.

That's one of the reasons I like the Royal Rayuda Lodge – it's so expensive you don't have to put up with people who think they're making a statement by sporting a Celtic ring tattoo or getting something pierced.

You may be wondering what I'm doing in Thailand in a five-hundred-pounds-a-night resort. The truth of the matter is I just had to get away. I was cracking up back there. I hadn't had a holiday in five years, and the last one I did have was in Pamplona. It was a long weekend with Scarlet. I'd said I'd run with the bulls although I had no intention of doing so. It all boiled down to the fact that I knew she'd punish me when I chickened out. And she did. During the actual running of the bulls, we were ensconced in the honeymoon suite of the Sanguesa Hotel where Scarlet was thrashing the shit out of me with a rolled-up rubber shower mat. Not exactly a get-away-from-it-all. So, this time around, I thought I'd splash out. This place is very exclusive, very expensive and very discreet.

'Thank you,' I tell the waiter when he returns with my drink. 'Oh, and those two people over there' – I point at the British couple on the beach – 'I think they're thieves.' He looks confused. 'Stealing?' I try, and he nods. You can never be too sure how good these guys' English is, but he seems to get my drift and reaches for his walkie-talkie as he wanders off.

Though I'm here to recharge the batteries, this break isn't entirely for pleasure. I'm also here to do some work. A little research. I have a new client, you see. Since I told Bill to shove it, I suppose he's my only client. But a client who eclipses every pathetic wannabe pop star, hopeless actor and unfunny comedian who's come crawling to my door over the past few years.

When he phoned the first time, I was convinced it wasn't him. Serial killers don't, as a rule, seek personal management. I just figured it was a crank call from someone who'd watched *The Church of Q&A* or had read about what had happened in the *Standard*. Either that or it was some smart-alec media jerk having an ironic little joke at my expense, maybe a journo attempting a scam in order to prolong my ritual humiliation. Regardless of the perpetrator, the more I thought about offering some advice to the Piper, the more it appealed to me. Though I was still convinced the call was the work of a practical joker, I found myself musing on my strategy if I did manage him. Over the next couple of days, I fell prey to fantasies involving my handling of the Piper's public image, and the flow of ideas released was so strong it made me realise I must have been chewing this subject over in my subconscious for some time.

While all this was going on in my head, Ralph and I were embarking on our new cohabitation in Calamity Towers. He's moved in, you see, although to say this implies he's made a decision to live with me and has brought his belongings with him. The reality of the situation is, after I'd taken him home with me that night with the intention of killing him, he never left. But any hopes I may have harboured that introducing Ralph into a domestic environment – even one as dysfunctional as Calamity Towers – would calm him down were soon dashed. He's taken to sleeping during the day and, at night, he wanders through the house, often in total darkness, wrestling with his demons. Sometimes when he's shouting and mumbling it's as though he's trying to communicate something, as though he has a message for me, and it's just a matter of my decoding it. But even without this strange feeling, I don't think I could kick him out. Not now. I need to ease my conscience about wanting to – or at least thinking I wanted to – kill him. I also need to check I don't have a recurrent urge. This latter reason for letting him stay troubles me somewhat. I try not to consider whether my subconscious is engineering his close proximity to me so that in the event of another murderous impulse it can find an immediate release.

Bill left a few messages on the machine before I came away which I chose to ignore. On the first couple he was trying to sound upbeat and nonchalant, but I could tell he was terrified that without me the whole shit factory would come tumbling down around his ears. Which with any luck it will. The later messages were more desperate, the last one in particular.

'Tobe, we need to talk,' he said. 'There are issues here that are bigger than both of us. You can't just turn your back on all of this. We've busted our balls building this company up and I'm not going to let you throw it all away just because of some imagined slight on my part. So you've ended up on TV. You were the subject of some unwanted press attention. So fucking what? You know the score better than anyone. Everyone'll get bored with it in five minutes and then piss off and leave you alone. Christ, Tobe, you're as tough as old boots. Stop behaving like such a poof.' His voice cracked on the 'oo' of 'poof' and then he slammed the phone down. I never did call him back. I was going to just so I could tell him where he could shove it, but then Hugo Blain was murdered.

I don't often travel by Tube but that afternoon I was on a mission. I was on my way to Scarlet's office. It was the first time I'd left the house for days, and I was using my delivery of a stack of mail that had arrived for her over the past couple of months as an excuse to also deliver a letter to her, a real letter, with ink on paper, from me. In addition to the letter, there was also a chance, albeit a slim one, that I'd bump into her in the reception of the *International Profiles* building. After our last phone conversation, when I'd confronted her about Hugo Blain, I felt I needed to make contact, however fleetingly, and try to tell her the truth about him and what a mistake she was making.

The Tube always brings out the worst in me. As the approaching train rattles towards me through the tunnel and the displaced air blows in my face, my nerves jangle and I feel faint. When the front of the train breaks free of the tunnel and bursts into the station, I fall prey to an increasing sense of fatalism and, as the driver approaches me illuminated in his little cabin, I experience a whirlwind of emotions. Part of me is paranoid there's a nutter standing behind me who will wait until the train is level with me and then push me over, and another part of me wants to jump in front of the train and know I've reached the point of no return, that there is no turning back and in a few moments I'll be dead on the rails. In these situations, it's like part of me is daring another part of me to make the jump and the dared part is playing a double bluff and saying, 'OK, I'm going to do it. Now how do you feel?' Thankfully there's always another part of me that is strong enough to override this mental struggle, but I feel it's best not to tempt fate. Besides, even if I didn't have these feelings, I'd still avoid the Tube on account of the inappropriate psychological attachments I sometimes make with my fellow passengers. Usually this takes the form of me latching on to a person in my carriage and obsessing about who they are, where they're from, what they do and – more than that – what they're *into*. There have been times when I've missed my stop just so I can remain focused on a specific target. The worst instance was when I ended up following a woman home once just because she looked a bit like someone from a sitcom I used to watch as a kid. I didn't do anything. I didn't speak to her, just stood on the opposite side of the road to her in some ghastly north London suburb as she took the keys out of her bag and disappeared behind one of a row of identical front doors. I felt like shouting to her, 'I can make you famous.' Thankfully for both of us, I didn't. Although I could have made her famous, of course, if I'd wanted to. But I'm not interested in conducting a social experiment, seeing if I can take a no one and make them a star. That's been done to death. It'd be more interesting these days to see if you could take a no one and not make them a star. With this woman it was just that she looked as though she should be a star. That was all, and momentarily, in my semi-deluded state, hypnotised by the train and the intensity of coincidence that I should have been seated opposite her, it felt right I should tell her.

So, there I was sitting on the Tube train on my way to Scarlet's office when I found myself staring at a photograph of Hugo Blain on the front of the *Standard* someone was reading. He was winking at me, or at least that's how it looked owing to a crease in the paper which opened and closed with the motion of the train. It was a shot of him either entering or leaving a social function. He was wearing black tie and grinning his everybody-loves-me grin. It took a moment for it to register. At first, I was more struck by the fact that it looked as though he was winking at me than the fact that he should be pictured on the front of the paper. Then I read the headline. TV PRODUCER SHOT DEAD.

The next stop was Baker Street. I rushed off the train, took the steps up the escalator two at a time and bought a *Standard* in the ticket hall. My hands were shaking so much I had a problem holding it still as I read: *Leading TV producer Hugo Blain was found dead on the steps of his north London home late last night. Police confirmed Mr Blain died from a single gunshot wound to the head. Detective Chief Superintendent Michael Ross, who is leading the murder investigation, said it was too early to discuss a possible motive for the murder.* And so it went on. I took the letter I'd written to Scarlet out of my pocket, tore open the envelope and read it through once again:

Dear Scarlet,

As a means of communication, words were never our strong point. I always felt our relationship transcended words and relied on some sort of psychic exchange. So it is only as a last resort I am forced to put pen to paper. I won't drag this out. I'll say what needs to be said and leave you alone. While I can appreciate your desire to distance yourself from my 'emotional wreckage', I fail to understand your methods. Whatever your relationship with Hugo Blain is, it is a mistake first and foremost. Whether you are genuinely giving me a final shot of pain as you said on the phone last week, which I doubt, or whether you have genuine feelings of affection for the man, which I find almost impossible to believe, you should at least be aware that you are being used as a pawn in a game that started over twenty years ago. Whether Hugo has chosen to tell you about our time at school I neither know nor care, but please understand that his pursuit of you and my appearance on that ghastly TV show, although seemingly unconnected, are, in fact, all part of Blain's on-going campaign to renew hostilities between us. Why he wants to do this I have no idea, but I suspect he feels I've become too big for my boots and it's time I was cut down to size. That's all I can think. I have successfully managed to avoid him for over twenty years, but he seems hell-bent on forcing himself into a leading role in my life once again.

Scarlet, don't become the plaything of Hugo Blain. I'm not trying to control your life or anything sinister like that. I just want you to know what you are dealing with here. You deserve the facts.

Love,
Tobe

I screwed the letter up and went to throw it in the bin. But there weren't any bins. They don't have them in Tube stations these days – too easy for a terrorist to conceal a bomb, and that's just what I felt like. I had to get rid of the letter. I ran up the stairs and found a bin outside the station. I stuffed it inside the newspaper and threw them both in the bin. But as I was walking away the thought of someone, somehow, finding the letter and making the connection with Blain's murder made me walk back and pick the screwed-up newspaper from the bin and take the letter out and tear it into little pieces. I took some of the pieces with me to put in another bin.

The journo in the *Standard* hadn't been slow to spot the coincidence that Hugo had appeared on *The Church of Q&A* the week before with the 'loathsome' Tobe Darling, the man who had suggested that a vicious serial killer was bringing happiness to people. The police would beat a path to my door pronto.

Thankfully, despite my jittery mental state after my initial discovery of Blain's murder, I did the right thing. I telephoned Charlie Gifford.

Gifford is mine and Bill's lawyer. Just as it is our job to come to the rescue of celebrities and members of the showbiz shit factory who have fallen foul of the media and therefore their adoring public, so Gifford works his magic for the same bunch when their extra-curricular activities fall foul of our guardians of law and order. Like all the best lawyers, he is totally bereft of any morals or scruples. So long as you're the one paying his exorbitant fees, it doesn't matter if you're Vlad the Impaler – he'll treat your accusers as though they are attempting to perpetrate the most appalling injustice. What's more, you always get the feeling with Gifford that even if you were accused of murdering his own mother, he'd whip you up a quick self-defence plea and convince all concerned that she had it coming to her. I didn't tell him about my phone call from the Piper, of course. I thought it was best left unmentioned. Gifford suggested I should be totally up front about everything and call the police. Offer to help. They might suspect me at first, but as I had done nothing wrong they'd soon realise this and leave me alone. This worried me somewhat because I had broken Gifford's first and, so he claimed, most important rule. I'd lied to him. Gifford doesn't give a shit about what anyone has actually done. So long as he knows what it is. Whatever you might have done, however bad it might be, Gifford demands to know the truth so that – as he puts it – he knows what he's supposed to be safeguarding.

When I walked into Highgate police station, where the murder inquiry was being conducted, and asked to speak to Michael Ross, the bloke in charge of the investigation, I was more than a little nervous. Ross seemed like a decent bloke, which made me despise him immediately. He asked me a lot of questions and I really laid it on thick about how I'd known Hugo at school and how, although we hadn't always been the best of mates, we had developed a sort of grudging respect for each other in recent years. He already knew about Hugo and Scarlet. He'd done his homework, but he seemed to relax when I spoke of things so openly. I told him almost everything, but I didn't tell him about my and Scarlet's unorthodox relationship or the bit about the telephone conversation with a man who sounded like Donald Duck and claimed to be London's premier serial killer. I figured these were pieces of information best left out, all things considered.

My confidence was bolstered by the knowledge that I had a watertight alibi. At the time of Blain's murder, I was in the Witherton, a private hospital (more like a luxury hotel) where I was recuperating after a minor operation to straighten my nose after the little Scottish bastard's attempts to rearrange it. Even with this alibi, I could feel guilt pouring off me in rivers of sweat. But despite my paranoia that I might blow it, I must have put on a convincing show, because Ross didn't ask to see me again, and the fact that he's allowed me to leave the country while the investigation is in full swing means he can't be too interested in me.

Once my initial pangs of guilt had subsided, I grew to like the idea of Hugo being dead. When all was said and done, he had it coming to him, and it meant Scarlet was that little bit more attainable. It also gave me an opportunity to phone her and offer up my condolences. She told me to fuck off, but I could tell she didn't mean it. Sure enough, on the day I left to come here, she called me and we arranged to speak on my return and maybe meet up. A couple of weeks earlier, this glimmer of hope of a reconciliation would have sent me into hours of obsessing on the best ways to capitalise on it, but since the Piper had made contact with me and proved his credentials, it became little more than a minor diversion from my on-going plans for his career. He was out there somewhere, a man capable of killing not only with the self-indulgence and ritualism of the serial killer but also, when required, the speed and ruthless efficiency of a hit-man and, in both cases, leaving behind not one scrap of evidence that could link him to his crimes.

I knew he'd call. It was just a matter of time. When he did I found myself talking not to Donald Duck as last time but to Droopy in all his cartoon glory. I've spoken to some big stars in my time but as we started talking – joke voice and all – it occurred to me he was probably the most famous person I'd ever spoken to.

'I'm impressed,' I told him.

'Don't be.'

'One minute you're the Piper, to all intents and purposes an out-and-out psychopath, and the next you're an assassin. Weren't you tempted to overindulge and do a bit of a Piper number on him?'

'There's no point confusing the boundaries. I didn't want him to be a Piper killing. It just wasn't right.'

'I take it this call cannot be traced.'

'It can be, but only as far as Bombay where I'm routing it via an Indian government call centre. I'm what people like you used to call a computer nerd. So, you don't have to worry about privacy. No one's listening. I'd know about it if they were.'

'Well, you've proved your credentials. What do you want from me?'

'When I saw you on TV that day, you fascinated me. At first I felt nothing but contempt for you, but then you started going on about me. You were everything I had never expected. You wrong-footed me. Initially I thought I might kill you as an ironic gesture. The one person in all the world who stands up for me and I kill him. I thought this might be a serious statement of intent like, "Look at me, I need no one, I kill the one person who openly admits to being a fan". But then I thought it might be interesting to start a dialogue with you and see if you could be of any use to me.'

It was impossible to detect any emotion, no way of knowing whether he was screaming the words like some frothing lunatic or muttering them quietly in a calm, measured tone. All I got was crackling, distorted Droopy. Despite the fear I'd felt when he said he'd considered bumping me off, I decided I'd front it out.

'I don't see what's in it for me. My advice is expensive, and if I were to have anything to do with you, I'd be an accessory to murder.'

'You're not interested in money, Tobe, and as far as getting caught is concerned, forget it. It won't happen.'

'So what makes you think I'd like to become involved in your career, if that's an appropriate term for what you do?'

'You're a man of vision and imagination. I've done my homework on you.'

In the space of two weeks I'd been well and truly evicted from my island of anonymity. I'd been researched not only by the usual media vampires but also by the most notorious homicidal maniac currently practising in the Western world. I was beginning to feel that my life was becoming an open book.

'Go on,' I told him, trying to sound as though I couldn't care less. 'Tell me about me, then.'

That's when he laughed. It seemed that the electronic gizmo he used to contrive the cartoon impersonations couldn't cope with laughter and sounded as though it were laughing of its own accord, entirely independent of any outside stimulus.

'This is a golden opportunity for you,' he said when he'd calmed down. 'You're bored with your job, you're tired of all the ambition and ego of your clients, so why don't you take up a new challenge and become a pioneer? I'll bet this has never been done before.'

He was right, of course. It was as though he had tapped into my subconscious. My life was shit. My attempts at satisfying my ceaseless psychosexual addictions were becoming more and more desperate. Scarlet had kept me from myself. She'd kept me from the edge and, without her, I was lost. I knew I had to let the Piper into my life. Giving yourself to your destiny is just the only way sometimes. *Che sarà sarà*, in the words of some old fart.

'Are you suggesting what I think you might be suggesting?' I asked.

'You decide,' he said.

'But surely you're driven by uncontrollable urges to kill and destroy. Surely you can't just switch it on and off.'

'Who's to say that to be a serial killer you have to be driven by uncontrollable urges? Don't judge me by the rules of criminal psychology and deviancy theories. Some kids dream of becoming famous footballers or pop stars; I dreamed of becoming a serial killer. Let's get this straight right from the start – I don't kill people because I have to. I could stop whenever I wanted. Nothing drives me to kill. As far as killing is concerned I am completely existentially free from all the guilt and the horror usually associated with it. I kill as an act of creation. I want to leave my mark on the world. I want everyone to know my name. The best any pop star or celebrity can hope for is the adulation of millions. Well, I want to go one better than that. Adulation ebbs and flows. Fans are fickle. No, I want to be feared by millions. Not like a fictional character in a film or a book, but because there's a very real possibility my next victim could be you. It's like the lottery. Only instead of a finger pointing at you, it's a big knife I'm holding, and instead of lavishing riches on you, I'm going to rip you apart.'

When I told him I would be leaving the country for a couple of weeks, he suggested we keep in touch via e-mail. As with his phone calls, which are diverted through so many countries' networks and accounts that to unravel them to their source would be impossible, his e-mail system is similarly tamper-proof. His e-mail address is thepiper@eviscerate.com. He finds this amusing.

At the airport, on the way out here, I bought a book called *Serial Killers, Society's Folk Devils* by an American criminologist called Irvine Mannesmann. It's basically a roll-call of all the truly great serial killers from Jack the Ripper right up to Enrique Hernandez, 'The Beast of Havana'. In the introduction, Mannesmann tries to make out that the book is a serious analysis of motives and psychology, but in reality it's all just jazzed-up tabloid reportage with as many lurid full-colour pictures of victims and scenes of crime as possible. The cover design is a bloody red handprint on a white-tiled wall. It was exactly what I was looking for. I don't want to study these men as a criminologist does. I have only a passing interest in why they do what they do. What I am interested in is their fame; why and how they became as famous as they did. You might be able to tell me about some seriously twisted maniac with a massive body count, but unless he managed to capture the zeitgeist, then I'm not interested.

With serial killers, as with all things, there are good and bad. I don't mean morally, of course – the only morality associated with serial killers is the fake moral outrage the media employ when discussing their crimes in order to excuse themselves and us, their consumers, from our enjoyment of all the gory minutiae – I mean good or bad as an aesthetic judgment of their work and contribution to the canon. Serial killing has had a tough time of it in recent years. There's been some fierce competition from spree killing, particularly in America. Spree killing is all about people breaking down mentally, reaching the end of the line, snapping, whatever you want to call it, and then going on a murderous rampage. It's nearly always just a suicide trip, only the suicide or suicides decide to take a few other suckers along for the big dirt bath. School kids make up the majority of the spree killers in America and, let's face it, American adolescents have got no class, even if they do occasionally accumulate impressive body counts. Someday soon, some American kid is going to wipe out an entire school with a bomb he's knocked up in his bedroom. Instructions on the Internet – you can see the headlines, but as always seems to be the way in these situations, the chances are he (she would be more interesting but unlikely) will either go up with it or top himself. The way I see it, the most fundamental rule to abide by if you want a successful career in murder, and the one all the American school kids appear to struggle with, is: always kill other people; don't kill yourself. What spree killing needs if it really wants to compete with serial killing is for someone to wipe out his classmates or neighbours or work colleagues and then decide they want to go on killing other people's classmates, neighbours or work colleagues, and carry out a succession of similar murdering sprees elsewhere. Like a sort of serial spree killer.

Competition aside, another problem facing the modern-day serial killer is the improvement in police methods of detection. With offender profiling, DNA testing and the advances in forensics generally, all the odds are stacked in favour of the boys in blue. Take Russia, for example. It's churning out serial killers nineteen to the dozen, but because the police force has finally got its act together, the killers are caught relatively quickly and carted off to jail, funny farm or government-sanctioned abattoir. Since Chikatilo, they rarely achieve even the most minor celebrity.

One way of achieving a high body count in relative safety from police intervention is to develop a 'house of horror' scenario and store your victims at home. This way, you can make sure the evidence of the crimes stays away from prying eyes. If your victims are also from a 'forgotten' demographic like down-and-outs and drifters, then you can remain at large for a considerable period of time. The problem with the 'house of horror' serial killer, however, is that storage of all the evidence becomes increasingly difficult (and malodorous) as time goes on, and as far as the celebrity angle is concerned, your impact is diminished by a lack of freshly killed victims, not to mention the fact that all your publicity comes in one hit rather than being allowed to develop organically over a period of time.

There's no question, when it comes to murder the nomadic serial killer is top dog. No other type of killer can generate the fascination, the intrigue and, most importantly, the fear he can. On the inside back cover of Mannesmann's book, I've scribbled the following list of rules which any aspiring serial killer would do well to study.

1. Get a name. Bestow one on yourself if needs be. Make sure it's something snappy and idiosyncratic that will be adopted by journalists and public alike.
2. Develop a dialogue with the media.
3. Encourage a gladiatorial contest with the police.

Mock them. Goad them. Exert your superiority over them.

4. Ensure that your crimes are truly savage and depraved. There's nothing like some good old-fashioned shock tactics to make yourself known.

5. Develop a 'signature' to your murders. This will add further mystery. The police will admit there is a signature but will not disclose details for fear of copycat crimes. The public's imagination will run riot. It also has a secondary purpose in that it means a copycat killer cannot come along and bag one of your kills.

6. Operate in a country that has a sophisticated news network where details of your activities can reach the largest possible audience. It's no coincidence that the countries with the most sophisticated broadcasting and publishing industries are the ones with the most famous serial killers. And if you're getting some excellent coverage, it's bound to make you up your game.

7. Don't get caught. After a few good years at large with a healthy body count, a high-profile arrest can create a media roadblock, but this is where most serial killers becomes unstuck publicity-wise. It's impossible to perpetuate the legend of the Mad Beast or the Monster when all there is in front of the camera is a dysfunctional dullard in a knitted tank top and spectacles. So don't get caught and, if you do, make sure you look and behave the part and, if at all possible, escape.

I toy with the idea of writing down a sort of hit parade

of all-time great serial killers, taking their details from Mannesmann's book and scoring them on style, body count and all-round story content. But the Scotch has made me drowsy and I close the book and rest my head back on the sunlounger.

SERIAL

'Mr Lowenstein will see you now,' says the man. 'Please
follow me.'

We set off down the corridor and through a door that
has the words P. Victor Lowenstein on it in gold letters
so large they barely fit within the door frame. The office
is enormous, with a huge collection of exotic potted plants
and, in the middle, a round desk with two chairs at
it. The far wall is a sheet of tinted glass, and there's a
door set into it that leads out on to a lawn on which
peacocks strut about with huge butterflies flapping to and
fro above them.

'Please take a seat,' says the man. 'Mr Lowenstein will
be with you in a moment.'

'Should I call him Mr Lowenstein, Victor or just plain
P?'

'Victor will be fine.'

The man leaves and I take a seat at the round desk
in the middle of the room. The walls are covered with

photographs of famous Hollywood actors and actresses. Most of them are taken at the Academy Awards, and big grins and gold statuettes abound.

A man whom I can only presume to be P. Victor Lowenstein saunters across the lawn and in through the door. He looks like a cross between a fat Robert de Niro and a sherry-advertising-era Orson Welles.

'Hey, Gus, how's it going?' he says.

'Fine, thanks, although it's Tobe actually.' My hand disappears into his and is neither shaken nor squeezed but momentarily moistened.

'I'm sorry,' he says as he lowers his gargantuan backside into a chair to the accompaniment of a loud farting noise which could come from the chair or could come from him – it's difficult to tell.

'So, Toby, whatchya got for me?'

'It's, erm, it's Tobe. T-O-B-E, Tobe.'

'OK, OK, I'm sorry.'

'That's all right. No problem.'

'Please call me Victor. V-I-C-T-O-R, Victor.'

'Right you are, Victor. Now, I've drawn up a list of the most likely candidates for the part and I thought we might just run through them and see if there's anyone you particularly like the look of.' I hand him a document on which there are some photographs with brief biographical details written next to each one. 'Before we start, can you just confirm at what stage you're at in development?'

'Development?' he says, as though this were the most absurd question he ever heard. 'There are so many green lights shining in my eyes at the moment I need a new pair of fuggin' sunglasses.' He roars with laughter at this and I let out a half-hearted chuckle just to show willing.

'And you're still going to call it *Serial*, I take it?'

'Uh huh. It'll make every other serial killer movie ever made look like a walk in the park. That's why the lead is so key.'

'OK, first up we've got a German by the name of Peter Kurten, otherwise known as "The Monster of Dusseldorf".'

'Don't like Germans, Gus.'

'It's Tobe.'

'Sorry.'

'Kurten's a pretty strong character actually, although his profile isn't as high as it might be. As a child he enjoyed stabbing animals to death while sodomising them. Now he's graduated to humans, he's developed a fondness for drinking their blood after he's killed them.'

'Nah, nobody wants another vampire movie.'

'There're a couple of decent Brits here either of which might be right. There's Peter Sutcliffe. The one with the beard there. He's also known as "The Yorkshire Ripper" and he's racked up a good body count, although he's a little difficult to work with, I hear. And then there's Dennis Nilsen below him, just there.'

'Looks like a producer I used to know at Paramount.'

'Yeah?'

'Good golfer he was.'

'Nilsen kills his gay lovers as a means of preventing them leaving his flat. He's arrested because a neighbour of his calls the drainage engineers to come and unblock a drain and, when they turn up, they find it's blocked with decaying human flesh.'

'Plumbing doesn't sell. Believe me. Got any Americans?'

'Plenty. How about that one there?'

'This guy here with the tattoos?'

'Carl Panzram, that's the one. He's a totally unrepentant psychotic who butchers people all over the world. On one occasion, in Africa, he hires eight natives under the premise of organising a hunting trip, then drugs them, rapes them in turn and feeds their bodies to the crocodiles.'

'Looks like a troublemaker to me. Never trust a man with tattoos, that's my motto.'

'Well, how about the one at the bottom of the page there. That's him. Albert Fish. He's the oldest man to go to the electric chair in the USA. According to the shrink who studies him, he's practised every sexual perversion known to man and a few others besides. Although convicted and sentenced to death for the murder of a little girl he chopped up and ate in a stew, it's thought he's killed many more. He's a religious nut, likes to beat himself and stick needles into his groin which cause the electric chair to short out when they fry him. Just look at that face – it's pretty scary.'

'Too old. We need someone younger. Someone who's going to make the girls horny.'

'In that case, how about Richard Ramirez just over the page there. He's known as "The Night Stalker".'

'Like the name.'

'Ramirez breaks into houses in the dead of night and shoots, bludgeons or mutilates the occupants depending on his mood. Sometimes he carves satanic messages on their corpses. When the judge sentences him to death, he comes out with a great line. He says, "Death comes with the territory. See you in Disneyland."'

'He's more like it, I'll grant you. Looks like trailer trash, though. Got anyone a bit more up-market?'

'How about a doctor?'

'A doctor could work.'

'How about this guy, then? Dr H.H. Holmes. He kills most of his victims in "The Castle", a house he has built opposite his surgery complete with secret passages, trapdoors, hidden staircases, soundproofed rooms that double up as gas chambers, and a dissection laboratory in the basement.'

'I like the story but I don't like his face. Too old-fashioned. No one has a moustache these days. Got anyone better-looking?'

'Albert de Salvo, "The Boston Strangler"? He's got a bit of a Sinatra look to him.'

'Nah.'

'In that case, if you want good looks, there's Ted Bundy.'

'What's his story?'

'Bundy is a charming, handsome, Ivy League type who studies law and dabbles in politics. But beneath the surface, he's one of the most prolific and savage serial killers of all time. Suspected of killing upwards of fifty women, Bundy is captured but escapes not once, but twice.'

'He's a definite maybe. Who's next? Got any real sickos?'

'They're all sickos, Victor, but if you want someone who's really off the deep end, how about Ed Gein over the page?'

'Looks like some sort of redneck.'

'Oh, he is. Only beneath the rustic exterior he's a real

grade-A psycho. Gein's got a thing about his mother, you see. Can't get over her death. So what he does is dig up recently buried women from the local graveyard who look a bit like her and makes clothes out of their flesh and kitchen utensils from their bones. Eventually his tastes turn to murder, and that's when they catch up with him. Gein's a genuine American original.'

'Looks too much like a halfwit for my liking. What about this one here?'

'That's David Berkowitz. He operates in New York City and shoots people with his .44 Magnum. Calls himself "Son of Sam" on account of his neighbour of that name who Berkowitz believes is transmitting orders to him via his pet dog.'

'That's pretty far out, but he's a bit fat.'

'OK, then, how about Charles Manson? According to his prosecutors, he thinks the Beatles are communicating with him on their *White Album* and are urging him to start a race war. His victims are high-profile Hollywood types—'

'Whoa. That's a bit too close to home. We don't want to upset the staff. What about this guy here?'

'That's Henry Lee Lucas. He confesses to killing hundreds but it turns out he's exaggerating. If you want a high body count then the next one down's your man. Pedro Lopez, also known as "The Monster of the Andes". When Lopez gets going, he's unstoppable. On occasions he's been known to average three killings a week and is thought to be the most prolific serial killer of all time.'

'Looks like a pinhead. What about this bald guy here?'

'That's the Russian, Andrei Chikatilo. He lures children

and young women away from railway stations into nearby woodland and subjects them to the most frenzied and barbaric attacks imaginable. It takes the authorities years to catch up with him, and he succeeds in putting Russia firmly on the serial killing map.'

'There's going to be a language problem I take it?'

'Probably.'

'Jesus, what's this guy doing on the list? We're not running a circus here.'

'That's John Wayne Gacy, also known as "The Killer Clown". He's a pillar of the community – successful businessman, local politician, he even (as you guessed) entertains sick kids in the local hospital. In his spare time he picks up young men, rapes, tortures and strangles them, and then buries their bodies in the "crawl space" underneath his house in Chicago. He may prove difficult as he claims he's got an alter ego who carries out the killings.'

'Yes, schizos are hard work. Directors hate 'em. They're too much alike.'

'How about Jeffrey Dahmer? He's a class act. When the police break into his apartment, they find it littered with human body parts which he uses as sex toys and sometimes food. During his trial he reveals that he has attempted DIY lobotomies on some of his still-living victims and poured acid into their brains in an attempt to create zombies out of them.'

'It's that moustache thing again, I'm afraid.'

'We could have him shave it off?'

'No, he looks like a nerd. Come on, Gus, who do you think should get the part?'

'It's Tobe, but never mind. My own personal favourite, and by far the most notorious serial killer of them all, is the one down at the bottom of the last page.'

'Jack the Ripper?'

'Yup.'

'But there's no photograph.'

'That is a bit of a problem. No one knows who he is, but believe me, when it comes to serial killers, this bloke's Elvis, the Beatles and the Rolling Stones all rolled into one, and what sets him apart from all the rest is he's a bona fide legend.'

'Who's his agent?'

'Again, that's a bit of a problem.'

'Come on, Toby, what gives? I'm trying to make a movie here. I need someone under fifty, good-looking, brutal, menacing and available.'

'OK, Victor. There is someone else who's not on the list, and although I don't have a picture of him either, I do know how to get hold of him. He's called the Piper. He's new on the scene but, trust me, he's going to be massive. He films his murders while committing them and sends the videotapes to the police and the media. I don't have a biog but I do have a list of quotes here so you can see the sort of man you're dealing with.'

I take a sheet of paper from my folder and pass it to him. It reads:

The words sick, twisted and depraved are not adequate to describe these crimes.

Chief Inspector Brian Woolcot, leading the Piper investigation

The level of psychopathy displayed by this person is beyond belief.
Harvey Johannsen (forensic pathologist), *Independent*

. . . the sort of carnage usually associated with the grossest of splatter movies.

New York Times

The details of these murders are almost too sick-making to contemplate.

Mirror

Serial murder doesn't get more shocking than this.

Newsweek

This killer has ensured London goes to the top of the 'no-go' holiday destination list.

Guardian

What this man has done to our son is too unbearable to contemplate . . . I hope he rots in hell.
Muriel Mahune (mother of the Piper's first victim, Ted Mahune)

By videotaping these murders and sending the tapes to the media, the killer has ensured his place on the league table of 'worst serial killers of all time'.

Time magazine

The most notorious serial killer since Jack the Ripper.
Mail on Sunday

Victor looks up from the sheet of paper and grins at me. 'I like the look of this fella, Gus. He's got style. I'll get my

145

people to speak to his people and see if we can knock out some kind of deal.'

'Great, I'm glad you like him. By the way, it's Tobe not Gus.'

'Ah, lighten up a little, why dontchya.'

SNELLING

Daytime napping in tropical climes breeds dreams to die for. I wake up with a start and look up to see that the British couple are still here. In fact, they're more than just still here, they're spread out on two sunloungers on the beach in my clear line of sight. I beckon to the waiter, who hurries over.

'They're still here.'

'They stay at hotel,' he tells me.

'Those two there?' I point right at them and the bloke looks up from his book and returns my stare. The waiter nods enthusiastically.

'Well, bloody hell.'

I put on my sunglasses and, safe behind the dark lenses, I stare at them for a while, trying to suss out the deal. Neither of them is old enough to be earning the sort of money they'd need to stay here. Maybe they're lottery winners or one of them's got rich parents. But the money's definitely on his side of the family because she's really cute and he's a dog.

147

He's up off his sunlounger now and heading towards me. Fuck him, he can't tell I'm staring at him. Can he? He's still approaching. Maybe he can tell. I pick up Mannesmann and pretend to read.

'Can I help you?' he asks me. I look up from my book, trying to wear as blank an expression as possible.

'I'm sorry?'

'You keep staring at us.'

'You know, I really don't think I am. But perhaps if you tell me where you were sitting before you got up I might be able to tell you whether I was looking in your general direction.'

'Have you got some sort of problem with us being here?'

'You're full of questions, aren't you?'

'Well, first you try to have us removed from the beach, and then you sit and stare at us.'

'Is that your girlfriend?'

'She's my wife. We're on honeymoon.'

'Congratulations.' This throws him a little and he manages a 'thanks' under his breath, his tough-guy posturing in ruins. I've got the upper hand in this exchange and my confidence soars. He might have youth and fitness on his side but he doesn't have the imagination to launch a dirty and downright unfair attack as I have. If he comes anywhere near me, he'll wind up falling and cracking his head against the ice bucket on the drinks table next to my sunlounger. Accidentally, of course.

'Bye, now,' I say, and give him a smile teetering on the edge between sincerity and sarcasm. He says nothing, just shakes his head and slopes off.

'Give her one from me,' I say as he's going. He stops,

spins around and this time I can tell he means business. He won't try anything physical, he doesn't have that level of commitment, but he's going to have a shout about things to make him feel as though he's defending wifey's honour. But he doesn't make it. As he takes a step towards me, a tall, slightly stooped figure dressed in baggy khaki shorts and a garish Hawaiian shirt appears from behind me and, pointing a long, nicotine-stained finger at him, says, 'Piss off, sonny.'

'But he . . .'

'I said piss off, now piss off.'

All the psychological mechanics of a potential fight are stacked in his favour. He's bigger, older, uglier and looks like he doesn't give a toss. The young bloke swears and flounces back to the missus. My defender watches him go, then turns around to face me and I get a good look at him for the first time.

'Tobe Darling, you old cunt. I thought it was you. Thought I recognised the voice.'

'Gary Snelling. Sounds like Smelling. What the fuck are you doing here?'

'Well, I'm not picking fights with British tourists, that's for sure, but other than that, pretty much the same as you I should imagine. Meet my friends.' I stand up and turn around to see identical twin sisters. They must be twenty-one at the most with catwalk model looks. 'This is Joi and Sai,' says Snelling. They both shake my hand in a businesslike manner.

'So you see, Tobe, I'm over here for a spot of rest and relaxation Thai-style. Know what I mean?' He laughs like Sid James.

I've known Gary Snelling as long as I've been in the biz. He's a freelance photographer. That's a nice way of putting it. If you're a celebrity, he's a telephoto-lens-wielding shit-eater who'll always turn up when you least want him to and you might not even know he has turned up until you see yourself on the front of the papers doing something you'd really rather you hadn't. Snelling put the rat in paparazzi.

He got his first scoop at the Brixton riots as an eighteen-year-old working for the South London Press. He was responsible for the throwing of more petrol bombs than anyone. He'd managed to gain access to a flat above one of the shops on the high street, and while a friend lobbed the bombs out of the window, Snelling took shots of each flaming petrol bomb arcing in profile against the scenes of rioting in the background. He won an award for the subsequent pictures which landed him a job with an Italian news agency called La Verità, the truth, a some-what inappropriate name taking into account their proven doctoring of pictures and dealings with the most intrusive and sensationalist among the world's media. La Verità's photographers are renowned throughout the industry for their tenacity and willingness to go to any lengths to get a picture. They trained him well, and he's been freelance now for about ten years. He's forty but could pass for a man at least ten years older. He enjoys life. He works hard, plays hard and screws as many good-looking women as his finances will allow, which is a fair few, especially in this part of the world. Hence the two-pack. I spend my life meeting people who try to give the impression they don't care what people think of them when in actual fact they feel every criticism like a dagger to the heart. But Snelling's about the only person I've ever met who really doesn't give a shit. He's going to do his own thing however gross and offensive people might think it is, and fuck you if you don't like it. He maintains his on-going moral bankruptcy with the commitment of a Zen master.

He takes a seat on the sunlounger next to mine while his 'special friends' take a walk on the beach.

'It's marvellous, isn't it,' he says, watching them go. 'In any other time in history, a man like me from working-class stock, and not particularly handsome working-class stock at that, could never hope to sleep with a really beautiful woman. Yet here I am spending every night with not one but two. Not a bad life, eh, Tobe?'

'Not bad. So you spend a lot of time here, then?'

'As much as I can. Maybe a couple of months a year. Sadly, I still have to work from time to time, but only on special assignments. I've just come from one in Milan. I was there for a couple of fashion shows. Just a bit of bog-standard celebrity snapping. It was as dull as fuck, to tell you the truth, but on the day I was due to leave I was walking through the lobby of the hotel when who should walk past me but Maria Slovo. You know, *Death in Paris*, *Seduction and Betrayal* and that thing with Alan Rickman last year.' Well, there she is taking the lift to her room. I thought, Shall I bother? And then I thought, Bollocks, I haven't earned anything else from the trip so I might as well.

'It cost me about half a million lire to bribe one of the hotel staff at the Hotel Alessandra to confirm she was even staying there, and another half a million to tell me which room she was in. As soon as I'd got my bearings I booked myself into a guest house on the opposite side of the street, making sure I had a room with a view of Maria Slovo's room in the Alessandra. The Italians love a net curtain but I was in luck; in fact, the pictures I got will keep me in the likes of Joi and Sai for a good long while. This is strictly shtum, OK, Tobe?' I nod and he lowers his voice to a gravelly whisper. 'I haven't done anything with them yet but I have in my possession about two hundred close-up clear-as-day pics of Maria Slovo and Sophie Moran – the blonde one from *Ballsup 1 and 2* and *The Zookeeper's Friend* – going at it on the bed, strap-ons, toys, the lot. It gave me the fucking horn, I can tell you.'

'What are you going to do with them?' I ask, laughing at the undisguised relish with which he tells the story.

'Don't know. Sell them, obviously. But maybe keep some of the more steamy ones back. They couldn't print them anyway. I've got loads like that. They're just too strong. I bung a few on the Internet occasionally if the price is right, but mainly I just hold on to them. One day I'll have an exhibition perhaps. Tell you what, though, Tobe, you wouldn't believe one snap I've got.' I know what's coming but then anyone who's known Snelling for any length of time will have heard this story on numerous occasions. None the less, I never tire of hearing him say, 'I've got a picture of Prince Philip's dick.'

I've never managed to see this glorious image myself but friends of mine have, and in addition to the wonder of seeing the Queen's old man's old man, you also have the enjoyment of Gary's velvet-lined presentation box in which he keeps it. As is only right and proper, I suppose,

on the lid of the box is gold embossed lettering which reads:
PRINCE PHILIP'S DICK.

'You heard what happened?' he asks me. I've heard what
happened a hundred times but I want to hear it again.

'No, I don't think I have.'

'Well, I got a phone call from a mate of mine, Danny,
who was working for the *Mirror*. Apparently they were
trying to develop this story about race fixing and illegal
gambling among the racing fraternity. Now I've never done
undercover work, it's not my scene at all, but their boy was
ill and Danny was desperate. So, I was given all the kit, the
specially mounted camera in the bag with the hole in it and
the tape recorder with microphones wired all over me, and
I put on some glad rags and went along to Ascot for some
big cup-day event, I forget which. I had VIP passes to get
me into all the various marquees and enclosures where
they suspected the dodgy dealing to be taking place but
I didn't manage to uncover anything criminal other than
the price of the drinks I started to consume. On one of my
trips to the loo, who should I find standing next to me at the
urinal but the Greek fella himself. Well, it was too great an
opportunity to miss so I hurriedly finished pissing and put
my plan, which was simple but highly effective, into action.
I faked a stumble and as I fell against him, I pointed the bag
with the camera in it towards his groin and managed to fire
off a couple of shots on the remote switch. On the first one
you can only see his hand and a stream of piss – the royal
wee, geddit? – but on the second you can see his helmet
as clear as day. Bloody marvellous.'

If there is a genetic tic in our national make-up which
has created the British obsession with crudity and finding

humour in all things lavatorial, Gary Snelling has received a double helping. I can tell he's been on the local weed. He laughs harder and longer than I do and tears well up in his eyes. When he's finished he says, 'Well, Tobe, it's bloody good to see you, mate. Are you here with anyone?'

'No, I'm alone. It's a sort of working holiday. I'm doing some research for a new project. Can't tell you what, though, Gary, because if I did I'd have to kill you and we don't want that, now, do we?'

Snelling gives it his best Sid James then says, 'Talking of killing, a mate of mine's in the Old Bill and he's working on the Piper investigation.'

As he says this, I nudge Mannesmann's book under the sunlounger with my heel, smile nonchalantly and say, 'Oh yes, the serial killer?'

'Yeah. I've been trying to persuade him to let me have a sneak preview of one of the scenes of crime but he won't play ball. I've offered him a cut of any money I can make off the pictures but he's surprisingly moral for a pig. Anyway, they think they had their first copycat killing the other day. Hotel room in central London – brutal murder and videos of it sent to the police and the press.'

'So what makes them think it wasn't a Piper killing?'

'Well, the thing is, they know it wasn't from the Piper because the recording on the video doesn't run backwards.'

'What do you mean, it doesn't run backwards?'

'That's what the Piper does. He records the killing with his digital camcorder but when he transfers it on to video he does it backwards, so the first thing you see is the dismembered corpse and then he makes it whole again, like he's bringing his victim back to life. They think he's making some statement about the direction of time or something. Anyway, that's how they know it's him, and obviously they won't release that to the public. Here, changing the subject, how about joining me at the bar on the cliffs? I'm dying for a drink.'

'Could do.'

'I'll just round up the girls.' He punches me on the arm playfully, and with a leering smile slicing his face in two says, 'Tell you what, Tobe, you should get yourself sorted out with a woman or two out here. These babies really know how to fuck.'

HEAD

I tried to explain to Oy that I had a hangover but she didn't understand, or if she did, she didn't care. She went at me with her usual vigour. Sadly, the communication of pain across my nerve centres was impaired by my hangover and I couldn't get off. It's a shame to see all that pain go to waste but you win some and you lose some. She seemed annoyed that her efforts had come to naught, and when she went to douse me with cold water she let go of the plastic bucket, which bounced off my forehead. Not the best remedy for a thumping headache.

Today is the fifth day in a row I've had a hangover. It's Snelling's fault – he brings out the worst in me. But I needn't worry because today is also my last day here. Tomorrow, it's back to Mud Island.

Instead of taking up my usual position on a sunlounger by the beach, I head back to my room. When I first arrived here, I had booked myself and Oy into two of the pavilions dotted among the ornamental pools in the nature reserve, but a couple of days later I became wary of the abundance of fauna and decided I'd be safer in one of the tree-houses. So Oy stayed where she was and I moved. They're not strictly tree-houses, I suppose, because they're not actually built in the branches of trees. But owing to their positions clinging to the cliffs that surround the lagoon, which are covered by creepers, vines and greenery of all sorts – including trees – you could be mistaken for thinking they were. Mine has a living area in which a wooden seat like an ornamental park bench is suspended from the ceiling by black chains opposite a huge wide-screen TV which receives every available channel in South-East Asia. Sliding doors lead out on to a balcony overlooking the lagoon and the curious rock stacks that break up the vast tracts of ocean beyond it. Against the wall to the left of the balcony is a kitchen area. I've only been here a week or so but already it's in a hell of a state. At first, I thought I would be able to cope with having the hotel staff come in to clean and tidy up but this proved to be impossible. On the first day here, when the cleaner, a middle-aged Thai woman, came in, I had a panic attack and had to ask her to leave. I called the management and told them that no member of the hotel's staff was allowed in my room under any circumstances. I figure at five hundred quid a night they should allow me to live like a pig if I want to.

I take the spiral staircase to the bedroom, lie down on the bed and switch on the laptop. YOU HAVE E-MAIL, it tells me. It's from thepiper@eviscerate.com. There's an attachment which I open first. As the pixels fall into place, I can see it's a photograph of a mutilated corpse. One of the Piper's victims, no doubt. It's a man, or rather it's the components of a man – head, body, arms and legs – dismembered and arranged into a star shape with the legs where the arms should be and vice versa. The man's head is placed on the middle of the torso, eyes open, and whether the Piper's done something to his mouth I don't know, but it looks for all the world as though he's smiling for the camera. As you might expect, there's blood everywhere, and in the bottom of the picture are the Piper's feet in white rubber boots, the sort surgeons wear. I study the man's face for a few moments, trying to imagine who he was and whether he ever imagined he'd wind up like this. Then I open up the message and read:

Tobe,

I trust you're still enjoying your holiday. I thought I might send you the attached in order to focus your mind as regards the mechanics of what I actually do. I don't want you going into all this with your eyes closed. I could have sent you far worse, like some live footage of me in mid-rip, so to speak, but I figured it was better to take one step at a time.

In your last e-mail you mention how you hate your ex-clients, hate them for their addictions, for the frailty of their hopes and dreams, their grotesque personalities; their inability to take the needles of celebrity out of their arms. It almost sounded as though you might feel the same for me one day once the novelty of being involved in my career had worn off. If this is the case, all I would ask you to remember is what it is that sets me and them apart, and that is strength of will. I doubt you can have any idea of the strength of will required to kill someone, not in self-defence or for profit or on account of inner demons or a derangement of any kind, but as an act of creation, as a piece of art rendered all the more epic by its divorce

*from sentiment and emotion. What I do is the ultimate
expression of artistic intent. I am holding a mirror up to
the putrescent soul of Western society and showing people
how life really is.*

Reply soon; this is lonely work.

P.

Most of his e-mails are like this, full of snippets from
some unimaginable manifesto with which he attempts
to justify his actions. This one is different in that he is
displaying a deeper level of insecurity than of late, and
this might be an opportunity to tell him a few home truths.
I click on the reply button and type in:

*It would take more than a gory photograph to make me
have second thoughts about our working relationship. Just
as you are no ordinary serial killer, please do not mistake
me for your ordinary personal management type. Your
assertions regarding art and artistic intent are all well
and good but if you really want to become a legendary
serial killer, then you've got a lot of work to do. There are
thousands of deranged lunatics out there, and think of all
those that have gone before you, such as Jack the Ripper,
Ed Gein, Ted Bundy, Andrei Chikatilo, Jeffrey Dahmer.
You're not in the same league as these guys. You've killed
three people. I'm inclined to say 'Big deal'. An important
rule when attempting any form of celebrity is: don't believe
your own hype. I'll be back in London in a few days and
we'll speak then.*

Tobe.

I click the Send button on the web browser and it's gone

down the wire. I lie back on the bed and shut my eyes, but as I start to drift off the phone goes.

'Hello?'

'All right, you old bastard?' It's Snelling. 'Sun's gone over the yard-arm or whatever the expression is. Wondered if I could tempt you with the hair of the dog.'

'Go on, then. Twist my arm.'

'See you poolside?'

'Yeah, give me a couple of minutes.'

I lean over to the laptop, open up the image of the Piper's dismembered victim and stare at the severed head, which grins back at me as though it doesn't have a care in the world.

HOME

The plane drops through a bank of cloud into Heathrow, where it's pissing down. Twelve hours ago, when I got on the plane, I had the hangover from hell after my farewell drink with Snelling, but I've been drunk again since then and now I feel leaden, weighed down by a suntan that doesn't suit me, a liver that feels like a cauliflower and a lethargy I just can't seem to shake. When I took my seat in business class I felt jumpy, but put it down to an occasional fear of flying. Mindful of my alcohol-ravaged innards, I ordered a tomato juice as soon as the plane levelled out. Then my thoughts drifted to the Piper, as they do so often nowadays, and it struck me for the first time that my involvement in his career might very well mean the end of the line for me. If relations between the two of us were to sour, he might very well kill me or, alternatively, if my complicity in his crimes were discovered by the police, I might very well be looking at a lengthy incarceration which could be a whole lot worse. Strange, I know, that I hadn't thought of these eventualities before but they just hadn't seemed to cross my mind. As soon as they did I realised tomato juice just wouldn't do and ordered a steady stream of tequilas until I passed out in my seat.

We taxi along the runway and come to a stop at the stand. I push my tongue around my mouth in a vain attempt to shift the scum that coats the inside and stand up before anyone else, before we're supposed to. I grab my laptop case from the overhead locker and head down the aisle. The cabin crew are in place, two on either side of the door, fake smiles beaming, all ready in place to tell me bye-bye like they really mean it.

'Don't bother,' I scowl at them as I hurry past; their smiles fade and they don't say a word.

Sod's law – I'm first off the plane but my bag is the last one on to the baggage carousel. When it finally appears, I snatch it up and make for the taxis. It's 8.15 a.m. Even if I'm lucky, it'll take at least half an hour to Ladbroke Grove. That's at least an hour's worth of potential conversation with a cabby. But I've come prepared – he looks like a chatty bastard so it's just as well – and as I settle back in my seat having told him where I want to go, I slip on the pair of headphones I swiped from the plane, and with the wire connected to nothing more high-fidelity than the inside of my pocket, nod my head occasionally to a make-believe tune as we head east.

What I am returning to or why I am even returning to it are questions I'd rather not answer. Love it or hate it – perhaps that should be hate it or hate it even more – Calamity Towers is my home.

In Desford Gardens, I pay the cabby, grab my bags and climb out. All the curtains at the front of the house are drawn. I take the steps to the front door, push the key in the lock and enter. I breathe through my mouth at first, fearful of the stench that'll greet the scent receptors in my nose if I do otherwise. In the sitting room I chance a sniff, and it's as bad as could be expected. My foot knocks against something on the floor and a black swarm of flies rises off it to reveal a fetid rat carcass. Horror-stricken, I jump back from it and head for the kitchen.

The mound of refuse by the back door has grown, which suggests Ralph has been using the money I left him for groceries. I can hear movement within it, faint scurryings and scratchings. There is an arrangement – you could almost call it a sculpture – of Mental Brew cans in the corner of the room. At some time or another, Ralph has also deposited the contents of his stomach here too. There are footsteps on the stairs. Tiptoeing not-wanting-to-be-heard footsteps. A floorboard creaks.

'Ralph?' I call. The footsteps stop. Silence. I put my head around the door and there he is, standing on the stairs with his back to me, motionless.

'Ralph?' I call to him again as reassuringly as possible. He spins around to face me. The expression on his face is one of abject terror. The first time he says it, no sound comes out of his mouth but I know what he's saying anyway. The second time he says it, he remembers to switch on the volume and it comes out loud and clear: 'Kelly!' With an athleticism I would not have thought he was capable of, he vaults the banister rail, and no sooner have his threadbare socks hit the floorboards than he's thundering towards me, arms outstretched. A normal person would attempt some form of deceleration before carrying out the hug that's clearly his intention, but not Ralph. He hits me full on and, with his arms clamped tightly around me, we careen into the kitchen locked together. We're horizontal when we hit the floor, and our momentum sends us sliding along it buoyed up on a slick of festering ooze. Fortunately, Ralph's head is extended beyond mine and it is this which strikes the leg of the table first and brings us to a halt. The impact doesn't appear to bother him any and he continues to shriek 'Kelly, Kelly, Kelly' into my face, his warm beery breath blasting up my nostrils.

'Ralph, get the fuck off me, you lunatic.' I manage to disentangle myself from him but it's a struggle. He's a strong bastard. No sooner have I done this than the phone starts to ring. As I jump up and hurry through to the sitting room, I can feel the slime from the kitchen floor seep through the back of my shirt and jeans.

I snatch up the receiver. 'Hello?' I can hear someone draw in a breath as though they're just about to speak but then nothing, as though they've thought better of it. The line goes dead. I dial 1471. Number withheld. There are twenty-eight messages on the answer machine. I delete them all and wander back into the kitchen, where Ralph is still lying on his back on the kitchen floor in among the empty tin cans, torn packets and congealed, mouldering foodstuffs. He's wearing my clothes. A pair of black Levi's and a grey T-shirt. He's muttering to himself incomprehensible words interspersed with the ubiquitous 'Kelly'. I look around the room. When Scarlet left me, I saw the steady deterioration of this place as an act of creation. I was creating disorder where once there was order, dirt where once there was none. The house was changing with me to reflect my own inner feelings, but now it's not even my mess any more, not all of it. This house is now worse than I feel. The whole point of it was it was meant to be the same. Ideally, I'd like it restored to how it was a couple of months ago, already a shithole admittedly, but more commensurate with my state of mind. It seems to have done Ralph the power of good, though. He has put on weight and his skin has lost some of its drunken rouge. He also appears to be of an altogether sunnier disposition.

When I go upstairs to my bedroom, he follows me. I pull a sheet from the stack in the wardrobe and spread it out on the countless sheets that have gone before. I turn on the TV and lie down on the bed. Ralph stands in the doorway and watches me. Once I'm settled, he climbs on to the bed and sits next to me. I fiddle with the remote control until I find a news programme. There's been another earthquake in Turkey. There's a special report on famine in the Third World. A notorious murderer in the US has been sent to the electric chair, and we see the supporters of the death penalty outside the prison holding placards with slogans like 'Frying tonight' and 'Burn baby burn' written on them. There's been a potholing accident in Dorset. Nothing about the Piper. The news has moved on.

The doorbell goes. I look at Ralph in the vain hope he might get it. He looks back at me and shrugs. I'll leave it. No one'll hear the TV from down there and if they do, well, so what. The guy presenting the news starts to tell me about NHS waiting lists and the doorbell rings again. This time it's a longer, more persistent ring. An I'm-not-going-away ring. This hardens my resolve to leave it. We're on to a dreary outside broadcast from some beleaguered hospital in Sheffield when I hear his voice.

'Tobe. I know you're in there.' It's Bill Barlow. What the hell does he want? Whatever it is, I don't want to find out.

'I called earlier, Tobe – I know you're there. Now open the door and let me in. We need to talk.'

He sounds desperate. I climb off the bed and crawl over to the window on my knees. There's a crack in the curtain and through it I can see him looking upwards at the wrong window. He looks pretty rough. He's let his hair grow and gone is his trademark two-thousand quid suit, replaced by a polo neck and black combat trousers that just don't suit him.

'Come on, Tobe, don't be so bloody ridiculous.'

I suppose I owe him a hearing if nothing else.

He's in mid-shout when I open the front door. His gut instinct is to hurl abuse at me, I can tell, maybe even hit me, but although either of these reactions would make him feel better in the short term, his long-term agenda is far more conciliatory. He's here to try to make me see sense, to win me back, so he struggles to mask his temper with a smile, but it comes out as more of a crazed leer than an expression of good humour.

'Where the hell have you been, Tobe?'

'Thailand.'

'What the hell were you doing there?'

'I was on holiday.'

'We have got to talk.'

'OK, but not here. You wouldn't like it in here. I've – how should I put this? – I've let things slip a little on the domestic front.'

'I really don't mind.'

'Believe me, Bill, you would. We'll go for some breakfast. I'm starving. There's a caff round the corner.'

Tony's is a down-at-heel greasy spoon which produces cheap, oily food that may be taken away or eaten in in an environment that smells of boiled cabbage, fried bread and cigarette smoke. It's the very antithesis of Notting Hill chic. But as is often the way with places like this in London, Tony's was hip for a brief period of time many years ago. From out of nowhere, trendies started turning up. I suspect some hack from a hip young glossy had given it a glowing write-up and the fall-out was that, for about six weeks, Tony's was rammed with media types all dressed in black. Thankfully, they soon realised there wasn't anything ironic, self-conscious or edgy about Tony's in any way, and just as suddenly as they'd turned up they fucked off again, thank God. Though it must have confused Tony, this sudden burst of enthusiasm after years of apathy, he didn't show it, just continued to greet the world in his customary curmudgeonly way. He doesn't look up when I order our breakfasts – a glass of mineral water for Bill and my favourite meal in all the world: a mug of tea and one of Tony's fried egg sandwiches – just runs his hand through his hair (which seems to contain as much grease as one of his breakfasts), and shuffles through to the kitchen. He grunts the order to some nameless, faceless being I have never seen who is, as far as I'm concerned, the Marco Pierre White of the greasy breakfast.

Bill and I have traded only awkward pleasantries on the way here, but when we sit down to wait for our food I can tell he wants to cut to the chase, although he doesn't quite know how to go about it.

'So, how was Thailand?' he tries.

'It was fine.

'I'm sorry I threw the phone at you,' I tell him. 'Although I'm not sorry about what I said.' To be honest, I could almost apologise for what I said as well, he looks so wretched. All my animosity towards him has dissipated.

'Well, I suppose you had your reasons,' he says like a sulky child.

'Of course I had my bloody reasons, Bill. You betrayed me. You chose to align yourself with an egotistical opportunist who wanted to resurrect a schoolboy grudge in order to engineer a publicity coup. Much good it did the fucker.'

Bill leans forward, suddenly intense, and says, 'Please God, tell me you had nothing to do with his death.'

'Oh, come on, Bill, I may be many things but I'm no murderer.'

'But you can't tell me you're not pleased he's dead.'

'Bill, you're right. I thought he was a cunt and I'm glad he's dead but I didn't kill him. Anyway, you didn't come here to talk about Hugo Blain, did you?'

'No, I just wanted to keep you up to speed with how successful you've been with your attempts to screw up my life.'

'Go on, then, Bill, get it off your chest.'

This makes him laugh, but it's the sort of laughter that if he allowed it to continue unchecked could develop into a sobbing fit. Thankfully, he doesn't.

'Don't play the psychoanalyst with me, Tobe. You're the most neurotic, fucked-up person I've ever met. I didn't come here to get things off my chest or to make me feel better, I came here our of desperation owing to your on-going professional ineptitude.'

I know what's coming. He's going to reel off my pieces of bad advice one by one. He's going to try to shame me with a catalogue of my cock-ups. Ever the traditionalist, he counts them out on his fingers one by one.

First up there's Dame Imogen Lescarre, an octogenarian ex-opera singer whose agent came to see me just after Scarlet left, which was around the time I started with all the bad advice. In what I can only imagine was a moment of lucidity in her on-going Alzheimer's, Dame Imogen had asked him to orchestrate a comeback for her. He said he knew it was hopeless but he'd promised her he would seek professional advice and was as good as his word. What I should have said to him was that Dame Imogen was a legend and any attempts to resurrect her career would tarnish that legend, so the best thing to do would be to allow her to bask in her former glories by engineering some recognition of her achievements at an appropriate awards ceremony. That way, she would have the opportunity to get up on stage once again in front of her few remaining peers and the opera cognoscenti and achieve some public recognition for her lifetime's work. That's what I should have said. What I ended up saying to him, however, was that there was a whole new market out there she could tap into and that he was wrong to doubt her abilities. By the time I'd finished with him, he was looking at the situation from the point of view of Mr Fifteen-per-cent again, and with the sort of money I was bandying around, he was soon convinced. What I said was needed was a high-profile television appearance in order to showcase her still-blossoming talents. It just so happened an old acquaintance of mine was putting together a charity gala performance at the Palladium in aid of some Turkish earthquake fund. I had a word with him and, although he was doubtful of Dame Imogen's abilities to entertain a tea party, let alone a global audience of millions, none the less, on my recommendation, he gave her the gig.

'And that's when it all went tits up,' says Bill, with reference to her performance on the show. 'She walked on to the stage to rapturous applause and then froze. Completely bottled it. No longer was she Dame Imogen Lescarre, opera legend, but Dame Imogen Lescarre, confused geriatric. Tobe, she pissed herself on stage. Thank God they managed to edit out her entire spot but Terence' – that's her agent – 'tells me the ordeal was so much for the poor old cow she's now little more than a vegetable. He's considering legal action. What the fuck were you thinking? Barlow & Darling was always about giving people the facts, not just some half-arsed bullshit dreamed up just so you can have a laugh at someone else's expense.'

'Bill, if you want an apology, then I'm sorry.' He knows I'm not thanks to my too thinly disguised amusement.

'Then there's Peter Dugdale and *Hoxton Square*. You were supposed to come back to me with some ideas about how we could counter the stories about his getting caught in the ladies' on Brighton seafront. That was weeks ago and still nothing.'

'Bill,' I interrupt, 'all you have to do in a situation like this is pay some mincing wannabe telly star to say that Dugdale's as camp as tits and they've been at it for months. Christ, Bill, this isn't rocket science.'

'People aren't that stupid, Tobe.'

'Believe me, nobody has ever lost money underestimating the intelligence of the great British public.'

'Well, let's forget that for a minute. What about Simeon Cruikshank?'

'He has a disproportionately large left nostril. What of it?'

'Correct me if I'm wrong here, please, but did you or did you not suggest that the star of *Popstar!*, Sonny Page, should save someone's life in order to give the show a publicity boost?'

'I did, yes.'

'Any particular reason?'

'I think it's a good idea.'

'Many people in this industry consider you something of a genius, Tobe, and even if you're not a genius, you're still one of the brightest, sharpest people I have ever met, and yet you can sit there and tell me the best way for one of our biggest-paying clients to restart the fortunes of his West End show is to have the star save someone's life. All I can say is Simeon Cruikshank is a bigger fuckwit than I gave him credit for because he's all for it. He phones me every day, Tobe, to find out how the plan's going. What the fuck am I supposed to tell him?'

'Tell him what you like. You seem to forget I've quit. I no longer work for Barlow & Darling. Barlow & Darling has ceased to exist. It's just Barlow and nothing. Bill Barlow Associates perhaps. Actually that's got a nice ring to it, don't you think?'

'For what it's worth, Tobe, I'm firmly of the opinion you're going through some sort of . . . nervous breakdown is too strong a term, but personal crisis or something, and for that reason I'm prepared to cut you some slack and let you have some space for a while. But as far as the rest of the world is concerned, as far as our lawyers and our clients and their lawyers are concerned, Barlow & Darling is still very much alive and well and is very much Barlow *and* Darling. Legally, you're as much a part of this company as you've always been. So, what I'm proposing is this – have some time off, have a sabbatical or whatever it will take for you to sort your head out. But in the meantime, at least give me a hand in sorting out the appalling mess you've created.'

Bill is a self-satisfied man. I don't mean in an egotistical way but in a content, at-one-with-the-world-and-his-place-in-it way. Now he's scared. He can see everything slipping away from him and he sees me as the cause. He feels he needs to bring all his personality to bear to win me back, but at the same time he's so scared by the sight of the abyss that, like a man suffering from vertigo, he's terrified he'll throw himself in. I ought to give him some advice. That's my job in life, giving advice. The trouble is, though I know what the good advice should be, I've gone so far down the road of bad advice I find it impossible to stop now.

'OK, Bill, I'll admit I've been off with the fairies in my professional judgment of late, and I'm not even going to attempt to explain what is happening to me on a personal, private, psychological level because I'm not even sure I know myself. So, we'll keep this simple. I'll accept your offer of a sabbatical. But it's going to have to be open-ended with no guarantees that I will ever come back. Now, if you'll agree to this then I'm sure we can come to an arrangement whereby I'll give you all the help you need to deal with the clients, on the condition that I have nothing to do with them on a day-to-day basis. If I never have to share a room with another paranoid showbiz scumbag as long as I live it'll be too soon. Perhaps you can get yourself some hotshot young suit who can dish out all the stuff I feed him.' I throw him a shit-eater grin. 'Just think of me as the oracle.'

He can't disguise the relief on his face as he says, 'OK, Tobe, it's a deal, but in the meantime what are we going to do about Dame Imogen? What are we going to do about Simeon Cruikshank, Sonny Page and Peter Dugdale? I haven't even mentioned Eric Massey and the Lifeboys. Jesus, Tobe, you told the man that "Honeygun" or whatever the godawful single is called was going to be a number one. It didn't even chart. What the hell am I supposed to tell these people?'

'Relax, Bill,' I tell him as Tony plonks my egg sandwich down in front of me. 'It'll all turn out fine.'

'God, I hope you're right,' he says.

I lift the top slice of bread from the sandwich, lance the yolk's scablike crust and stir in some tomato ketchup so the filling resembles a bloody, pustulant wound.

GOING DOWN

I was so paranoid about making this trip I became convinced that if a cabby asked me what I was up to I'd blurt out the truth, that I was on my way to a rendezvous with Britain's most notorious criminal. Hence the Tube. Ladbroke Grove to Baker Street on the Metropolitan & City line, then the Bakerloo line to Charing Cross. Just like a regular commuter. Completing the last part of the journey on foot, I pass the Whitehall Theatre, the last outpost of the West End before the blank windows and grey net curtains, statues of earls and dukes, poppies at the Cenotaph, black spiked railings and Union Jacks flapping in the wind herald my arrival in the heart of the British establishment. Not exactly the sort of place you'd expect to find a vicious serial killer, but he's here somewhere, behind one of these austere façades.

Albion House is exactly where he told me it would be in his e-mail, and unlike most of the buildings on Whitehall it has a panel of name-plates and buzzers by the door. As instructed, I press the buzzer marked Wormald Holdings.

'Hello?'

'Hi, it's Tobe Darling.'

'Come in, walk to the end of the corridor and take the last door on the left. Through the door you'll see a filing cabinet. Open the third drawer down and you'll find a Walkman. Put the headphones on and press Play.'

So this is what he sounds like without the electronic cartoon impersonations. Just dead normal. He has one of those accentless Middle England voices. No hint of a regional dialect and altogether more composed and measured than I'd expected.

The door clicks open. In front of me there's a long corridor with striplights running along the middle of the ceiling like dazzling white lines on an upside-down road. The door swings shut behind me and all is quiet save for the sound of my shoes on the brown linoleum as I walk down the corridor. The office I enter has a desk in the middle of it with nothing on it but a blotter pad yellowed with age and an old-fashioned angle-poise lamp. It doesn't feel like a real working office but rather the set of an office in some cheap TV sketch show. In the corner of the room there's the grey filing cabinet he mentioned, next to which there's another door the same as the one I've just come through. I open the third drawer down as instructed and there's the Walkman. With the headphones on and the tape running, I wait nervously for the sound of his voice.

'Hello, Tobe. Thanks for coming. I'm afraid you still have some travelling time ahead of you because while I told you I live in Whitehall, which I suppose I do technically, what I omitted to tell you is I actually live beneath Whitehall.

A long way beneath. Now, I'll provide you with all the instructions you require to reach me and if things get a little hairy at times, never fear – so long as you do what I say, you'll be fine. Now, open the door by the filing cabinet.' I do as he says and find myself in a room so small it is little more than a cupboard in the middle of which is a spiral staircase leading down through a hole in the bare concrete floor. 'Close the door after you and go down the stairs.' As I start down the steps, my movement triggers a series of lights that illuminate my way. 'Under the bottom step of the spiral staircase you'll find a torch and taped to the torch you'll find a key. Turn on the torch and you'll see a passageway ahead of you. Walk along it until you find yourself on a metal walkway.' This walkway comprises lengths of metal panelling welded together end to end and suspended by long crooked brackets from the ceiling of what appears to be a huge subterranean cave. All around the sound of dripping water reverberates. It's only when my torch picks up a series of red-brick arches and Gothic buttresses on either side that I realise it can't be a cave, it's all man-made.

'Take it nice and slowly,' he tells me through the head-phones, 'and whatever you do, don't drop the torch. In a moment or two you should see there's a break in the walkway across which you'll need to jump. This isn't particularly hazardous but be careful because if you do fall it'll mean curtains, I'm afraid.'

Added to the sound of dripping water all around is the sound of me hurling obscenities into the darkness. Aside from certain sexual practices for which I have developed a fondness, I don't do hazardous. Anything more

177

hazardous than cutting my toenails and I'm out of the door.

I shuffle along the walkway, my eyes glued to the rusty metal sheeting in front of me. The air tastes oily and stale, something between a school chemistry lab and a compost heap. When the Piper gave me an address in Whitehall at which to meet him, it seemed to soften my mental image of him. I found myself thinking of him as some sort of gentleman criminal, a Raffles type living in an oak-panelled drawing room taking tea in his silk smoking jacket and dividing his thoughts between the murder of his next victim and the *Times* crossword. But now I'm teetering along a flimsy metal construction that looks as though only the rust and corrosion are holding it together I feel a whole lot different about him.

'Stay calm,' he tells me. 'Don't worry – it's not in my best interests to hurt or injure you in any way.'

And then I see it. It looks as though the metal sheeting has given way under the weight of something heavy, a fat bloke like me perhaps, and left a gap of about five feet across which I'll have to jump. I switch off the tape and stand there shining the torch at the twisted broken metal framing the abyss across which I must make my leap of faith. My stomach churns, sick with fear, and my legs tremble. Every second I stand here motionless weakens my resolve. I have to do this, I can't go back to the way I was. I take a few paces backwards in order to give myself sufficient space for a run-up. The entire structure feels as though it might give up the ghost and collapse under the pressure of my feet pounding along it before I hurl myself across the gap and crash-land on the other side, breathless and relieved.

I switch on the tape again and find myself hoping for some sort of congratulation or at least recognition of the strength of will it took for me to make the leap. But it clearly means less to the Piper than it does to me and, apropos of nothing, he starts off on some sort of history lecture: 'People have been digging away under London for years. Initially, it was through a desire to improve their environment and to try and put some distance between them and their sewage. The ruling classes had decided it just wouldn't do for the seat of the great British Empire to smell like a public lavatory. Hence the enormous construction projects that took place in the eighteenth and nineteenth centuries in order to develop the extensive network of sewers that remain in operation to this day.' He sounds like the narrator of some Open University documentary, and were it not for the fact that I might miss some important piece of information regarding my route, I'd turn him off.

'Once they'd solved the sewage problem, they then turned their attention to the transportation of people and started on the underground railways, some of which – but not all – are incorporated into the modern-day Tube network. By the Second World War, the government had begun to concentrate on the problems of sheltering large numbers of people underground during the Blitz, and once the war was over and the Cold War had begun, construction continued on what had become known as the "citadels". These were a series of large-scale bunkers that could house entire communities for long periods of time in the event of a nuclear strike and were interconnected by underground railways. Of all the Cold War citadels constructed beneath London, the one you are about to enter, the Churchill Citadel, is the largest and deepest of them all. There is a neighbouring citadel beneath Parliament Square of which the Cabinet War Rooms are just one minute part. This was to be home for the government in the event of nuclear war, but the Churchill Citadel was funded by private individuals, nobility mainly. The area you are currently in was originally constructed in the war as a huge dormitory and canteen to house American troops. It was subsequently used as a service area for the machinery required in the construction of the Churchill Citadel. At any moment, you should see the end of the walkway.'

I can just make out a glistening moss-covered brick wall about a hundred feet ahead against which there is a metal staircase housed in a rusting cage that plunges downwards into the darkness.

'Take the steps down until you reach a blue door at the bottom. Pause the tape until you get there.'

I do as he says and start my descent. After a couple of minutes, the rusted cage gives way to brickwork painted in thick gloss paint the likes of which can be seen in a thousand schools, prisons and army barracks throughout the land. It's government paint, paint that pays no heed to the whimsies of fashion, paint that's meant to cover the surface beneath it for as long as possible. Scratched into the paintwork here and there are graffiti, but they're not the graffiti of modern day. There are no obscenities scrawled just for the hell of seeing what they look like. Instead, there are just names and dates. 'Hodgkiss 1949,' reads one.

The blue door turns out to be a door not unlike a prison door, except there is no peep-hole. I roll the tape again.

'Take the key that's taped to the torch and unlock the door. Even down here, I like to maintain some level of security.'

Once I've opened the door, the sound of running water is so loud I have to turn up the volume on the Walkman so I can hear him say, 'In addition to the sewers, railway lines and giant nuclear bunkers, I forgot to mention there are also underground streams and rivers which have been plumbed into the mains of the city like subterranean canals. This is one of them. It is in fact what remains of a stream that once flowed about two hundred feet above where you are presently standing but was rerouted in order to provide the Churchill Citadel with drinking water, once purified, and also electricity through hydroelectric power.'

By the light of the torch, I can see the stream as it roars past in a cave that's been blasted out of the rock and disappears into a tunnel about eight feet in diameter set into the wall to my right.

'You'll see there's a stack of small inflatable dinghies. Take one and put it into the water. Push yourself off and let the current carry you into the tunnel. On the right-hand side of the tunnel there's a rope threaded through a series of rings. If you grab hold of this, you can control your progress along the tunnel. After a couple of minutes, the tunnel will open out into a sort of basin across which you'll see there's a rope which you must grab hold of to pull yourself to a halt. Pause the tape until you get there.'

This is a nightmare. I am not the sort of person who should be doing this. In addition to vertigo, I also suffer from seasickness and have a massive aversion to carrying out any activity that involves leaving *terra firma*. But needs must and all that, so I pick the uppermost dinghy from the pile and set it down in the water. As I do so, I come face to face with the huge rat sitting in it. I jump back, letting go of the dinghy as I do so, and it disappears into the tunnel carried away on the current, its loathsome occupant staring at me as it goes. Why the Piper and I couldn't have met in a quiet out-of-the-way pub somewhere I don't know. I grab hold of another dinghy and, having checked I will be its only passenger, set it down in the water and climb in. As I cast off into the tunnel, the dinghy scrapes against the rough stone wall and it sounds as though at any moment the fabric will tear and I'll be deposited into the cold grey water. I manage to grab hold of the rope secured to the side of the tunnel, which is sodden and slimy, and let it run through my trembling fingers. My eyes strain into the thin shaft of light thrown by the torch, and it feels as though I'm being flushed down a giant toilet. As I come out of the tunnel into the basin I let go of the rope on the wall and position myself ready to reach up and catch hold of the other rope he mentioned strung from left to right on a level with my head. As I grab hold of it, the dinghy is pulled from underneath me by the current and I'm left dangling with my legs in the water. Fearful of dropping the torch, I clamp it tight in my jaws, pull myself up by both hands and manoeuvre myself along the rope until I'm clear of the water and can drop to the ground. My heart is hammering in my chest and my legs tremble against the cold wet material of my trousers. I take the torch from my mouth and run the tape on the Walkman, which has thankfully escaped a dousing in the water.

'If you walk at right angles to the stream, you'll see some

steps leading up to a door. Go through the door and along the passage – mind your head, it's very low – and you'll come out in a room against the back wall of which are three goods lifts.' I do as he says, my shoes squelching on the rough uneven floor. 'You are now directly beneath St George's House, which was to be the main pedestrian entrance to the Churchill Citadel. Sadly, it's not available to the likes of you and me and we have to use the slightly more obscure back entrance, as you've just discovered. Head for the smallest of the three lifts on the far left and slide open the door by pulling the handle to the right. Don't be fooled by appearances, it will get you down in one piece. I service it myself. Step in and slide the door back after you. Once inside, you'll see a lever not unlike the levers they used to have in railway signal boxes. There's a handle on it you must depress before you pull it towards you. It's a little stiff so give it a good yank.'

Once in the lift, I pull the lever and for a moment nothing happens. Then, to the accompaniment of screeching metal all around, the lift descends.

'Tobe, you are now entering the Churchill Citadel. Think of it as an inverted skyscraper thirty-eight storeys deep. In the event of a nuclear war it was to have housed one hundred and eighty families with sufficient utilities and food to keep them going for well over a year. I'll sign off now. Pull the brake on when you reach the thirty-second floor and I'll see you there.'

The lift's erratic descent makes me think of the depth of the shaft and how the only thing stopping me from falling hundreds of feet is a rusty old cable that could shear through at any moment. I take off the headphones and, in order to check the lift's ability to stop, pull on the brake. I come to a juddering halt on the sixth floor. I know it's the sixth floor because there's a number six in peeling paint on the wall just outside the lift. I shine the light into the darkness but can make out nothing more than a passageway with narrow doors leading off it. I pull the lever back and the lift continues its descent. By the time I reach the thirty-second floor, it's become considerably colder and, what with my nerves and sodden trousers and all, I start to shiver as I slide back the door and step out.

There's no one here. I thought he might at least have met me at the lift. There's not even a light on. In fact, the thirty-second floor appears to be identical to the thirty-one other floors I've just passed.

'Hello?'

Then I see I was wrong. There is a light, a faint one coming from under the door at the end of the corridor. I walk towards it and try the handle. It turns and, expecting the hinges to be old and worn like everything else in this place, I give it a good shove, whereupon it swings open freely and slams against the wall. There's a man standing on a chair. He's tanned with blond spiky hair and is dressed in white linen trousers and T-shirt. There's a noose around his neck, and I can see it's attached to a metal ceiling joist. Our eyes meet. The beginnings of a smile form on his lips as he kicks away the chair, which clatters into my shins and knocks me down. As I fall I drop the torch. The only other light in the room comes from the solitary low-wattage light bulb in the middle of the ceiling. The man knocks it with his shoulder as he swings from the rope, which creates the illusion that he's stationary and it's the room that's moving around him. I try to stand up but I misjudge it and he bumps into me and knocks me down again. I fall against the upturned chair, and when I stand up again I take hold of it and turn it the right way up. He knocks into it again and it spins away. For what seems like an age, but is probably no more than a couple of seconds, it feels as though I'm trying to solve some giant three-dimensional puzzle, my one arm around his waist trying to reduce his momentum and the other outstretched, making a grab for the chair. Once I've managed to bring these two seemingly hostile entities together, I hoist him up on to the chair. He leans against me heavily while I reach up to his neck and pull the noose open. Free of the rope, he slumps against me and we both collapse on to the floor panting from the exertion.

'Are you OK?' I ask once I've caught my breath.

'Yeah, I think so,' he says, his voice as hoarse and strangled-sounding as you might expect but still recognisable as the voice on the tape. 'I'll have some bruising for a couple of days, I expect, but nothing major. Not enough drop on the rope, you see. Certainly not enough to break my neck. It was a good noose, though. It would have asphyxiated me in no time.'

'What the hell were you doing?' I ask as I scramble to my feet.

'I was giving you a choice, Tobe.'

'What sort of choice?'

'Well, it's simple. You could have saved the lives of my future victims. Or you could have saved me, which you did, and therefore become complicit in all my future murders. I think it's what you guys call a contract. So, now we have one.'

'Right.'

'Look,' he says, standing up, 'I even had handcuffs on so that it was as authentic a hanging as possible. The key's in the corner over there. Will you do the honours?'

I've got to think fast about this. Do I want to take his handcuffs off him? He's got to be nuts, but then how could I have thought otherwise?

'What would you have done if I hadn't saved you?' I ask him as a way of buying some time.

'What? Is that some sort of riddle? I'd have died, of course. Just take it as a sign of my commitment. I hope you'll show the same commitment to me now we're going to be working together.'

Sod it, there's no point not unlocking him. By the looks of him he could easily get the better of me even with his hands cuffed behind his back. I fetch the key and unlock him. He rubs his wrists, holds out his right hand and says, 'Pleased to meet you at last, Tobe.'

I shake his hand and say, 'Yeah, likewise.'

'You've heard a lot about me,' he says and laughs. 'Come on, I'll show you around.'

He pulls open a sliding door to reveal a huge room that looks like part of a multistorey carpark. Gone is the dusty Ministry of Defence paintwork, to be replaced by bare stone walls in which chrome halogen lights are sunk. Running along the full length of one of the walls is a narrow – perhaps two-lane – swimming pool which is lit from beneath the water so that its ripples are magnified and projected on to the walls and ceiling.

'Sorry about the journey, by the way. I hope you didn't think it too melodramatic as an introduction to me and my world. Plenty of symbolism, eh? Especially for a man in my line of work. Overtones of Dante and Cocteau, don't you think?'

'Very much so, yes.' That's the ticket, Tobe, keep agreeing with him, at least for the time being. He's full of the joys of spring now, behaving like a stuntman who's just carried out a particularly tricky stunt which, when you think about it, he is, I suppose.

'Excuse the smell of chlorine,' he says. 'I try to use as little of the stuff as possible but it's impractical to dispense with it altogether, even if it is only me who uses the pool. Swimming is a passion of mine and the pool is the reason I chose this floor rather than any other. Also, it's nice to be near water, don't you think?' He looks at me for a reaction and I smile and nod. 'Now, this is where I spend a great deal of my time,' he says, leading me towards an enormous black leather sofa in the centre of the room, positioned in front of a cluster of television and computer screens. About half of them are switched on and show news programmes and share prices; one of them plays MTV, one of them – a computer screen – has a screen saver of an axe cleaving open someone's head, and it runs forward then stops and runs backward all in slow motion; another shows an episode of *The Simpsons*.

'This is my lifeline to the outside world, my umbilical cord through which I can receive information regarding the scurryings of humanity above. My only concern about setting up home down here was that I might not be able to receive telecommunications and broadcast signals.

Thankfully, before they called time on the construction of the Churchill Citadel, they had installed a link to a surface aerial situated within its own reinforced concrete bunker on the Embankment. This has remained fully operational to this day and gives me access to all the terrestrial, satellite, digital and telecommunications networks I might require. Unfortunately, the link had only been made to the top of the Churchill Citadel so I had to drop a cable down to the thirty-second floor, but once it was in place I was fully operational. I must confess, in the past couple of years I've become something of a self-taught electronics and computer whizz. The thing I love about the digital revolution is not only can you earn a living from the comfort of your own home, but if you're that way inclined you can start your own revolution as well. It's given the little man a voice.'

'Is that how you see yourself, as the little man?'

'Maybe I did for a while, but not any more. You seem to forget I'm a celebrity now, and with your help,' he says, patting me on the shoulder and grinning, 'I'm going to become a megastar.

'Ever dabbled on the stock market?' he asks me, nodding at the computer screens.

'No, I've never felt inclined. It's all just numbers to me. I've never been interested in numbers.'

'Maybe if the numbers were translated into tangible property then you might have more respect for them. For me, it's just a lucrative hobby.'

It's difficult to believe that not ten minutes ago this man was dangling from a rope, killing himself.

'Do you want to see something?' he asks, as though

he's a mischievous schoolkid who's got a matchbox with something nasty in it and he wants to share it with me as long as I don't tell sir. He sits down on the sofa and starts moving the computer mouse, and my eyes follow his to a screen on which he's opening folders. When he's found the file he's looking for, he positions the cursor over it and turns to me once again and asks, 'Are you sure you've got the stomach for this?' I nod, trying to appear as nonchalant as possible, and he double-clicks on the file. A piece of video footage starts to play. There's no sound. The camerawork is a little shaky but the image is unmistakable. It's a head and a pair of arms arranged so as to resemble the skull-and-crossbones emblem. Written in blood on the wall behind it is THE PIPER. A white-gloved hand reaches out and erases the letters one by one, wiping the blood back into the neck stump with its index finger until the wall is clean. Then the hand picks up the head by the hair and carries it across the room to a headless body which is absorbing blood out of the carpet. As the head is reattached to the body by the chopping of an axe, he turns to me, and like a kid watching a favourite movie, says, 'You're going to like this bit; this is the only one I've done where I managed to film the actual murder itself. With the other two, I just filmed the dismemberment, as I had to kill them both first before I could get the camera set up. With this fellow, I got him to allow me into his room. I told him I was a plumber come to fix the shower. So, when I come out of the bathroom with the camera running, you get to see the whole thing. Look.'

As with the head, the arms are chopped into place on the body's bleeding stumps. Then the axe is replaced by a filleting knife which is thrust into the corpse's chest, where it absorbs blood from a stain on the shirt. For a few seconds, the camera is pointed at the carpet, and then it's shaken around as the man comes back to life, twitching at first and then becoming increasingly conscious and mobile until he's wrestling with the knife and struggling with it, jumping to his feet as he does so. Once standing, he manages to throw the knife from this chest and lurch away, spinning around. He glances over his shoulder, a fearful grimace mutating into a good-natured smile, then he turns his head away before the camera pans back and a door closes in front of the lens.

'So, what do you think?' the Piper asks as he closes files on the screen.

'Nice.'

'Yeah, I think so. It'd be good if I could develop another means of filming the action. It all becomes rather jumpy with the camera mounted on my head. I know, Tobe, maybe you could come and hold it for me.'

'Yeah.' I laugh nervously.

'God, look at your face. You look terrified. I wouldn't really ask you to hold the camera, Tobe. You don't look like the sort of person who'd respond well under that sort of pressure. Better to leave that sort of thing to the professionals. Do you think it was gory enough? I worry sometimes I don't do enough with the bodies.'

'In what way?'

'Well, I kind of feel if you're going to be a great serial killer then you owe it to your public to indulge their fantasies a little. I want the Piper's killings to be something special. If the word goes out there's been a Piper killing and the police turn up and there's just another dead body, they're not going to be impressed, and you have to remember the police are your mouthpiece to the media. They see dead bodies every day of the week. Murders, suicides, accidents, natural causes, serial killings: dead people, over and over. So, I kind of think it's important my bodies stand out from the pack.'

'It makes sense,' I tell him. He throws me a big grin like a kid who knows he's being naughty but is happy about it and proud of himself none the less.

'Come on, Tobe, let me show you the rest of the place.'

I follow him to the area directly behind the bank of computer monitors and television screens where there is a selection of exercise machines and weight-training equipment positioned in front of a mirrored wall.

'I spend two hours a day here without fail and, with my swimming, which takes up about another hour, I like to feel I am fitter than the average man of my age.' He looks me up and down. 'Take much exercise yourself?'

'What do you think?'

'Maybe not. I like to pursue a vigorous exercise regime.' I know what's coming next. Like all fitness freaks, he is obsessed with all the numerics of his work-out and starts on about how many reps he does on this machine and how many minutes he does on that machine, and his heart rate, and this and that and on and on. I switch off.

Next up on our grand tour is the kitchen area – all chrome and stainless steel, and spotless. As a house of horror, this place just doesn't cut the mustard. There are no heads simmering in saucepans, no severed limbs, no bin-bags full of body parts. As he begins to tell me how much he likes to cook, a grey cat – some sort of Burmese, I think – jumps on to the hob in the middle of the kitchen.

'Get down,' he shouts, and claps his hands. The cat jumps down and pads towards him. All his aggression melts away and, assuming a baby voice, he says, 'Who's my little fluffy-woo? Who's my little fluffikins?' He picks up the cat and, as it purrs in his arms, he says, 'Who's my little fluffy-friend, mmm?' And he nuzzles his nose against the fur on the cat's neck.

I feel embarrassed and awkward, as though I'm imposing on a personal and intimate moment.

'It's a nice cat. What's she called?'

'It's a he, and he's called Guts.'

'Sorry. I kind of think of cats as she's and dogs as he's. I suppose it's because I've had neither. Good name, though, all things considered.' I smile at him but he doesn't return it, and as he sets the cat down on the floor he says, 'The cat's called Guts because he never stops eating. Talking of which, have you eaten?'

It's a hell of a question. Have I eaten? I haven't eaten and I'm hungry but do I want to accept this man's food?

'I'm fine, thanks.'

'Well, I'm going to make something. You're very welcome.'

'What did you have in mind?'

'I thought we might have the cat.'

'You're joking, right?'

'No. Cat meat is very nutritious. It's only tradition says we shouldn't eat our household pets. I was saving Guts especially for you.' He grins. 'Of course I'm joking. I wouldn't eat Mr Gutzoid Scooby Cat.' We're back to the bonkers voice momentarily before he says, 'Come on, Tobe, keep up. I thought you had dealings with the comedy industry.'

'Sometimes, although your average comedian is a miserable bastard as a rule.'

'Another day, another *douleur*,' he says, and giggles at his joke before asking, 'Glass of champagne?'

'Thanks.'

He takes two champagne glasses from a cupboard, pulls a bottle from a huge chrome fridge, opens it and pours some out. He passes me a glass and says, 'Here's to us.'

'Cheers,' I reply, and take a sip.

'I was going to rustle up a little stir-fry. I'll make enough for two, so just see how you feel. I'm vegetarian so you don't have to worry about any meat of dubious origin.' I force a laugh, as though this were the last thing on my mind, and take another sip of champagne.

'So I suppose you'd like to hear a little bit about me. How I came to be in this line of work?'

I get a lot of this with new clients. They seem to think I need to know every last vestige of their personal histories as background information for my task of selling them as pop stars, actors, comedians or, in this case, serial killers. I don't. But I must confess to having more than a passing interest in this guy's story. I have a feeling his biography may be a little different from the rest.

'I grew up in the Midlands. My parents were teachers. My mother taught PE and my father taught history. I had a normal childhood – nothing would have led even the most probing of shrinks to so much as hazard a guess at what I might end up becoming. I did well at school. Got good

O-levels and A-levels. I could have gone to university, Oxford or Cambridge even, but I took one look at the other kids from my school who were heading off there and decided I couldn't handle another three years with the likes of them. So, I joined the army and went off to Sandhurst. I had no concept of what the armed forces actually did other than what I'd watched in war films. I just thought it'd be exciting. Like the joke, I wanted to travel the world, meet lots of interesting people, and kill them. The killing bit particularly appealed to me. As I've told you before, when I was a kid I dreamed of becoming a serial killer. Not for me the posters of footballers and pop stars on my bedroom wall. Just a scrapbook with newspaper cuttings about the latest psychopath to grab the headlines. So, when other kids went on about the lack of freedom I'd face in the army, I knew they'd got it all wrong. As far as I was concerned, you were granted the ultimate freedom. You had the freedom to kill. In certain situations, you were positively encouraged to do so. What other job could give you that freedom? In my mind, being a soldier was an almost mystical occupation. Nothing else even came close.'

He's cutting onions and garlic on a chopping board and the knife is a blur across the tips of his fingers. He reminds me of some smug celebrity being interviewed at home, talking about his life for the nth time, reciting the script he's recited a thousand times before.

'So I climbed the tree. I was ambitious. I won't bore you with regiments and ranks and so forth. It'd probably be pretty meaningless to you anyway. Now, as you are no doubt aware, in 1982 the Argentinian military junta decided to invade the Falklands. Next thing I know, I'm on a ship heading south towards a series of events that would change my life and the lives of many others who came into contact with me, for ever.

'What my Falklands experiences did were to show me a side of myself I didn't know existed. The thing about the army is you spend a long time training for a situation that rarely, if ever, happens. And when it does happen and you're in combat, you never really know how you and the men around you are going to react. Everyone reacts differently. Some bottle it straight away, but it's never the ones you think it'll be. Others, perhaps those guys who you thought weren't up to it, are as steady as a rock. The real test is when you see another man, especially if he's a friend, getting his legs blown off by a landmine and he's crawling towards you screaming. Happened to me. My best mate Lenny. As I say, people react to it in different ways.' He's stopped chopping now and stares at his fingers thoughtfully.

'How did you react?'

'I shot him straight through the forehead. Did us both a favour.' He resumes his chopping in silence and I wrestle with the dilemma of whether to say anything – offer him my condolences perhaps. Before I can make a decision, he says, 'Lenny wasn't the only man I killed that day. A couple of hours later, we were approaching an old deserted quarry. I felt almost certain it would be empty because it provided virtually zero cover. There were just a few low shrubs and bushes. I was leading some men around the western edge of the quarry when I saw them. There were four of them in total. Two of them were squatting down tending to a casualty and a fourth was standing with his back to the others, struggling to light a cigarette in the high winds. Our eyes met. I don't know whether he was going to try to surrender. I didn't give him time to make that decision. I'd shouldered my gun before he'd even let go of the cigarette. I shot him straight through the forehead, and just as it was with Lenny earlier on, the bullet punched out the back of his skull. It felt good. It felt as though we were quits. It was revenge, or that's how I justified it to myself. I would have been quite happy to have opened fire on the others in the quarry but it was obvious they weren't going to put up a fight and were, in fact, desperate to surrender. I felt exhilarated by my killing of the Argentinian and looked forward to repeating the experience.

'Thankfully, I didn't have to wait long. A few days later, we retook the islands. I was put in charge of one of a number of units whose purpose was to round up all the Argentinian troops who were separated from the rest of their men and still at large on the islands. For most of us, it was an exciting time. The war was over, we were convinced of our hero status back home in the UK, and the Argentinian stragglers put up no resistance whatsoever. But for some reason I didn't share the general feelings of euphoria. I found myself thinking about killing Lenny and the Argentinian. Instead of feeling horror for what I'd done, I found myself mesmerised by images of the perfect round bullet holes in their foreheads, and the bloody eruptions of brain and skull from the backs of their heads which looked like flowers, their petals opening up, reaching out to the sun.' He looks up from his cooking with a nervous expression, as though he's fearful of my mocking him for his flights of fancy. I try to maintain an expression of solemnity and he says, as though I'd interrupted him, 'Bear with me, Tobe. I know this must seem strange after dealing with your show business types, but it's better you know all this stuff. Anyway, one day, at the start of the clean-up operation, we came upon an abandoned farmhouse.' He scrapes the onions and garlic and chopped vegetables into a wok he's been heating on the hob and the oil spits and hisses. He shakes the wok backwards and forwards, causing flames to jump and billow and cast an orange glow against his face. 'It was late in the day,' he continues, 'and the men were tired. So, I let them have a rest while I had a recce around the farmhouse. I've always been an inquisitive bastard. It was obvious the occupants had been moved out by the Argentinians at the start of the conflict, so I started going through the drawers and cupboards, looking at photographs and letters, trying to get some mental image of how people might live in a remote farmhouse in a godforsaken place like the Falklands. So convinced was I that the farmhouse was empty I attributed the faint sounds of movement above me on the first floor to a bird that had got in through a broken window, or a rat maybe. When I made it upstairs and opened the door to the bedroom from where I'd heard the noise, you can imagine I was more than a little surprised to find a room full of Argentinian soldiers. There were nine of them. I didn't count them at the time; I was told it was nine later. Doubtless they were more frightened of me than I was of them. Some were sitting on the floor, others, maybe two or three, were lying on a large bed in the middle of the room. The ones on the bed were injured, covered in bloody makeshift bandages. I don't know what they were all doing there. Perhaps they'd been separated from the rest of their men during battle and decided to shelter in the farmhouse until they were either relieved by their own troops or had an opportunity to surrender. But why they didn't make themselves known to us beforehand, I have no idea. Maybe they didn't know the war was over, us only having retaken Port Stanley a couple of days before. I just don't know. But for whatever reason, there they were hiding away in the bedroom of this farmhouse. It was like destiny had handed them to me on a plate. I opened the door and nine pairs of eyes met mine. A couple of them raised their hands in surrender but by then I'd shouldered my gun. There was a brief moment of collective realisation for all of us. We all knew what I was going to do. A couple of them shouted at me but I wasn't going to be stopped, not by my own victims. The bullet wounds grew out of their bodies like roses. I kept my finger on the trigger until the magazine was empty and it all went silent again save for the rolling of the cartridge cases on the floorboards and the sound of the men coming in from outside and rushing up the stairs. I wanted to savour my handiwork, but I wasn't given the chance. They wanted to know what had happened. For a moment I felt like clicking another magazine into the gun and taking them out as well just so I could have some peace and quiet. Thankfully I didn't. That would have got me into some serious trouble. As it was, it didn't look good. One of the Argentinians had both legs missing and must have been half dead already. Difficult to claim he was trying to kill me. The thing is, no official complaint or charges were ever levelled at me. When I returned home, the powers that be told me that in view of my otherwise excellent record they were going to turn a blind eye to the whole situation. I literally got away with murder. We were at war. I was young and hot-headed. Over-exuberant, they called it. I was discharged – honourably. I'd carried out an atrocity and I walked just because I'd got the right clothes on and done it at the right time and in the right place.'

He mixes the rice that's been boiling in the saucepan next to the wok and adds it to the vegetables before stirring it all around with a large wooden spoon.

'So what does a hot-headed young twenty-three-year-old do when he's got himself a taste for killing? Answer: he tries to find himself another job that will allow him to kill. And that's exactly what I did. Through various army contacts I had, I managed to land myself a job with an organisation called the African Security Federation. It's an organisation that safeguards the interests of various multinational corporations whose activities in Africa are of a somewhat controversial nature: oil and mineral mining companies, nuclear power companies, that sort of thing. The ASF is like a private militia and equally well armed. In addition to providing a buffer between their paymasters and organisations that might be resistant to their often highly environmentally damaging and illegal activities, the ASF also arranges contract killings utilising the services of men like me. Most of these contracts are commissioned by unscrupulous African governments keen to rid themselves of troublesome elements within their own countries.

'My first job for the ASF was one of these. It was the assassination of a union leader in the Ivory Coast. I wasn't told why he had to die, or in fact any information about him whatsoever, other than the details I required for the hit. As with all my jobs, I was sent a folder containing photographs and details of the target's day-to-day movements. This one was a fairly easy hit for which I was thankful. It required an easy head shot from a tower block overlooking a political rally where the target was speaking. This being a government job, I was given a police escort there and away.

'In time I built up a reputation for taking on assignments others wouldn't. Some guys won't take out women, for example. It doesn't bother me. I've done four; three deliberately as targets of respective hits and one who was the wife of a target who went up in a car bomb I'd planted. Their three kids went up with them. Unfortunate, I grant you, but it comes with the territory.'

He scoops the rice and vegetables from the wok and shares them out between two plates. He passes one to me and we sit at a pine table to eat.

'There you go,' he says, his fork poised, 'all made from the finest organic ingredients and not a piece of meat in sight. Get stuck in.' We eat in silence for about half a minute before he says, 'I killed forty-seven people before I decided to become a serial killer,' and I find myself nodding in approval. 'By the early nineties I was the ASF's top man, or at least the ASF's busiest man. I'd go anywhere and kill anybody. The way I see it, a lot of it boils down to hormones. I can't help my hormones just as you can't help yours. Evolution has left us a legacy from prehistory. Our bodies were designed for the life our ancestors lived tens of thousands of years ago when the environment was a whole lot different from what it is today. Our bodies haven't changed since then, neither have our hormones.

Men are designed to kill. They are predatory. Humans are pack animals. The responsibility of feeding the pack falls to the dominant males. Some of those dominant males are better at killing than others and these get the pick of the females. Their genetic line is assured.'

'And what about you?' I interrupt. 'What about your genetic line?'

'It's all taken care of. I don't even know how many kids I've got. My refusal to take any contraceptive measures whatsoever – perforated condoms being my favourite trick – combined with my seeming inability to make a commitment to a woman for longer than a couple of weeks means I've got kids all over the place.'

'Surely some of them were aborted?'

'I'm sure some of them were but I'm also sure a lot of them weren't. It's one of the bonuses of living down here and assuming a number of bogus identities – it means no one can find me to slap another paternity suit on me. I figure I've done enough for those kids. I've given them life – what more do they want?'

I'm about to suggest they might want a father but decide against it and say, 'Surely the desire to kill – for you or anyone – isn't confined to genetics?'

'No, of course it isn't, but much of the propensity to kill is, and when this is combined with certain key influences and behavioural characteristics then a serial killer may be created. In such instances, I'll agree with the most conservative exponent of law and order that you can't allow maniacs to wander the streets killing people. That is not acceptable. Lock them up and throw away the key. I'm all for that. Better still, if your laws will allow it, kill them. But, you see, I'm not a maniac. I'm not driven to kill. When serial killers kill people, it is through a massive loss of self-control. When I kill, on the other hand, it is the ultimate expression of self-control. I am never more in control. I am making an existential decision. It is an affirmation of my freedom that I can kill without guilt and without remorse. I feel no anger or hatred for the people I kill. I feel nothing. If anything, my feelings towards my victims err more on the side of affection. My killing of a person is a union of destinies that becomes an act of transcendence for us both. Killing someone for no reason whatsoever – no fear, no hatred, no jealousy, no curiosity, not even an aberrant motive like cannibalism or sexual thrill, just for the sheer fact of doing it – well, that goes beyond being a social experiment, it's a' – he puts down his fork and looks up at the ceiling as though conjuring up some former enlightenment – 'it's a work of art.

'During my first few years with the ASF, it was different. I was confused. Remorse was my greatest fear. I still felt the occasional pang for the Argentinians in the farmhouse and the family in the car bombing I mentioned earlier. But in my darkest moments I was able to soothe my angst with the knowledge that I was only doing my job. Just as the perpetrators of war crimes can build up a culture of justification around their crimes, so I could always fall back on the notion that in my worst excesses I was either killing in the name of Queen and country or for financial gain. Both of them solid, tangible reasons. But as time went on, I felt an increasing desire to make an ideological leap and carry out my first murder for which there was no justification or motivation outside of my own desire to do it. I saw it as a quest for existential freedom. Society always differentiates morally between different kinds of killing. Murder is deplorable, while killing an enemy in battle, on the other hand, or as an act of self-defence, is fine. Every premeditated killing has a belief system behind it. The perpetrator of the killing feels, even if it's only for the most fleeting of moments, that what they are doing is right and just. It seems to me the larger the number of people who agree with you, the more likely you are to get away with it. Be applauded for it, even. I decided I wanted to carry out a killing where there was no such belief system, where the act and the perpetrator of the act were morally autonomous of one another, therefore allowing the victim to become a canvas on which the killer, as artist – me – could paint an image of the futility of mankind.

'I was living in South Africa at the time. I had a ramshackle old beach house a couple of hours outside Cape Town. I was driving into town one day and there was a young guy in his twenties with a backpack hitchhiking along the coast road. I pulled over. Turned out he was an Australian. We set off for town together. He was keen to chat. Wanted to know who I was and what I did. So, I told him. I knew he wasn't going to live so there was no point keeping anything from him. It helped to harden my resolve as well. He was fascinated to meet a real-life assassin and fired questions at me. What did it feel like to kill a man? That sort of thing. We got on well, or as well as two men can when one of them intends to kill the other in a few minutes' time. He told me mine was the first car that had gone past and because he'd allowed the whole afternoon for his journey, he'd now be early for his friend who he was meeting at a youth hostel on Long Street in central Cape Town. I could tell from his clothes and his hair and the fact that he called me "man" that he was a stoner. So, I told him I was early for an appointment as well, and suggested we go for a smoke as a pleasant way of killing some time. He agreed. He was a big bastard. I knew I'd have a struggle on my hands, but I also knew killing him was something I just had to do. I don't think I've ever felt so nervous. Even under fire in the Falklands. My hands were sweating on the steering wheel. As we drove along the road at the foot of Table Mountain, my mind was racing, trying to think of ways of disabling him before I could kill him with my bare hands which, by the way, I'd decided was another way of proving my integrity as a killer as opposed to a hired hit-man.

'There were a few other cars around but by the time we reached the end of the road, they had all turned off into lay-bys in order to admire the view of the city stretched away beneath us. I noticed he hadn't followed my example and put his seat belt on, so I virtually stood on the brake pedal. We skidded for a few yards and then the tyres bit into the tarmac and we screeched to an abrupt halt. I'd wanted to throw him forward so he'd crack his head against the dashboard or windscreen in order to daze him before I set about strangling him. The trouble was, I never got the chance. I'd overdone it on the brakes, you see, and he was catapulted through the windscreen in a shower of glass. He missed the bonnet altogether and hit the road head first. When I got out of the car and took a look at him, the top of his head was caved in like the top of a boiled egg when you've whacked it with a teaspoon. There was blood everywhere and one of his eyes was hanging out of its socket on a thread of cartilage or vein or something. I felt so angry with him that he should have died like this in what was little more than a stupid accident that I kicked him in the head. This succeeded in snapping the eyeball free of its connecting tendril and it ended up staring up at me from a pool of blood on the road. I felt affronted by its gaze and I stamped on it.'

I'm about to spear a button mushroom with my fork but think better of it and push it to the side of the plate.

'Because of all the glass and blood everywhere, I decided I'd be as well to play along with the illusion that we had had an accident. All I had to think up was a reason as to why I'd had to brake so suddenly. I like to think my reason was pretty inspired. A couple of weeks previously there had been a feature on the television news about some sightings of leopards in the Table Mountain region where it was thought there hadn't been leopards for years. So that was it – a leopard had run out in front of the car. Honestly, Officer. The authorities swallowed the story hook, line and sinker. I even ended up in the local paper, whose journalists appeared to be far more interested in the leopard sighting than the death of the young Aussie kid.

'A few days later, the ASF called me up and told me I was needed in Algeria to kill a bent government official or, as was more likely to be the case knowing Algerian politics, a straight government official. As much as I was desperate to get out there again and see whether I could kill without guilt, there was no way I was going to turn down work.'

He stops to take a mouthful of food and I ask him, 'Why

didn't you at least kill this guy with your bare hands so you could practise for the real thing?'

He shakes his head as though I've missed the point entirely, and when he's finished chewing he says, 'When you're hired to kill someone, your reputation rests on your ability to do the job as quickly and efficiently as possible. You go in, do the job and get out with the minimum of fuss. You don't start messing about strangling people when you're working for an organisation like the ASF. So, I went to Algeria and killed the government official. He lived unguarded in a remote village outside Algiers. I remember going to his house, knocking on his door and, when he answered, emptying a revolver into his head. Quick and easy. I was back home in the Cape by the next morning with nothing else on my mind but thoughts of killing someone for myself. So, as before, I set off towards Cape Town in my car. The windscreen had been mended but there were still droplets of blood on the roof lining. This time I came across a couple of backpackers, a girl and a boy. I drove past them at first because I was looking for one person on their own, but after a couple of miles' worth of consideration I thought to myself that if I was serious about it then why not two at once? That would really test my mettle. I turned the car around and decided I'd leave it up to chance. If they were still there when I got back then destiny decreed it should be so. And they were, so I gave them a lift. They didn't seem to find it strange I'd doubled back for them or, if they did, they didn't mention it. They were brother and sister, as it turned out, not girlfriend and boyfriend as I'd first thought. They introduced themselves as Marie and Jean-Claude or something typically French like that. I told them I had to stop off at my brother's house on the way into Cape Town and they said fine. I knew where I was headed. I'd been to this place a few weeks before, just driving around one afternoon, and had thought to myself how remote it was. No houses, just deserted beaches for miles. Whales breed along that stretch of coast and often launch themselves out of the sea and crash back into the water in a flurry of foam. It's an amazing sight. I'd sat there watching them for hours.

'When I got to the rocky headland, it was completely deserted as before. Not a soul in sight, just the three of us sitting on a slab of rock wedged between the sky and the ocean. I spun around in my seat so I was kneeling on it facing into the back. They were giggling about something. The boy was about twenty-one and his sister was a couple of years younger. They were young and healthy and had everything to live for and, as far as I was concerned, everything to die for too. The boy said something like, 'Where is your brother's house?" He was just beginning to realise there was something wrong when I grabbed him and his sister by the hair and cracked their heads together, and I kept cracking their heads together until they were both unconscious. They might have been dead for all I know, but I still stuck a knife into each of their chests to make sure. The girl had managed to scratch my arm pretty badly. I had to fix a tourniquet to it to staunch the flow of blood, which made digging the grave pretty difficult. But I got there in the end, pushed their bodies in, and that was the end of that. As far as I'm aware, no one ever found them. There'll be a family somewhere in France wondering what happened to their son and daughter. I can picture them sitting there in some French town wondering when the kids are coming home.' He takes a final mouthful of food and pushes his plate away.

'I drove off. Got back on the main road and went home, where I drank some Scotch and stitched up my arm. There.' He holds out his arm and shows me the crescent-shaped scar just above his wrist. 'I'd crossed the line. Now I just had to wait and see if I could weather the storms of guilt and remorse. It was make or break, but I'd prepared for it and it wasn't as bad as I thought. I've always believed the path to freedom is the conquering of one's fears. My greatest fear in life was remorse, and I'd finally nailed it. For the first time in my life, I felt free and happy. I knew I didn't *need* to kill, but if I did kill, for whatever reason, I could do so without fear of my conscience getting the better of me.

'For about five years I killed just the people I was paid to kill by the ASF. It was a busy time. I made a lot of money. And I became bored. I decided I'd make a trip to the UK. I hadn't been back for years. After visiting my parents for a few days, I decided I'd look up some old friends. One of them was a guy called Ewan who I'd known in the Falklands. We met in a pub in Clapham. It turned out he'd had a pretty rough time of it after the war. He'd drifted from one dead-end job to another, his self-esteem diminishing with each one. He was living with his elderly father, who had recently suffered a series of strokes which had left him partially paralysed, and he couldn't be left alone for more than a couple of hours at a time. So,

Ewan asked me back to the flat they shared for a drink and to reminisce about old times. He kept apologising for the state of place on the way there but his apologies didn't prepare me for the squalor they lived in. It smelt like a sewer. His father was a perfect advertisement for euthanasia, voluntary or otherwise. The poor old sod was having terrible problems with his bowels. It was obvious he was in dire need of a colostomy bag or something, but his pride had prevented him from taking the plunge. His pride, however, didn't prevent him from calling Ewan through from the living room every so often to "press the button", as he called it, which entailed Ewan sticking his finger up his arse to find a pressure point which, when pressed, would help him go. Ewan had to press the button about three or four times a day. It was demeaning. I would have been quite happy to have left and never come back were it not for the talk I had with the old boy. I was trying to make polite conversation with him and asked him what line of work he'd been in. He told me he'd worked for a building company after the war which was principally contracted to the Ministry of Defence. It turned out he'd been a site foreman on the Churchill Citadel. He was still technically prevented from talking about it by the Official Secrets Act but he didn't seem to care and enjoyed the opportunity for a chat. I'd been to the Cabinet War Rooms as a child and, later on, when I was in the army, I'd heard tell of nuclear fall-out shelters beneath London, but I'd never imagined there was anything so huge as this. I was fascinated by what he told me and I asked him if he thought it would be possible to gain access to it. He said he'd thought about this at length and decided that, though it would be impossible via the main entrance in St George's House, it might be possible to get in through the cellars of Albion House, an old office block owned by the government which was let to private businesses. When I subsequently enquired of the letting agent whether any of the offices on the ground floor of Albion House were vacant, he told me they all were.

'I acquired the lease on the office you came through earlier under a false identity. Ewan came with me on my first foray underground and it turned out his dad was right. Once we'd taken a pickaxe to the cellar wall in Albion House, we managed to get into the central access shaft through which you passed earlier, and from there down to the stream where we inflated the dinghy the old man had told us to bring with us, and found our way to the service lifts above the citadel. These were completely inoperable but we'd come prepared with climbing gear and abseiled down one of the shafts. We didn't make a full exploration on that visit – we were far more concerned that, having found our way in, we should be able to find our way out again.

'I became obsessed with this place and soon decided I wanted to make my home down here. I employed Ewan to help me carry out the work that was required to make the place habitable. It took eighteen months. So as to not arouse suspicion, we arrived every morning in our suits and, in the evenings, we'd wash and change out of our overalls back into our suits again before leaving.'

'Why this floor?' I ask him as he takes a sip of his champagne. 'Why not one nearer the surface that's easier to get to?'

'As I mentioned before, I wanted the swimming pool.

I knew I was going to have to spend long periods of time down here so I thought I might as well make it as comfortable as possible with all the amenities I require. This place is my first real home and a perfect location, I think you'll agree, for a man in my line of work. I can appear from nowhere, kill someone, then lose myself in one of the busiest city centres in the world before quite literally vanishing off the face of the earth.'

'So what happened to Ewan?'

'Poor Ewan, he had an accident.'

'A real accident or couldn't you afford for anyone other than yourself to know where you lived?'

'When you've killed as many people as me you don't have to euphemise about death. If I'd killed Ewan then I'd tell you. It's no skin off my nose. Death doesn't hold the same horror for me as it does for you. Sadly, Ewan fell down the lift shaft one day while trying to fix up the lift. No murder, Tobe, just a straightforward accident.'

'What happened to his father?'

'I did the only decent thing I could do under the circumstances. I put him out of his misery.'

'Like a sick animal.'

'Yes, Tobe, like the sick animal he was. I went around to see him after Ewan's death and told him what had happened. He knew it was the end. I did him a favour. It was a mercy killing.'

'So, you've given me all the background, how you developed the ability to kill without remorse and why you're living hundreds of feet underground in a deserted nuclear fall-out shelter, but perhaps now you'd like to tell me why you've decided to become a serial killer. You've admitted you don't need to kill, so why do it?'

He smiles at me as though he's amused by my childlike bluntness and naïvety. 'If you've got a gift then I think you owe it to yourself to use that gift. Your gift is that you have an acute understanding of the workings of show business and the creation and management of our so-called stars. You don't waste your gift, you use it, and because of it you earn a big salary and are admired and respected by your peers. My gift is that I can kill without remorse. So what I am doing is using the gift I've been given both as an expression of my existential freedom and as a means of creating something that will stand the test of time, something lasting in a world of impermanence, a phenomenon, a legend that will resonate throughout history. This isn't so much crime, as art. I see myself as the ultimate art terrorist. That guy with his chopped-up animals in formaldehyde, what he does is only shocking to people with limited imaginations. I'm all for shocking the squares, but how much better to shock the whole of society to its very core. I think, if you really want to be subversive, then how about a freshly killed and dismembered human body? Now that's what I call art.'

'So how do you see yourself, as serial killer or artist?'

'I don't really care what labels people want to pin on me. All I know is I'm transcending the shallow, hopeless cult of celebrity and showing all those losers just what they really are – bubbles, little bubbles that look pretty for a moment then float away and, pop, they've gone. There's nothing left. No substance, nothing. With me, on the other hand, my legend will reverberate throughout history and no one will ever know who I was or why I did what I did.'

'Just like Jack the Ripper?'

'If you like, yes. Are you a fan?'

'It's a great story. To my mind, he's the one to beat. But while I can understand his nickname, I can't understand yours. Why "The Piper"?'

'You're probably hoping for some cryptic explanation along the lines of "I see myself as a latter-day Pied Piper" or "a piper at the gates of dawn" or something to do with "he who pays the piper calls the tune", but you see, it's nothing that clever. In fact, it's nothing. Nothing at all. I just like the name. It's got a certain enigmatic quality to it and I didn't want to let the papers come up with something bland. Before the police released the details of my graffiti, one of the papers called me the Five-Star Killer on account of the hotels where the killings took place. I was all set to write to them and put them straight before it caught on but, thankfully, I didn't have to. Now, people obsess about what the Piper means as though it's a clue to my identity. And it isn't, so all the better.'

'I must admit to being a little confused. You seem to have all this well and truly mapped out and know exactly what you're doing. I don't understand what you want from me.'

'Oh, come on, Tobe, you're not telling me there aren't a few angles I haven't thought of. You've been doing this sort of stuff for years. OK, so you're not in exactly the same line of work as me but the same rules apply. There must be stuff I can do to etch my deeds even more deeply into the historical consciousness.'

Broadly speaking there are two types of client I have to deal with. The first type wants to hear what I've got to say because they're devoid of ideas, don't know how to move on and need some advice pronto. The second type wants to hear what I've got to say not because they lack their own ideas but because they want to reassure themselves they've already got the whole situation covered and that their ideas are better than mine anyway. I have a feeling this guy falls into the latter category.

'It's not as though you really need me,' I tell him. 'As the old adage goes, if it ain't broke, don't fix it. However, if you want to know what I'd do if I were involved in the management of your career, then I'd develop a clear plan of where you're going and where you want to be farther down the line. Let's face it, you've established the brand perfectly. That's the hardest bit done. There isn't a man, woman or child in this country who doesn't know who the Piper is. You've achieved more fame, more notoriety and more global media coverage than your average celebrity chump could hope for in a lifetime. Now, you have to set your sights on finite goals and set about achieving them one by one. I think your first goal should be to take serial killing to a new level. As much as you claim that what you do is art, to the average bloke in the street you're a serial killer first and foremost, and with that label comes a lot of baggage. Serial killer stories, both factual and fictitious, have been around for so long that people have a sophisticated knowledge of what a serial killer does and how he behaves. I think you've got to start playing around with the format. Body count has never been the most important factor in the fame and notoriety of a serial killer. It's style that counts, although in the long run, if you take my advice, your body count will most likely eclipse the most prolific of killers anyway, but first things first.

'You have to make sure the public don't get complacent about what you do. Always remember there are countless celebrities backed by the massed ranks of the global entertainment industries vying for your airtime and print space. Owing to the nature of your activities, you're also competing with wars, famines, droughts, mass murders, terrorist bombings, royal weddings and celebrity deaths. You've got to stay newsworthy, and that means you've got to be adaptable in order to keep grabbing the headlines. This isn't the Victorian England of Jack the Ripper's day. You've got to do a whole lot more before you disappear and bequeath your legend to mankind. Killing in hotels was a great idea, as was the nationality of your victims. I read somewhere the other day that as a result of your handiwork, tourist bookings to London from America are down by forty-eight per cent. That's pretty impressive. Using music business terminology here, you've broken America. But I think now's the time to change your modus operandi. You should start to move away from hotels and from Americans. For starters, every hotel worker in London is on stand-by in the hope that they can be instrumental in your capture. This isn't through any selfless desire to rid the world of a vicious maniac, but rather so that they can have the chance to snatch their brief moment of fame. The stakes are high. Whichever have-a-go hero manages to nab the Piper stands the chance of achieving their fifteen minutes, and for the vast majority of lumpen proles in this country, that's about as good as it gets. So, don't give them the chance. While the authorities have their eyes focused on West End hotels, I think you should go and kill someone in their own home. You've already terrified the visitors and potential visitors to London; now you should switch your focus to the residents. You can go back to hotels at a later date and maybe target another nationality like the Japanese, but for the time being aim at the domestic market. Just remember you'll need to continue to grab those headlines, so don't just kill any old Londoner, kill someone in the public eye. That way, the media will go into a feeding frenzy. If you could kill a politician or a celebrity or someone in the royal family it'd be great, but initially set your sights on someone only marginally famous, and then work up to the big names from there. So, this is what I think your short-term goal should be.'

He nods his head and raises his eyebrows as though to say, 'Yes, and?'

'As far as your long-term goal is concerned, I think you should aim to move away from the constraints of the serial killing genre and move into other areas such as spree killing, mass murder, even terrorism. Fame isn't about admiration or respect. Nowadays, all it boils down to is people's awareness of you, and people will never be more aware of you than when they're frightened of you. Imagine how scary motiveless terrorism would be. Terrorism with no cause. Blowing away hundreds, maybe even thousands, of people for no reason whatsoever. No dodgy political motives, no ranting letters outlining some crass political cause, no coded bomb warnings, just boom, bye-bye. And think of the video footage you could send to the police. You could run the explosion backwards in slow motion and give it a classical soundtrack. Tchaikovsky perhaps. Just a thought. What you have to remember is there are no rules any more in show business, art, call it what you want. All the boundaries are coming down. Just as pop stars become artists or film stars, and television turns members of the public into celebrities, I don't see why you can't transform yourself from a serial killer into something else entirely.'

THE ALBATROSS SUITE

'Bye, Tobe,' he said, and let go of the dinghy. I was carried off on the current and, just as he'd told me I would, I drifted through under a low arch into another tunnel which carried me along past a tiny gravel beach covered with rats, their squeaks echoing against the enclosed brickwork and making me shudder. I tied the dinghy up to some railings on what appeared to be a section of canal towpath and pulled myself out. Any relief I might have felt at having finished my navigation of the underground stream was tempered by the knowledge that I now had to complete what he'd told me (with undisguised relish) was the most dangerous part of the journey. This involved climbing up a rope ladder to the start of the metal walkway across which I'd come earlier in the day. Vertigo set in about halfway up and I kept getting the shakes so badly I had to stop every few feet to try to control my hyperventilation. Near the top of the rope ladder my arms fell prey to excruciating cramps which I convinced myself would send me tumbling on to the cold stone floor at any moment. By the time I made it back on to the walkway, my relief was such I felt like crying. From there, I found my way along the passageway to the spiral stairs, then back into the offices of Wormald Holdings and out on to Whitehall and a ruddy London sunset.

There were two e-mails waiting for me on my return to Calamity Towers, one from Bill and one from Scarlet. I toyed with the idea of deleting Bill's straight away but decided against it and opened it instead. He was apologising for his sulky behaviour when we met for breakfast at Tony's caff. He said he was on the case as far as the Simeon Cruikshank/Sonny Page press scam was concerned and was looking forward, yes, looking forward, to seeing me soon. Creepy twat.

Scarlet's e-mail read as follows:

Tobe, hope you enjoyed Thailand. We said we'd meet up on your return so let's. I've booked the Shrubbery on the 3rd at 1 p.m. Let me know if you can't make it, otherwise I'll see you there. Who knows – might be like old times. Remember the Gardens Hotel?
  Love,
  Scarlet

A few weeks ago this conciliatory tone of hers would have made me obsess for hours as to what it implied. Now, I just don't know. The attraction I feel for her is as intense as ever, but whether I need her as I once did is another matter. I thought I did, I thought I couldn't live without her. But now, perhaps, I can, and that knowledge calms me and gives me strength as I sit waiting for her in the Shrubbery.

She's late as of about ten seconds ago. Between the two of us, tardiness is a privilege that only Scarlet can enjoy. Many's the time I've arrived a few minutes late at a proposed rendezvous such as this only to find she's been and gone. Hence my uncharacteristic earliness whenever I meet her. Not that being early bothers me unduly when seated in a quiet corner of this theatre of the absurd, watching the antics of the media and showbiz players. It's kind of amusing, especially as about half of them have found themselves on the opposite side of a desk to yours truly at some time or another during their frantic attempts to climb the greasy pole. For them, it's like visiting the doctor:

'For God's sake, you've got to help me, Doctor.'

'Well, what appears to be the problem?'

'I'm just not fucking famous enough.'

'Well, let's see what we can do.'

The thing is, although they all recognise me, and know only too well who I am, it's like I'm the clap doctor: they won't acknowledge me lest it appear to be an admission of some dark secret we share.

Seated at the table next to mine is Richard Hoare, the BBC executive, a man who takes the word smug to new extremities of meaning. He's wrested a bottle of champagne from the waiter so that he can make a big show of popping it himself. He doesn't want to risk losing the attention of his three guests for as much as a second. He pours the champagne, one glass for a mousey-haired woman with a shark nose who laughs like she's chewing carrion;

another glass for Mark Steinberg, the pink and bloated manager of a large stable of TV presenters who front teenage magazine-style programmes with about as much intellectual clout as a fart gag; and a final glass for the focus of both Hoare's and Steinberg's grovelling attention, Talatha Resnick, who it is rumoured is destined for great things at the BBC kids department. Looks like a contract's already in the bag by the way these two oily old sods are salivating over her. Talatha's looking good, it has to be said, with her lithe body squeezed into a pink crop top and combat pants. She's got a pierced navel which glistens silver against the tan skin of her flat stomach, but there's something not quite right about it. She's got one of those poppy-out belly buttons that are not button-like at all. It's like a pink acorn and – it makes me wince even to look at it – the silver bolt is stuck right through it.

The waiter snaps my attention from it.

'Can I get you a drink?'

'Yes, I'll have a tequila on the rocks, please.'

As he goes to fetch it, I turn my attention away from Talatha Resnick's pierced intestines and survey the rest of the room. There's Edward Morrow, the theatre critic, seated with his new beau at a table in the window. He's screwed up more careers with his vitriol than any man in London. He was involved in a notorious incident a couple of years ago after the first-night party for *Rodney King!*, the musical that dealt with the LA riots. He'd invited a young bloke from the chorus back to his house in Hampstead forgetting that this was the same guy who eighteen months before had starred in the musical *A Punk Rock Robin Hood!* and whom Morrow had described as having the voice of a tortured coyote. This was about the nicest and most constructive comment in his review and, thanks to opinions such as this, the show closed within a month of opening. So the story goes, Morrow settled back on his sofa waiting to be orally pleasured by the young singer, who grabbed the offending organ and sank his teeth into it. He admitted afterwards he'd wanted to bite it off altogether but was prevented from doing so by Morrow beating him over the head with a framed photograph of Dame Margot Fonteyn. The whole of the London theatre industry took sides. On the one side you had the old queens of the Shaftesbury Avenue mafia who felt as though they were not only defending the status quo but also one of their own, a man who had helped to perpetuate their culture of complacency for years; on the other side was the new wave of the arts world for whom the young thesp's chomp was seen as striking a blow – if you will – for artistic freedom.

At a table in the centre of the room is Roger Manley, the record producer, with his new protégées, Yo Yo Yo – Lisa Yo, Trisha Yo and Jasmine Yo – the gangsta rap band with a difference. The difference being they're female, all straight out of drama school, and the nearest they've come to South Central is a wine bar on the King's Road. In their videos and press shots, they're all homeboy swagger and pimp roll, while in here, away from the cameras, they all sit upright with straight backs just as they were told to in their posture classes and hang on every word that comes out of Manley's mouth. On the opposite side of the room, partially obscured by a huge tropical plant, is Christie Marcuse, the former porn star who has just landed a role in the next Spike Lee movie and looks set to be the first actress to successfully make the transition from porn to mainstream Hollywood. What she probably doesn't realise is that, despite the increase in her salary, credibility and self-respect, she's probably halved her audience. The man she's having lunch with is an old accountant of mine. I ponder on what this means for a moment, before the sight of Scarlet makes me jump. Her beauty always catches me off guard. It's as though her image in the here and now can't be saved to memory, not entirely. There's always a certain element that eludes capture, and it is the intensity of this mystery ingredient in her appearance which makes me catch my breath whenever I see her. And, when our eyes meet, I'm possessed. She pins me out, spread-eagled, ready for dissection. She opens me up, pulls my ribcage apart as though it were a just-cooked *moule*, thrusts her hand in and grabs hold.

'Hello, Tobe.'

'Hi, Scarlet.'

'I see you received my e-mail, then?'

'Looks like it.'

'I'm glad.'

'How're things at work?' I ask her after she's ordered a glass of champagne from the waiter.

'Same shit, different day,' she replies with a shrug. 'I hear you and Bill are getting divorced.'

'Not entirely. I'm staying on in an advisory capacity. I just won't get involved in the day-to-day running of the business.'

'And how is the business?'

'Not bad as far as I know. My trouble is, I don't care about it any more.'

'Don't lie,' she says with a derisory smile.

'It's true.'

'No it isn't. You care, you always care. You spend your life slagging everything off but, deep down, you'd be lost without your job. You love all those feelings of superiority you have over the people you deal with.'

Two minutes into our rendezvous and already Scarlet is telling me what I feel. This follows a pattern, but what confuses me is it's the pattern we established as part of our relationship. Our on-going relationship. She's behaving as though we're still together. I think I'll play along with it just to see where we're headed.

'You know as well as I do, Scarlet, the celebrities of today have become society's village idiots, not that that necessarily affects people's fascination with them, especially as your average joe in the street is little more than a village idiot himself. But everything's so competitive and serious nowadays. I've had enough. I want to do something new and challenging.'

Our drinks arrive and I break off while Scarlet clinks her champagne flute against my tumbler and says, 'Up yours.'

'And yours.'

We both take a sip and she says, 'I must admit, I'm beginning to tire of the whole deal too. I was in New York the other day interviewing Bruce Willis, and I was thinking to myself that a few years ago I'd have stayed awake for a week thinking about an assignment like that. Now, it means nothing. I found myself struggling to be civil to him.'

'Ever thought of getting out?'

'Nope. Not at the moment. Maybe one day. Maybe if I have kids.'

Kids? I've never heard Scarlet mention the word before in anything other than the most derisory tones. This is uncharted territory.

'I thought you hated kids.'

'I do, but that doesn't mean I never want to have one. I even thought for a brief moment I might have one with Hugo. He seemed like a man who might be good at dealing with that sort of thing. You know, responsible, would have coped if I'd decided to bugger off and leave him to it. But that's not to be now, is it?'

'Any news on the investigation?'

'None. It's a mystery.' She takes a big gulp of champagne and says, 'I wasn't seeing him, Tobe. He asked me out on numerous occasions. I went to dinner with him a couple of times and he made a pass at me on the last occasion which I brushed off, and that was the sum total of our relationship.'

'I believe you.'

'I should bloody hope so. He's not – sorry – he *wasn't* my type, and while I'll admit I did enjoy the fact he'd bullied you at school, that was the extent of the interest I felt in him.'

'Bullied me at school?'

'That's what he told me.'

'He didn't bully me at school. Well, maybe he did a bit.' I think of him dead in his coffin beneath a ton of soil and I'm glad. 'That appealed to you, did it? That he'd bullied me?'

'Yes, I have to say I think it did. It made me think of

how much I enjoy bullying you.' Did you get that? Enjoy not enjoyed. No past tense.

'What are you saying, Scarlet?'

'Oh, I'm not saying anything, Tobe. You know me. Actions speak louder than words. Always have when it's come to us.' Then her expression softens and she says, 'Remember our first date here? When we retired to the Gardens Hotel and I stripped off and so did you, and you must have thought your luck was in, and I just knocked you out cold. That was so funny.' She giggles. 'Who knows, maybe we could relive our past? What say you, Darling?'

It occurs to me this could just be an attempt to mess with my head, so I smile and turn my attention to the waiter, who is hovering over us hoping to take our order.

The thing about Scarlet is, she has a problem with serving staff. Always has. She is convinced that waiters and waitresses hate her, and indeed anyone they serve, because they've got the shit-end of the stick in the server-servee relationship. Therefore she greets what she perceives to be their thinly disguised derision with a condescension that drips with malevolence.

'I'll have the salad of root vegetable,' she says to him as though he were educationally subnormal and might benefit from a surfeit of enunciation and volume, 'followed by the lamb.' Just as she says lamb, there's a disturbance on the table to our left, where Mark Steinberg has knocked his glass of wine into Talatha Resnick's lap. She doesn't look too bothered about it but Steinberg is mortified and is on his feet calling our waiter over for a cloth and raining apologies down on La Resnick. Our waiter stands his ground for the few seconds it takes for the Shrubbery's accident and emergency unit to spring into action, and a waitress is dispatched at high speed with a cloth. During this time, Scarlet has not moved her eyes away from the waiter's face. The only change in her expression is that her eyes have got that little bit wider with each passing second, so when he turns back to look at her, she's glaring at him.

'Sorry, madam. Your main course?'

'I've told you my main course.'

'I'm sorry, I missed it.'

'No, *I'm* sorry you missed it. I'll have *the lamb*.' She enunciates this as though he were a myopic lip-reader trying to make out what she's saying from the other side of the room.

'How would you—'

'Rare,' she interrupts.

'And you, sir.'

'I'll have the scallops followed by the chicken with truffles.'

'And the wine?'

'We'll have a bottle of the Fleurie,' says Scarlet, handing him our menus and the wine list.

'And I'll have another tequila,' I say.

Scarlet appears to relax now the waiter's gone. She drains her glass of champagne and says, 'Now, where were we?'

'Reminiscing.'

'God, I never thought when I first met you I'd know you long enough for us to one day end up reminiscing.'

'You didn't like me much, did you?'

'Still don't,' she says, grinning, 'although – don't ask me

why – there's something about you I kind of like having around. It's not love or even affection, not in the traditional sense. I suppose it's that I just love to hurt you. Not in a vindictive way and probably not in the way you would want it to be to satisfy your own needs, but I just can't help myself.'

'What are you saying?'

'I'm saying we might try to take things one step at a time.'

'Towards what end?'

'Towards a new start?'

The twists of life confound me. There I was thinking I was all alone in the world, that my sexuality was cast adrift on a rudderless boat, and ahoy there, the good ship Scarlet heaves into view once more. I've got my girl back. I think. If I want her back, that is.

The waiter returns with the drinks.

'Wait there,' I tell him as he puts the tequila down in front of me, and I raise the glass to my lips and knock it back in one. 'Another one, please,' I tell him, and off he goes.

'You're such a fucking slob,' says Scarlet. 'I don't know how you can live with yourself.'

'It's all in the wrist,' I tell her.

The starters arrive along with the Fleurie and another tequila which bypasses my mouth altogether and splashes against the back of my throat, such is the speed with which I throw it back. I'm about to order another one from the waiter when Scarlet tells me, 'Leave it,' and there's such venom in her voice that I let him go without saying another word. 'If you're going to get drunk,' she says, 'at least do it with some style. Don't just send the damned waiter backwards and forwards to the bar. I can't enjoy my meal with him hovering around us all the time.'

I get stuck into the Fleurie instead, and by the time our mains have arrived I've ordered a second bottle. Scarlet's drinking heavily as well, and by the end of the meal the disparaging remarks we're making about our fellow diners have become louder and more vicious. We order a couple of brandies, and while the waiter goes to fetch them Scarlet tells me, 'I feel like making a scene.'

'What sort of scene did you have in mind?'

'One where I punch you.'

It'd be pointless to try to dissuade her; she's got that look in her eyes. Besides, it might be fun.

'Go ahead, then, punch me.'

'We'd better stand up.' As we do so, she unleashes a straight-arm punch that catches me under the chin and sends me careening into the table next to us, where I crash-land into their newly served desserts. Hoare, Steinberg, the woman with the shark nose and Talatha Resnick are all on their feet.

'I'm so sorry,' Scarlet says to them, 'I don't believe you ordered the fat bastard.'

Lying as I am across the table on my back, I'm only a couple of feet away from Talatha Resnick's pierced poppy-out belly button. A hush has descended on the entire restaurant as everyone tries to catch a glimpse of the disturbance.

'Jesus Christ,' I shout, 'that's not a body piercing, that's a fucking hernia kebab.'

Scarlet grabs me by the front of my shirt and pulls me to my feet. Steinberg and Hoare, trying to outdo each other with their indignation, start summoning waiters. Scarlet tells them to 'fucking calm down', while I contemplate the tartlet of pistachio and crème fraiche stuck to my sleeve.

'Good scran here, eh, Sharky?' I enquire of the woman with the nose as I scoop some up with my finger and plant in on my tongue.

Richard Hoare turns to Scarlet and has the stupidity to give her the 'I've never been so insulted in all my life' routine to which Scarlet replies in a booming voice, 'I have it on good authority that this man' – she points at him – 'this man here has the smallest penis in London. It is what is known as a micro-penis, and if it were so much as one millimetre smaller he'd officially be a woman.' Hoare's indignation dries up and he stands there with his mouth sagging open. Still holding me by the front of the shirt, Scarlet leads me towards the door. 'Get your credit card out, Tobe,' she tells me, 'this one's on you.'

The manager intercepts us in the lobby. I give him my credit card and Scarlet tells him to put the bill for Richard Hoare's table on it as well. I'm not arguing. Once we're all paid up I follow her out on to the street, where she hails a cab. 'The Gardens Hotel,' she tells the driver in the same fuck-you tone of voice she reserves for waiters and serving staff. As we set off, she pushes her hand down the front of my trousers and starts squeezing my balls just hard enough to prevent it from being pleasurable. We don't make any other contact. I let out the occasional groan when the testicle-grinding becomes too intense or one of her fingernails snags on my scrotum. The cabby watches us in the rear-view mirror, so much so he nearly crashes into a dispatch rider on St Martin's Lane. We pull up on Auster

Street and Scarlet removes her hand from my trousers. I pay the fare and we climb out. But instead of heading towards the Gardens Hotel, she leads me towards the dry cleaner's opposite.

'Where are we going?' I ask her.

'You'll like this,' she tells me. 'The Gardens management, in their infinite wisdom, have deemed me worthy to use the special entrance reserved for the use of those residents who require the utmost discretion. I kind of figured we might end up here so I made a reservation.'

She takes me by the hand and leads me through the bogus shopfront to a door in the back room. Having typed a code into a keypad, she leads me through the door, down some steps and along a narrow corridor, then up some more steps and out of a door into the still, quiet interior of the hotel. There's no one around.

'Why are we doing this, Scarlet?' I ask her. 'We're not famous. It doesn't matter if the whole of London sees us coming in through the front door.'

'We're doing it,' she says, 'because we can.'

She leads me to a door on which there's a brass plaque with the Albatross Suite written on it. She types in another code into the keypad by the door – or maybe it's the same code, I'm not checking – and we're in.

'When I was planning our little rendezvous this afternoon,' she says as she starts to undress, 'I thought I might book us into the same room we had on our first visit, and then I thought, cobblers to nostalgia, let's go for some real luxury. So here we are.'

I must admit I'm not overly concerned about the décor at

this particular moment in time while I'm hurriedly pulling my clothes off, but I won't tell her that.

'How about a little room service?' she asks. 'We can have whatever we want. Fancy a threesome? How about a foursome? Better still, how about watching me do it with someone else? Now that'd hurt, wouldn't it? Some good-looking bloke giving me what you can't give me while you sit there and watch and feel inadequate.'

'I don't think so somehow, Scarlet.'

'Me neither.'

Scarlet's naked now and standing opposite me, waiting for me to get my socks and boxer shorts off. She's always managed to keep in good shape. Goes to the gym, swimming, yoga, all that. My body is shapeless and flabby in comparison, and I feel ashamed of it, so much so that when she punches me in the stomach it feels as though I deserve it. As I double over, she puts me in a headlock and steers me through into the bathroom where, with her free hand, she puts the plug in the bath – it's a big marble corner bath – and turns on the taps. While she waits for the bath to fill up, she wraps the shower curtain around my neck and starts strangling me with it. I thrash around and manage to up-end myself into the bath and smack my head against the marble surround. I don't have time to ponder the skull-cracking pain before she's in the bath with me, legs astride me, turning me over on to my front. There're about six inches of water in the bath by now, enough so when my head is on its side against the bottom, my mouth and nose are entirely submerged. I rear up out of the water momentarily, just enough to take a half-breath before she puts her foot on my head and more or less treads on it, crushing it against the marble. There's running water thundering in my ears from the taps, and blood – mine I presume – like an expanding cloud in front of my eyes. I hope to God she's taken into consideration that I didn't manage to get a full breath back there. If she's thinking I can last for a full lung's worth then she's going to end up with a corpse on her hands.

She's certainly rediscovered her zeal for all this stuff, I'll give her that. Really putting her heart and soul into it she is.

I think I'm drowning.

LIVE AND DIRECT

There are crowds as far as the eye can see, steam rising off them into the cool night air where helicopters hover, their laser-white arc lights cutting shafts through the darkness like iridescent antennae. Against the barrier at the foot of the stage, a line of security guards, burly men with shaven heads, make no attempt to disguise the brutality of their methods, beating people back with baseball bats and pickaxe handles. The roar of the crowd reaches an ear-splitting crescendo as the stage explodes into light and a solitary figure – the Piper – appears from the side and takes centre-stage. He's wearing an orange boiler suit, white rubber boots, and on his head he wears a black Balaclava on the side of which a digital camcorder is mounted. Images from this are projected on to enormous video screens on either side of the stage, along with footage relayed from other cameras mounted on hundred-foot-long robotic arms that swoop and dive all around him. He points at a youth in the crowd and the security guards allow a sweaty young fan to break free of the barrier and make a dash for the stage, clambering up on to it then turning to the crowd to jump up and down excitedly, his hands raised in triumph, the most important moment in his life played out in front of the assembled masses and countless millions watching at home on their televisions. The Piper reaches into a pocket of his boiler suit and pulls out a cheese wire and hoops it around the youth's neck. As he pulls on the handles, the youth's outstretched arms flop to his sides and he slumps backwards, his dying face projected in pixellated close-up on the screens, blood spouting from his neck. The Piper lets go of the cheese wire and wrestles with the corpse, twisting the head until he succeeds in his endeavours and manages to pull it from the body with the spinal cord still attached, holding it aloft like a trophy. He places the end of the spinal chord into his mouth and feeds it in as though he's swallowing a sword. Down it goes until the butchered stump of the youth's neck is resting against his Balaclava-covered face, giving him the appearance of having two heads, one growing out of the other. He holds his arms out, assuming the shape of a crucifix, and starts to spin around, the projections on the video screen becoming dizzying and disorientating as he does so. When he stops, he grabs hold of his victim's head and pulls the spinal cord out of his mouth. Taking the end of the cord in his hand, he swings it around and around, as though it were a stone in a sling, and then lets it go so that it arcs out over the crowd, where thousands of hands reach out to catch it. One of the cameras is extended on its robotic arm so as to get a close-up of the fighting that has broken out as the fans try to claim their prize. The Piper takes a bow and then points to two more fans – a boy and a girl – doing battle with the security guards. They too are allowed on-stage and run towards the Piper, who pulls out a chainsaw from a holster mounted on a belt around his waist, starts it up and takes the girl's head off with one swipe, sending it bouncing away, her Piper baseball cap still in place. The Piper spins around to face the boy, who makes no attempt to avoid the chainsaw thrust between his legs and forced upwards. The cameras zoom in as he is torn apart from his groin to his skull. The two halves of his body remain together for a moment and then the Piper does a pantomime blow by puffing out his cheeks and stamping his foot, and they fall trembling to the floor. The chainsaw ends up going the same way as the head and spinal column, thrown high over the crowd towards countless hands that reach up to catch it, even though to do so will mean certain amputation. The Piper pulls off his Balaclava and takes a bow, but when he stands upright again I can see it's not the Piper receiving the hysterical adulation of his fans, but me. And then the footage stops and starts to play backwards again, as it always has done and always will do, on a never-ending loop in some long-lost compartment of my brain.

POWER TOOLS R US

The sheets have been tucked in around me with such force that I feel trapped beneath them, and succumbing to a panicky flash of claustrophobia, I rip them off.

'Scarlet?' I enquire of the empty room, but there's no reply, just the perennial hum of hotel central heating and plumbing. I swing my legs around and stand up. I feel shaky on my feet and my head aches as I walk through into the bathroom. On a chair in the corner are my clothes, neatly folded. Everywhere is spotless. You'd never imagine a violent act had taken place here only a short while before. When I catch sight of myself in the mirror, I can see there's a plaster stuck to the side of my head. Cautiously, I peel it back and see that it's been placed over a split in the skin about an inch long which I must have sustained when I fell and cracked my head in the bath.

I take a shower, dry myself and get dressed. As I'm making my way through the passageway to the bogus dry cleaner's we'd come through earlier, I realise I am not alone. Coming in the other direction is a tall man in a camel coat who is clearly drunk, so much so that his companion, all blond perm and lipstick and young enough to be his granddaughter, has to hold him up. I recognise him. He's the novelist Dickie Malachi. I read one of his books once. It was good. Some sort of spy thriller, if I remember correctly. I press myself up against the wall of the passageway in order to allow them to pass, but Dickie wants to speak to me. Leaning against his young companion, who is obviously less than impressed by his behaviour, he tells me, 'All this fun's got to come to an end one day. It can't go on for ever, can it?' Despite the hands tugging at his coat, Dickie wants an answer.

'Who knows? Maybe it will. It bloody well ought to.'

This pleases Dickie and he says, 'That's the spirit. Fuck 'em all.' He then proceeds to laugh at the top of his lungs as he allows himself to be led away. I take the steps up to the dry cleaner's and out on to the street, pulling the door to after me.

A cab approaches, its yellow FOR HIRE sign lit. I stick my hand out but I'm beaten to it by a woman in a business suit on the other side of the street. But here's a first – although the cabby was clearly intending to stop for her, as soon as he sees me he changes direction and pulls over to my side of the street.

'Desford Gardens, off Ladbroke Grove,' I tell him, and get in. It always wrong-foots me when cab drivers do something out of the ordinary. I prefer it when my prejudices are confirmed rather than contradicted. He doesn't even attempt to chat to me. The bastard.

The journey home allows me to ruminate on the situation

with Scarlet. I'm ecstatic, of course. At least, I think I'm ecstatic. This is what I've hoped and prayed for for the past five months. But there's a feeling of hesitancy too. As though it's all come too easily. More than that, it's as though I've made a fresh start, and if I get back with Scarlet I'll be squandering my chance of a new life. Scarlet is one of two possible futures for me now. The second one being my work with the Piper. If I am to become involved in the Piper's career and become an anonymous pioneer working far out on the edge of the show business industry, I know I must eschew the sort of emotional intensity Scarlet arouses in me. I have to keep a clear head. I have to get my act together.

The cabby's taking me a strange way home but I can't be bothered to question him about it – he'll only have some bullshit story about the traffic, like they always do. Only, hold on, this isn't right. We're not even on the road any more. We're running along a narrow tarmac strip in the shadow of the Westway.

'Where the hell are we going?' I ask him. He doesn't answer. I try to slide open the glass partition but it's locked shut. I try both of the doors but, as I kind of knew they would be, they're locked too.

We're pulling up now under the Westway and the grey concrete caught in the headlights is covered in street gang graffiti. I half expect to see shadowy figures standing around a fire in an oil drum. But there's no one, just me and the world's first silent cabby. He's a big bloke. Must be at least six feet, and although he doesn't look like the hard-nut type, he does look perfectly capable of beating the crap out of me should this situation degenerate into a physical confrontation. He pulls on the handbrake and turns off the headlights and I figure now's the time to try to prevent him from doing to me whatever it is he's brought me here to do. If I can work out what that is, of course.

'Listen, mate, I haven't got any money on me but you're very welcome to have what I've got. Take my wallet and I'll get out here and make my own way home.'

'We've met before.' He's softly spoken but his tone is self-assured and menacing.

'I don't think we have,' I say, trying to sound as friendly as possible. 'I don't even live in London. The last time I was here was when I was a kid. I'm down here on business—'

'You pissed in the back of my cab.'

'When?' I hurl back at him with the righteous indignation of a five-year-old who's been caught lying.

'About a month ago. Now, don't waste your breath because I know it was you.'

'How can you know it was me when it wasn't me?' I'm trying to maintain a conciliatory tone. 'I was abroad a month ago.'

'I said, don't waste your breath. Now I'm not going to hurt you. Not so long as you co-operate.'

'But I didn't piss in your cab. I don't know what—'

'Shut up!' Spots of phlegm spray against the windscreen as the ferocity of his outburst almost lifts him out of his seat. This explosion, coming as it does after his calm measured tone of only moments before, makes me think he's a complete fruitcake and I'm in serious trouble here.

'So what do you want?'

'A favour for a favour is all I want.' He has regained his

composure now and his voice is so soft it's little more than a whisper. 'You do something for me and I'll do something for you.'

There's a thunk as he flicks a switch and the doors are unlocked. I toy with the idea of doing a runner but I'd only have a couple of feet head start if I did, and before I can make a decision he's out of the door and into the back, pulling down one of the fold-up seats opposite me.

'It's simple,' he says, seated and facing me. 'You either do what I want or you get hurt.' And then, as an afterthought, he adds, 'Badly.'

In my head, he's tied down across the bonnet of his cab and I'm approaching him with a chainsaw. He's crying and begging me for mercy. I take his genitals off with one fluid sweep and he screams as plumes of blood erupt from the wound. I place the chainsaw against his chest and push. It glides through the bone, showering me with gore, and I don't finish pressing down until I can feel the blade's teeth snag against the metal of the cab's bonnet. But it's little consolation – back in the real world he's fumbling in his pocket and, just as I'm beginning to wrestle with the ghastly thought that maybe he's brought me here to pleasure him, he produces a piece of folded cardboard which opens out into a creased black-and-white publicity photograph of a girl of seventeen or so wearing the anodyne smile of the terminally under-talented. In the white border at the bottom are the words Sonia Maguire, and beneath them, smaller, Roger Wilton Entertainments and a mobile phone number. He taps a nail-bitten finger against her forehead and says, 'She's going places, this one, I can tell you.'

'That's great.'

'She's just as good as all that crap you hear on the radio. Better in fact.'

'I'm sure she is.' He could tell me she's the greatest chanteuse since Edith Piaf and I'd agree with him.

'I know who you are. I saw you on the TV and read about you in the papers afterwards when there was all that stink over what you'd said about the Piper. Tobe Darling, the man who chooses to piss in the back of my cab. So, to make amends for what you did and to stop me from kickin' your fuckin' head in, maybe you'd like to give me some free advice.'

'What do you want to know?'

'I want to know what I should do to get this girl her break into show business and put her where she rightfully belongs.'

'Which is where exactly?'

'On the radio, on the TV, on the, er, Internet.'

I look at the girl in the photograph again. I can see her future singing in pubs and down-market nightclubs around London. Doting father, family and friends, chicken 'n' chips in a basket. Maybe if she's lucky, an appearance on *Stars in Their Eyes*. He's looking at me awaiting an answer, a pearl of wisdom perhaps that will give him the edge over all the other hopeful fathers with big dreams for their little princesses.

'How long's your daughter been singing?'

'Oh, she's not my daughter.'

'I'm sorry. Your sister? Girlfriend?'

'She's my client.' He points to the bottom of the photograph. 'I'm Roger Wilton. Roger Wilton Entertainments is my company. As you can see, it's only a part-time venture at the moment, but when I'm established I'll be able to give up the taxi driving. Although it's handy for contacts, I'll give it that. I've had some of the biggest names in the music industry in the back of my cab.'

This is just all too grotesque. I have to get away from this man.

'I'm going to be sick,' I tell him.

'What?'

'I'm feeling unwell. I'm going to—' I fake a heave and he's got the door open for me immediately. As soon as my feet have touched the ground, I'm off.

Athletics was never my strong point. I'm breathless after about ten yards but the sound of the taxi's engine being started and the crunch of gravel as it accelerates towards me make me double my efforts. There's a one-storey brick building to my left with a carpark adjoining it. The taxi's close behind and I cast a stumbling shadow in its head-lights. There's a wire fence around the carpark. I head towards it and, with the taxi's bumper no more than ten feet away, I launch myself at it. My momentum and trajectory are just enough to carry me over the top and I crash-land on the other side. Once I've dragged myself to my feet, I notice it isn't a regular carpark. All the cars in it are black cabs. I've seen this place before from the Tube which runs overground near by. It's like a canteen-cum-social club for cabbies, and through the window I can see them all sitting there at tables, eating, drinking tea and, as you might expect, bloody talking. Roger Wilton Entertainments has sped away, but I'm not out of the woods yet. It feels as though I've been dropped behind enemy lines and at any moment a series of spotlights will click on, an alarm will sound and a legion of cabbies will descend upon me like a pack of dogs, hungry for revenge. All those years of non-communication, non-payment of tips and the occasional in-cab urination will come back to haunt me. Thankfully, I make it to the main road in one piece and point myself in the direction of Calamity Towers. A couple of taxis go past but I don't hail them. I think I'll walk home.

As I turn into Desford Gardens, I can see a man standing on my front steps speaking to someone – Ralph, I presume – through a thin opening in the door. I move a little closer and can see it's my bloody neighbour, Michael Willoughby. Surprisingly, Ralph has the chain on the door just as I told him to if anyone called. This is a good sign. This is the first time he's actually managed to carry out an instruction, however basic. I toy with the idea of turning around and walking away but decide against it. I can cope with Willoughby. As I approach, I hear him say, 'Make sure he calls me straight away.'

'Ah, Mr Willoughby,' I say, and he spins around. 'How marvellous to see you.'

'Tobe Darling,' he says, as though he's uttering an explective. 'I think we need a bit of a chat, don't you?'

'I'm afraid it's going to have to be hello and goodbye.'

'There's going to be no goodbye from me until you've agreed to transform the patch of jungle behind your house into a garden.'

'Come on, open the door,' I tell Ralph, but his eyes dart from my face to Willoughby's and back again, his eyebrows dancing manically above them. 'Kelly?' he asks of both of us.

'Don't fuck about now, Ralph. Just undo the chain and let me in.'

'Unless you procure the services of a gardening company to chop it all down, or at least those parts of it overhanging your neighbours' gardens, you will leave me no alternative but to engage my solicitor to force you to do so. This isn't just me who's behind this, you understand. There are five of us on the residents' association immediately affected by your thoughtlessness. There's Lucy Harrington, the Millburns, Christopher—'

'Can't we talk about this in the morning? Ralph, open the door.'

'Who is this person?' asks Willoughby.

'He's my butler.'

'Your butler?' he says, as though this were the most ridiculous thing he's ever heard, which it might be, all things considered. 'But he doesn't appear to understand a word of English, just keeps calling me, "Kelly" over and over.'

'Oh, he does that to you too, does he? Ralph, open this door now or I'll cut your halfwit head off and shove it up your arse.'

For some reason this does the trick, and he opens the door. Willoughby sticks to me like glue as I go in and, by the time I've turned around to shut the door behind me, he's standing in the hall. He doesn't give a toss, I'll say that much for him.

'What the hell do you think you're doing?' I say as he saunters into the living room in front of me. Ralph has made some rearrangements since I was last in here. He's turned the two sofas over on to their fronts and pushed them together so their backs are touching. They make a little shelter over which he has thrown some curtains, and it's into this that he now retreats, crawling backwards, muttering to himself. There's food in varying stages of decomposition, bottles, cans, the bodies of a couple of dead rats Ralph has taken to shooting with my old air rifle; jars, boxes, broken glass, masonry dust from some seemingly pointless holes he's gouged in the wall; and in the far corner of the room, in front of the smashed glass of the French windows, there is a bizarre construction about six feet high comprising the wood from a number of picture frames and pieces of shattered furniture, all glued together into an awkward structure that has a sort of completeness, a self-containment and reason for being, that suggests Ralph is possessed of more than the brew-ravaged sanity-deficient headful of slop you might have expected. But only just.

'What the bloody hell is going on in here?' asks Willoughby with a barely disguised note of relish in his voice, as though this vision of domestic carnage is welcome confirmation of his beliefs about me. 'Is this some sort of social experiment? Are we on television? God, man, how did you let it get this bad?'

'Listen, Michael, I didn't invite you in here to make comments about how I choose to live. In fact, I didn't invite you in here at all, so do me a favour, will you, and piss off.'

He spins around to face me. He's been building up to this, I can tell. He's got his finger pointed at me and his anger is all ready to blow. But his left foot is sending him messages informing him that what it is resting upon is worthy of further investigation. It's one of the dead rats.

'Jesus Christ!' he shrieks, and jumps back.

'Don't worry, it's dead,' I tell him. 'My friend here kills them for me. Now, before you start on about you and your little chums on the Desford Gardens residents' bollocks, let me warn you, if you don't get out in the next five seconds, I'll be forced to kill you in the most appalling manner imaginable.'

'You media types think you're so bloody hilarious, don't you,' he says. 'I don't mind if you want to try and lead some alternative lifestyle. That's fine by me. You can do what you like as far as I'm concerned. If you want to live like some pseudo-anarchist in your two-million-pound house, that's all well and good. A bit pathetic, if you ask me, but you didn't so I'll just reiterate that if you don't stop behaving like a jerk about your garden then I'll get my lawyer on to you.'

I swing the bolt croppers out from behind my back and hold them up to his throat. His Adam's apple is pinched between the open blades. He starts to shout something but a moment later, after I've pulled the handles together, it all goes silent. Blood squirts from his neck and he raises his hand to the wound in a futile attempt to staunch its flow. He knows he's in trouble. He makes for the door but I'm too quick for him and block his way, the electric drill raised in front of me, pointed at him like a gun. He goes to punch me but I spear his fist with the drill bit and he backs away, making silent screams. I fly at him, knock him over on to his back, straddle him and start to push the drill into his chest. He holds his hand up to try to stop me but I drill straight through it. Just as he begins to lose consciousness, I push the drill into his face. There's a high-pitched whine followed by a burning smell as his teeth shatter against the bit. By the time I've pushed the drill as far as it'll go into both his eyes, his body does little more than tremble.

'Nobody wants this to turn nasty, Tobe,' he says, trying to instil a more conciliatory tone into his voice. 'I don't see why we can't just put this behind us and get on with being neighbours. I can't pretend for one moment that I find your domestic environment anything other than abhorrent, and to think you live like this so close by is frankly disturbing, but I still think we can at least be civil to one another. You have until Friday to sort out the garden. I trust you'll have the good sense to do so. Goodbye.'

I greet his little speech with silence in the hope that it will convey the utter contempt I feel for him. Ralph, on the other hand, pops his head out of his makeshift shelter and tells him, 'Bye, Kelly.' Willoughby emits an exasperated sigh and leaves, slamming the front door behind him.

PUBLIC RELATIONS

I read her e-mail again:

> *Tobe,*
> *You probably don't remember much about our time together in the Albatross Suite but believe me, it was most fulfilling. Bad luck about the head wound. Let's do it again soon.*
> *Love,*
> *Scarlet*
> *PS: I hope it hurts.*

I close the laptop and place it back on the bedside table. It's 3 a.m. Can't sleep. Ralph is downstairs in his sofa cave. Every now and then he shouts something in his sleep. When he first came here this used to unnerve me no end, but I've grown accustomed to it now. About an hour ago, I heard him get up and wander through the house. I think he must have been stalking a rat because I heard a shot from the air rifle and then he turned in again.

There's nothing quite so desperate and fearful as the sound of a telephone ringing in the dead of night. It's always bad news. I snatch it up.

'Hello?'

'It's Bill.'

'What's wrong?'

'We're totally buggered.' He sounds as though he's been crying. Bill's not the crying type.

'What's happened?'

'You really want to know, Tobe? You really want to know what you've done?'

'What I've done? Bill, for God's sake, are you going to tell me what this is all about?'

'OK, all right, try this for size. This evening, Sonny Page, our client, a man whose career we are, or rather *were*, in the process of doctoring, was due to save his next-door neighbour from a house fire, thereby grabbing himself some headlines and also some much-needed publicity for the show *Popstar!* in which he is appearing. That's what was supposed to happen. Wasn't it, Tobe?'

'I don't know.'

'What do you mean, you don't know? It was your fucking idea.'

'Just tell me what happened.'

'Page lives in a row of cottages off Brick Lane. We met there. It was just the four of us. No one else knew about it, or at least I hope to God they didn't. There was me, Page, a friend of his called Sammy Earle, whose house on the opposite side of the street we were going to set fire to, and Simeon Cruikshank, who was behaving like a little child he was so excited. It was meant to be foolproof, but they got their timings all wrong. Sammy Earle was to go to his house over the road. He'd already cleared out all his belongings and was set to make a killing on the insurance in addition to the five grand Cruikshank had promised to give him. He was to light a fire in a wastepaper basket under the window in his front bedroom. He'd then go downstairs, having shut the bedroom door to contain the fire, and wait for Page to rescue him. In the meantime, Page was to knock on all his neighbours' doors shouting "Fire", making as much commotion as possible and thereby ensuring as many eye-witness reports of his act of heroism as possible. While this was going on, on mobiles phones he'd acquired under false names Cruikshank and I were to telephone the news desks of all the national papers as though we were neighbours of Page's, or eye-witnesses, reporting that the actor was currently locked in a life-and-death struggle to free a man from a terrible house fire. It all went according to plan until Page spent too long knocking on doors rounding up his eye-witnesses. I suppose people were wary of being woken up late at night, and by the time he'd roused a handful of people and told them he was going into the blazing house to rescue Sammy Earle, the fire was out of control. To make matters worse, as he was about to run in, one of the people he'd managed to rouse, this big bloke with ginger hair, grabbed hold of him and tried to hold him back. By the time he'd broken free, the fire was raging. He dashed into the house through the front door which had been left open for him, and I could see him and Earle through the doorway but they never made it out. The ceiling collapsed on them. Tobe, they're both dead.'

'So what happened to Cruikshank?'

'He completely freaked out. I didn't know he had a dodgy heart. He had some sort of seizure. He took some tablets but they didn't do any good. One minute he was rubbing his chest and the next he was rolling around on the carpet going blue. I tried to revive him but he just died. It was like some sort of bizarre nightmare. I've never hurt anyone in my entire life, yet in one night I've been involved in the deaths of three men. Jesus Christ, Tobe, what the fuck are we going to do?'

I don't like this 'we' he keeps coming out with but maybe now's not the time to mention it.

'Where are you?' I enquire, trying to sound as calm as I can.

'I'm at home. When Cruikshank keeled over, I panicked and legged it. I don't think anyone saw me. I don't know. The fire brigade were trying to dig them out. It was chaos.'

Incredulous though I am that Barlow should even have considered this most ridiculous of plans, let alone put it into practice, I am very conscious that I must think fast and consider the implications vis-à-vis me and saving my neck. Barlow's fucked, in all probability. I can't see him walking away from this. But there's no reason why I shouldn't.

'Have you phoned Gifford?' I ask him.

'No. I thought you ought to be the first to know.'

'I'll call him.'

'Tobe, what are we going to do?'

'The first thing we're going to do, Bill, is we're going to stay calm. This is just a horrible accident, nothing more.

Gifford'll sort it out. I'll call him and explain everything. It'll be fine. Trust me.'

He doesn't reply.

'I haven't let you down yet, have I?' In truth, I've probably let him down dozens of times in dozens of ways, not least by giving advice to our clients that is deliberately negligent and, in this instance, downright dangerous. Just as I'm thinking this he blurts out, 'No,' and I chuckle to myself. 'Let me get on to it straight away, Bill, and I'll call you back.'

Like all good lawyers, Gifford is on call twenty-four hours a day, and when you phone him – even in the middle of the night as now, when other, lesser men would sound groggy and put-out – you can detect excitement in his voice, as though he's sitting ready at his desk, shirt and tie on, poised to sort out your problems. Gifford loves his work like no man I've ever known.

'Charlie, it's Tobe.'

'What can I do for you, Tobe?'

'It's Bill, he's in trouble. He just called to say that some publicity scam he's dreamed up has gone horribly wrong, resulting in the deaths of three people.'

'Go on.'

'It was a totally hare-brained scheme from the start. I can't believe he even thought it might work. It involved staging a house fire so one of our clients, the actor Sonny Page, could play the hero and rescue someone, thereby attracting some favourable press both for himself and the dire show he's appearing in. Something like that. I couldn't really work out what it was he was talking about. I think he's had some sort of nervous breakdown.

What I find particularly alarming is he keeps trying to make out it was my idea. Now, you know me, Charlie, I may have some unorthodox ways of doing business, but having my clients save people from house fires as a means of generating publicity? I don't think so.'

ACCESS CULTURE

I'm sitting in the toilet in the offices of Barlow & Darling. I'd planned on never setting foot in this place again, and I wouldn't have were it not for a certain amount of nervous circumspection on my part. Bill phoned me up, you see, and asked me if I'd see Tom DeMournay for him, and I don't want anyone thinking I'm not looking out for my poor sick business partner as he struggles with nervous breakdown, mental illness and, in his few brief flashes of lucidity, the realisation that he is responsible for the deaths of three people.

On the back of the toilet door there is a framed black-and-white photograph of the table Bill and I hosted at the Brits a few years ago, back in the days when we were full of ambition and optimism and the sort of outlook that makes you want to put black-and-white photographs of yourselves on the back of your toilet door. There's Janet Humboldt, head of Cosmos Models, pressing her industrial lipstick against Bill's cheek while Tiggy Ironside,

255

the doyen of the celebrity shit factory in New York, looks on wearing a grin like a wound. Marty Blanche, the UK publisher of *International Profiles* (and Scarlet's boss), is deep in conversation with his wife, the actress Patsy Gunn, and Bill's squeeze of the time, the pop star Heidi Janus. Henry 'Slugger' McKay, a big cheese at Global Artistes Management, has his arm around Scarlet as they share a joke, and there's me at the end speaking to no one, staring at the camera wearing a fake smile. It's funny how time peels away your self-image. At the time, I remember feeling like a master of the universe, but looking at me now I appear more like a frightened kid trying to keep up with the big boys. Not that they are necessarily the big boys these days. The relationship between show business and the media has changed. The media are all set to go it alone. They don't need traditional celebrities any more. There are millions of people out there who can be stars. Suddenly, we're all players on the global stage. All this real-life television, all these docu-dramas, docu-soaps, docu-this, docu-that; it's all just the tip of the iceberg. Traditional entertainment is changing. People don't want storytelling any more but access, whether it's access into the lives of extraordinary people or, as is more likely, access into the lives of Mr and Mrs Joe Public next door.

It's twelve noon. Right about now, in Bromley in south-east London, Paul Craddock, a fifty-eight-year-old businessman, and his wife Pauline will be coming face to face with the most famous person they'll ever meet. About three months ago, they scooped an eighteen-million-pound lottery win and decided to go public, so public they hired themselves a press agent despite the fact that they were already extremely wealthy on account of Paul Craddock's hugely successful road haulage business. The press have been only too happy to pander to the Craddocks' desire for publicity, turning up to snap them in their palatial house as they pose with oil paintings and sports cars. They clearly thought they could build themselves something of a media career, but what they hadn't bargained on was that in no time at all they would become media hate figures. This isn't so much because of their inappropriate good fortune – although that undoubtedly rankles with a lot of people – but more to do with their appearance on various chat shows of late, on which they have been unapologetic and boorish about their wealth as a sort of two-fingered salute to their critics. There's only one thing the British public likes less than a smartarse and it's a pair of them, and so, for once, my client and I thought it might be good to give the British public what it wanted. I must confess to feeling somewhat excited by the outcome of all this. I can't wait to see how the tabloid press will cover the brutal murder of their two favourite hate figures. Mind you, these are the first murders I have been involved in with the Piper and it's nerve-racking, not least because the Craddocks were my choice of victim. I have chosen that they should die and I'll have to live with it.

Initially, I suggested he should maybe try to kill someone else today in addition to the Craddocks so that he could achieve the 'triple event' – three in one day – but I decided that making the jump from unknowns to celebrities (of sorts) was a big enough hook for the press in itself rather than trying to up the body count as well. Being over-ambitious is dangerous in this line of work. Thankful though I am that he has decided to move his theatre of operations away from West End hotels, I'm still nervous about him getting caught. When we discuss this, he is quick to point out that any fears I might have regarding his possible capture are based on assumptions that he conforms to traditional serial killer patterns of behaviour. He assures me the only pathological trait he does display is his destruction of all evidence linking him to his deeds. He literally bathes himself and his murder scenes in disinfectant, and since one of the tabloids happened to mention what brand of disinfectant it was, its sales have rocketed five hundred per cent.

When the Piper carries out a killing, he plans it meticulously beforehand. He'll have every eventuality sussed out. Given that he uses an extensive array of disguises, should he be picked up on surveillance cameras either entering or leaving the scene of a killing, the authorities will never see the same man twice. His disguises are elaborate, involving body padding, so that he's never even the same shape twice. The only way he could be apprehended is if he were stopped either directly before or directly after one of his kills and was caught in possession of his bag of tricks. For such an eventuality, he carries a cyanide capsule. 'They'll never take me alive,' he told me with a grin when I visited him in the Churchill Citadel, and I don't have any reason to doubt it.

What is so refreshing about my involvement with the Piper as opposed to all the helpless chumps I've dealt with in the past is that I don't have to indulge in so much of the usual personal management bollocks – the ego massage, exaggeration of talent and, more often than not, barefaced lying: 'You're a star, David, the new book/ series/film/show/record is brilliant. Well done.' Then there's the tedious admin, the dull day-to-day negotiation with the arseholes involved in broadcasting, films, publishing and, worst of all, music. As it is, with the Piper I advise and suggest and that's it. The Piper's brand is fully established. You'd need Coca-Cola's yearly advertising budget to buy that kind of exposure. So all I have to do is carry out a little tweaking here and there. There's not even any money involved, no contract, nothing. Just a gentleman's agreement and that's it.

The killing of the Craddocks will be the Piper's first cross-genre foray into killing someone in the public eye. Killing a famous person is always a winner when it comes to attracting media coverage. Look at Lennon and Versace. As far as I am aware, no serial killer in history has set out to kill someone famous just so as to improve their own media profile. When the Piper kills the Craddocks, as always, he'll write his name on the wall in his victims' blood, but this time, beneath it, he'll also write, 'IT'S YOU'. All the thousands of photographs of the Craddocks taken before their murders which captured the images of happiness and good fortune on account of their lottery win will become horrific reminders of their savage deaths. People will look at photographs of Paul and Pauline Craddock in years to come and in their faces they will see the handiwork of the world's most famous serial killer. And if we can suss out a safe way of doing it, there'll even be a souvenir programme of the event in the form of some footage of the killing which they can download from the Internet.

I want to find ways of exploiting all the images and

footage of the murders he has collected. Everyone knows of their existence because of the videos that have been sent to the media, and their obvious censorship has had the effect that all censorship does, and created massive demand. I've been telling the Piper to utilise his computer expertise and develop a way of posting images on the Internet and creating viruses that will distribute the images organically. We're even looking into the possibility of webcasting a live killing – Pipercam™ maybe – although the man himself is concerned that, because the footage won't be playing backwards, it'll confuse his signature and open him up to more copycat killings. But our methods of recording and distribution are ultimately unimportant so long as they are safe and effective. What counts is the end result, which is to tap into the global obsession with horror and supply the demand. Want to see what your fellow humans are capable of? Well, now you can. This will be outlaw publishing the likes of which the world has never seen before. We will allow people a glimpse into the dark corners of their souls. We will bring snuff to the masses.

Reverse product placement is another area we're exploring. This is a form of corporate blackmail in which multi-nationals pay so that their products are not featured in our recordings. Instead of collecting the money ourselves, which might open us up to possible detection, we will instruct the companies to make donations to the causes of our choice. Imagine the scenario; a multinational ham-burger retailer is contacted and told: either you give so many million quid to these worthy causes or, during his next killing, the Piper will stop what he's doing mid-kill and in among the entrails and viscera he'll whip out one of your hamburgers and chomp away on it, all the while explaining how good it is and how he prefers it to all your competitors' hamburgers because it comes the closest in taste to human flesh. It's not exactly an 'on-brand' message. And as for the nominated charities, would they take the money? Would they legitimise the killing of a few in return for the saving of many? I can hardly wait to find out.

Taking the Piper on tour is another possibility. As with the early rave scene, we will only announce the location of one of our events on the night in question so as to keep people guessing and throw the nation into a blind panic. *Tonight, it's Norwich!* But throughout all this career development, we have to ensure we remain focused on the most important ingredient of the legend, and that is knowing when to stop. Lucky for the Piper, I suppose, that unlike pop stars and film stars, who have to die – as a rule – in order to achieve iconic status, he can just stop when he's at the peak of his career, give it up, walk away, and his legend will be assured.

The thought of having to listen to Tom DeMournay from Quorum Publishing rabbit on about his bloody new magazine *Sorted* is almost too unbearable to contemplate, but I might as well get it over and done with. I wash my hands and make my way back down the corridor to the meeting room. Sadie is serving coffee. We haven't spoken since I punched her that day. I didn't get a chance this morning because I met DeMournay on the way in.

I retake my seat opposite him, fix him with a stare and say, 'The question you've got to ask yourself with a magazine aimed at this market is, will it be tits out or tits in? You can have all the incisive journalism you want but the tit question has to be answered before we can move on anywhere.'

DeMournay and his company Quorum Publishing have been knocking around for about ten years now. He has a couple of half-decent computer games mags and plenty of ideas above his station. The fact of the matter is, DeMournay is a nearly-man. He's been involved in more projects that have nearly made it than any man I know. There's no faulting his tenacity, though, and now he thinks he can break into the men's magazine market. I haven't the heart to tell him he's got more chance of making a killing opening a department store in Knightsbridge. More than anything, I'm amazed he has decided to come to Barlow & Darling in the first place. It's not as though we're cheap, after all, and you'd think any publisher worth his salt would rather die than be seen to ask the opinion of a man like me. But seeing as he has, I'll give him an opinion. It might not be a very good opinion, it might not even be my opinion, but if he wants an opinion then he's come to the right place.

'Come on, Tobe, there's more to publishing a men's magazine than tits. This isn't porn, you know, this is aimed at the discerning male. We've got some real heavyweights aboard. We've got Lucien McAvoy doing a series of pieces looking at different forms of drug-running throughout the world. We've got Ruth Horobin as agony aunt, and Ruth will be doing some extensive research into the male orgasm. We've even got Chip Tate, the journalist who infiltrated the LA hard-core porn industry and ended up starring in about fifteen movies he claimed were all done in the name of research. This is mainstream stuff. This is what guys want to read about. They want sport, for sure, they want fast cars and gadgets, but they also want to know about serious issues such as mortgages and luxury holidays. We're not going to talk down to them. We're not going to treat them like kids. These guys are the you and me of tomorrow, Tobe.'

They might be the you of tomorrow, I'd like to say to him, but they are certainly not the fucking me, and do I look like the sort of jerk who has ever given a flying one about the latest gadget? Instead, what I really say is, 'I'm not being flippant about the tit situation, Tom. I'm merely suggesting that this is a pertinent issue that will speak volumes regarding where you see yourself in the market. A magazine has to be confident about its reader. You have to decide whether your reader is the sort of man who picks up a magazine with the philosophy that he wants to read about what's hot in the worlds of fashion, showbiz gossip and sport, or whether he's the sort of man who wants to read about what's hot in the worlds of fashion, showbiz gossip and sport but also wouldn't mind having a tommy tank over the Scandinavian bird on the centre spread. Now, Tom, which is he?'

DeMournay goes off on one about demographics and market share and I switch off. I nod and give him a look that says, 'I hear you, it's all going into my big clever brain, and all the time I'm thinking about you and your situation,' when in reality my mind's over at the Craddocks' house in Bromley. If all's gone according to plan, Mr and Mrs C should be undergoing a spot of dismemberment by now.

'The thing is, Tom,' I say, trying to look as pained as I can, 'I don't think I'm going to be any use to you on this one. I presume you've heard what's happened to Bill?'

'Sadie mentioned he had the flu.'

'Bill hasn't got the flu, Tom. We've kept Sadie in the dark on this one. You must have heard about Sonny Page getting killed trying to save a neighbour from a house fire a couple of days ago?' He's nodding at me. 'Well, that was no accident. It was a media stunt that went horribly wrong. He was meant to save his neighbour, be hailed as a hero and, in so doing, capture the headlines and give *Popstar!*, that dreadful show he's starring in, a much-needed profile boost.'

'That's terrible. Even so, it worked. Apparently *Popstar!*'s sold more tickets in the past couple of days than it has done in the rest of the run. The only thing they've got to do is find themselves a new producer and leading man.'

I assume a grim expression as though I find this comment tasteless in the extreme, and DeMournay apologises and asks, 'So what was your involvement in all this?'

'I had zero involvement, thank God. If I'd known Bill was going to attempt anything so ridiculous I would have pulled the plug on it immediately. Totally off the record now, you understand, like we never had this conversation?'

'Of course, Tobe,' he says, not even attempting to hide the leer of anticipation on his face.

'Bill's been under a lot of pressure recently. I've been trying to dissolve the partnership, you see. I want out but he doesn't. Recently, it's as though he's been trying to impress me with how well he can run things and he's come up with a whole string of bizarre, totally impractical ideas, none of which I really thought he would ever put into practice. So you can understand my alarm. Bill's my friend as well as my partner, and as much as I don't want to work with him any more, it doesn't mean I'm not concerned for his mental wellbeing. Up until now, the police seem to have been thinking it was a genuine accident, but I'm just terrified that as they dig deeper they'll discover the truth and that'll be Bill's career down the pan. It's really difficult for me at the moment because if I jump ship now, it'll look as though I'm abandoning him in his time of need. So, I've got a lot on my mind and I'm probably not in the best shape to be advising you on a project of this importance.'

'Jesus, Tobe, I didn't think things were so bad.'

'Tom, I'm convinced *Sorted* will be snapping at *FHM*'s heels within months, so I don't think you've really got any cause for concern. But as for Barlow & Darling, it's the end, I'm afraid. I'd appreciate it if you'd keep it to yourself for the time being at least.'

'Of course, my lips are sealed. But how is Bill?'

'Not well at all.'

This is true. It's only a matter of time before Mr N Breakdown comes knocking on his door, and when he does I'll make sure I continue to play the concerned friend and business partner and keep on telling whoever will listen that the whole Sonny Page house fire thing was his idea. Should Bill then decide in his disturbed state that he wants to confess all, I'll deny everything. Besides, all the people who knew of my involvement are all dead. They won't send him to jail; he'll most likely end up in some exclusive laughter emporium, and what's one more headcase in the bonkers world of showbiz, eh?

'I'm so sorry, mate,' says DeMournay. 'If there's anything I can do . . .' You'll do all I need you to, I think to myself, and give him one of those melancholic smiles which hopefully conveys the impression I'm on the verge of tears.

'Obviously if I can come up with any more angles on this one I'll be in touch. Just remember, when it comes to entertainment, there are two perennials that must never be overlooked. Sex and death. You can't have one without the other.'

'You're a good man, Tobe.' Oh, if only you knew the half of it.

'Good luck, Tom.' You loathsome creep.

I open the door and there's Sadie standing at the end of the corridor holding his jacket.

After he's gone I return to my desk to check my e-mails. As I hear the lift doors close, it strikes me that Sadie and I are now alone here and there's every likelihood of some sort of confrontation. I can hear her footsteps as she goes back to her desk before setting off down the corridor towards my office. As she comes through the doorway, I look up from the computer and say, 'Sadie, we need to talk.'

'What about?' she asks.

'Well, if you remember rightly, the last time I was here, I, er—'

'You punched me.'

'I did, as you say, punch you, and it was inexcusable.'

'No problem.' As always she is totally expressionless, gives nothing away.

'No harm done, then?' I ask.

'None. Now, while you are here, I need to tell you we have had a series of telephone calls from Eric Massey. He wants to arrange another meeting with you regarding the

Lifeboys. Their "Honeygun" single was released a week last Monday and as of Sunday had failed to break into the top one hundred. He feels there may have been an angle that has been overlooked.' He's right, of course. The angle that has been overlooked is that he's a fuckwit and the Lifeboys are a bunch of talentless, plug-ugly losers.

'Also Rudi Schneider called from New York. He was promised some advice regarding *Hoxton Square*.'

'There's no point giving me any more messages. I won't be able to do anything about them anyway. Sadie, I'm sorry to have to tell you that, as of today, Barlow & Darling has ceased to exist. Bill's going to be out of action for a long time and I'm going to move on and do something new. You've done an amazing job holding the fort here and I'll give you a glowing reference, of course.'

'Fine.'

'We'll pay you all the redundancy pay you're entitled to and probably a good lump sum on top of that as a sort of golden handshake. You've been great here, Sadie, and it's a sad day.'

She stares at me, and I feel as though I should say something more but I don't want to do anything that might incite her wrath.

'I'll get my things,' she says, and walks out of the room.

'You have e-mail,' says the voice on the computer. It appears I have accumulated eighteen messages since I last checked my mailbox the day before last. Most of them are work-related, which I will ignore, or else junk mail from various sites I've visited in my on-going cyber-trawl through the more sexually degenerate of the world's websites. Nothing from the Piper. In his last message, he said he wouldn't be in touch again until after the Craddock job, but our correspondence of late has been so regular and lengthy I almost expect a message from him every time I check my mail. There is, however, a message from Scarlet which reads:

Tobe,
   I've booked the Albatross Suite from 2 p.m. on Friday. The code for the door is 1123. Surprise me.
   Love,
   Scarlet
   PS: Maybe I'll do you some serious damage this time.

Good job I checked my e-mail. She'll be there in just over an hour's time.

I don't hear Sadie coming back down the corridor to my office because she doesn't have any shoes on. In fact, when I look up I can see she's not wearing anything at all apart from an expression of grim determination and a black rubber strap-on.

'Sadie, what the hell do you think you're doing?'

She makes no reply, just walks up to me, pulls me out of my chair and slams me across the desk. There's no point struggling; she's twice as strong as me. With one hand, she presses my head against the blotter pad. With her other, she opens the buttons on the front of my jeans and pulls them down. I suppose this is all my own fault really. This is what happens when you don't check out someone's references properly both employment-wise and sexually. I was so down about Scarlet leaving me that when I discovered

Sadie's tastes in sexual confrontation were similar to mine – though by no means compatible and becoming less so – I leaped at the chance of getting on the receiving end of some pain. I was so pleased with the attention I was receiving from her that I didn't bother to lay out any ground rules. Didn't impose any boundaries or codes of conduct. Not that they would do me much good now. My trousers are around my ankles. She's searching for her target and, oh my God, there it is. I've always been a one-way traffic sort of guy arse-wise. I hope that for Sadie at least this is a symbolic gesture and she doesn't feel that either of us has to achieve any sort of physical climax. I guess I'll have to wait and find out.

CLOSURE

The pain I'm feeling you-know-where means I don't want to walk any farther than I absolutely have to. I hail a cab and, as it pulls over to the pavement, I take a good look at the cabby and only once I'm sure it isn't Roger Wilton Entertainments or any other nutter who I might have offended in the past do I climb in and tell him, 'Auster Street, Covent Garden.' Up ahead, I can see Sadie walking along the pavement. Not fifteen minutes ago, we were still locked together, acting out our strange sexual ritual. She was like a silent machine throughout. Only when she had deemed our coupling to be at an end did she speak. Whispering into my ear in a flat monotone, she said, 'Dirty pig boy,' and with that she was off. I heard her put her clothes on, collect some things from her desk drawer and leave. She's almost level with the taxi now. Slung over her shoulder is her bag containing the strap-on, still warm from my arse, no doubt. This is the first time I've ever seen her outside the office, in the real world, or as real a world as a Soho street can be. She's dressed all in black and looks like some sort of Gothic Amazonian. Then it occurs to me I'll probably never see her again. This mysterious woman who has inflicted so much pain on me, who I've punched and who has in turn violated my derrière with a length of moulded plastic. As the taxi passes her, I turn around in my seat and our eyes meet through the back window. No sooner has she seen me than she looks away again, betraying not a hint of recognition.

'That'll be four-twenty, mate,' says the cabby as we pull up in Auster Street. I pass him a fiver and tell him, 'That's fine, thanks,' as he reaches for some change. It doesn't sound right coming out of my mouth but it's too late to take it back. I make for the dry cleaner's and key in 1123 on the keypad by the door as per Scarlet's instructions in her e-mail. The door clicks open and I hurry in, down through the passage underneath Auster Street and up into the Gardens Hotel. I knock on the door of the Albatross Suite but there's no reply, so I key in the number again and, once through the door, head straight for the minibar and dig out a couple of miniature tequila bottles, empty them into a glass, lie down on the bed and flick on the TV with the remote control. There's a spiteful-looking woman newscaster – a definite pain freak – and she's going on about some famine in Africa. We get some footage of some emaciated African kids sitting in the sun with flies buzzing around their eyes and then, without missing a beat, she switches to a piece about the actress Trudi Malone attending the première of a new movie in Leicester Square last night. And there she is posing outside the Odeon wearing what is little more than a glittery swimming costume that leaves both her buttocks exposed. This outfit – a blatant attempt at a 'that dress' – was designed for her by some tosser called Cuthbert Mélange, as though I could really give a shit. I turn off the TV, lie back against the headboard and my thoughts turn to Scarlet's imminent arrival and what she is hoping to achieve by this renewal of hostilities. Her behaviour of late has made me realise how much I've changed since we were last together. I've gone from hating myself to, not so much liking myself, but achieving some sort of grudging acceptance of who I am and what I need at least. And just as I'm beginning to learn about what I need, I'm also learning about what I don't need, and what I don't need any more is pain. Not mine anyway. This probably doesn't bode well for a new start in our fractious union, but then who am I to say? Scarlet's the boss. And here she comes; I can hear her fingers tapping in the number on the keypad outside the door. The door opens and in she walks.

It's as though someone's stopped the film of my life, spliced in the film from someone else's and restarted it. At first, I think to myself that she looks very tall, very full of figure, very different, very unScarletlike, and then my brain quits trying to equate the person who's coming through the door with its expectations of who it thinks should be coming through the door and accepts that there is only one certainty in this equation, and that is that whoever is coming through the door wearing a garish pink-and-tartan golfing outfit, a holdall slung over their shoulder, is not, nor ever has been, Scarlet Hunter, my Scarlet, my fellow traveller around life's strange cul-de-sac.

'Who the hell are you?' says a voice from my mouth that sounds a bit like mine only more nervous and hollow.

'You flatter me,' says the Piper, closing the door after him. 'I've always thought this was one of my poorer disguises.'

Every sphincter muscle in my entire body contracts simultaneously as the gravity of this situation dawns on me. I'm in a hotel room in the West End of London with the most notorious West-End-of-London-hotel-room serial killer that ever lived.

'Hi,' I boom, the inappropriate volume of this greeting a stark contrast to the whisper that follows it, 'How are you?'

'Good, thanks.'

He throws his holdall into the bathroom, where it hits the tiled floor with a metallic clank. He heads towards the minibar, flings it open, grabs a beer, twists the top off and, with his head thrown back, downs half the bottle in one gulp.

'I've been dying for that,' he says, wiping his mouth with the sleeve of his bright pink cashmere sweater. He exudes the aura of a man who's just had a great sporting victory and is flushed with success and preoccupied with reliving his glorious moment.

'Where's Scarlet?'

'She couldn't make it.'

'What do you mean?'

'Relax, Scarlet's fine. She's probably at work doing whatever it is that Scarlet does. Magazines, isn't it?'

'Yeah.'

He stares at me with his eyebrows raised, as though expectant of further questions.

'So what are you doing here?' I ask.

'I thought it might be good to have another meeting. Face to face. Isn't that what you people do, have meetings all the time? That e-mail you received from Scarlet, I sent it. It came to you via Scarlet's mailbox but really it was me all along. Did you know her password on her mailbox was "Darling"? I bet you didn't.'

He finishes his beer and lobs the bottle at the waste-paper basket in the corner of the room. It misses its target and bounces off the wainscoting to land on the carpet unbroken.

'How did you manage to find out about this place?'

'Oh, you showbiz types are such crazy guys,' he says in a mock American voice. 'You seem to think your little secret clubs and venues are so impenetrable and impossible to infiltrate, but for someone like me, they're a cinch.'

'How did it go with the Craddocks?'

'Like a dream,' he says, pacing to and fro, 'although I must confess to having been a little nervous about killing two at the same time. You see, there's always a vague possibility that while you're busy with one of them, the other might catch you unawares. I took the woman first. She answered the door. She'd had the door open for all of two seconds before I'd snapped her neck. Her husband was in the toilet taking a shit. When he pulled the chain and came out, he didn't even look surprised to see a stranger in his house. He probably thought I was a delivery man or something. It was only when he saw his wife lying on the floor with her head pointing the wrong way that he reacted and dived back into the toilet, bolting the door after him. I knew I had to move fast. He could have had a phone in there with him. So, I took an axe out of my bag and smashed the door in. There he was, cowering by the side of the toilet bowl. I cleaved his head open with one blow. It was like chopping logs. The only thing that put me off killing him was that he looked a bit like my dad, so I messed his face up a bit. Then I got changed into my operating outfit and started to carve them both up. I'd just managed to get his legs off with the saw and was halfway through his arm when the phone started ringing. It really put me off my stride, and it rang for ages as if the person on the other end knew they were there. When it finished ringing I was sweating. I left old man Craddock the way he was and quickly set to work on his wife. I got her head off and drop-kicked it around the room a couple of times, then wrote my signature on the wall in her blood and IT'S YOU beneath it as we'd discussed. Then I sprayed everywhere with disinfectant and left. It wasn't ideal but the telephone ringing had unnerved me and I wanted to get out of there as fast as I could. It was like it was a bad omen.'

He sits himself down on the edge of the bed, watching me, a half-smile on his face.

'So, I suppose we ought to discuss our next step,' I say.

'*Our* next step?' he says, laughing. 'You really do see yourself as some sort of Svengali figure, don't you? Like you're the Colonel Parker to my Elvis.'

'Not at all,' I say, trying to maintain as nonchalant a façade as I possibly can. 'How about we discuss *your* next step, then?' He nods his head, still grinning at me.

'So,' I say, trying to appear thoughtful and not in the least bit frightened, 'killing the Craddocks was your first move away from traditional serial killing into other types of murder.'

'Oh yes, I'm adding some more strings to my bow as you suggested. Maybe now I should make myself available for children's parties. How's that sound? Maybe I could develop a cabaret act and take it around all the working men's clubs? Get a couple of dolly birds as my delightful assistants? Is that the sort of stuff you had in mind?' The laughter's gone by now and only a sneer remains.

I've been in some tight corners in my career, situations when clients have disagreed with a piece of advice and taken it as a personal affront that I should have even suggested it, but nothing like this. There's never been the feeling that if I said the wrong thing, I might very well end up dead. Maybe if there had been I might have done a better job. In recent times, the people who've come to see me have been so confident of my abilities even when I've been feeding them bullshit just for the hell of it that they've sat there and accepted it. Now, I need to do some work, employ some psychology perhaps, but before I can think of anything, the laughter's back – for which I'm thankful to some small degree. 'Hey, Tobe, maybe I – sorry, we – should release a novelty record? What do you reckon?'

'I reckon you should stop taking the piss.'

'I'm sorry, Tobe, I'm in a silly mood. It's just sometimes I think you've mistaken me for someone I'm not. It's as though you think I'm one of the vacuous cretins you normally get to deal with. At first, I kind of liked the idea of being treated like some extreme form of celebrity. Now I'm not so sure.'

'Hold on a moment. I was under the impression you had made contact with me because you wanted to transcend your role as a serial killer and go one step farther.'

'I did.'

'Then why have you got a problem all of a sudden with the idea of messing around with the format, blurring the boundaries, confounding people's expectations?'

'I haven't, Tobe, I was joking. I'm sorry. Take it easy.'

'Oh, I'm fine.'

'You know what, Tobe, sometimes I think you're more detached about all this than I am. Have you, for example, really sat down and thought about the direct result of my actions? The horror, the grief, the tragedy. Think about Paul and Pauline Craddock's kids – they're grown up but, none the less, have you actually thought how they will feel when they discover their parents all chopped up?' He's staring at me.

'Of course I've thought about it.'

'I doubt you have.' He grits his teeth and stares at me mock-demonically before laughing and saying, 'I like you, Tobe. You're my kind of guy. You really don't give a shit, do you?'

I attempt a chuckle but it comes out all wrong, more like a series of coughs.

'I've got to take a leak,' he says as he stands up and makes for the bathroom.

So, what do I do now? And should I even stop to think about it? It's about ten paces to the door. I could probably cover the distance in a couple of seconds. Part of me is screaming out to make a run for it and another is urging me not to, that it would be the most dangerous thing I could do.

I pull the cord on the chainsaw and it snarls into life. He backs away from me and I can see he's saying something –

his mouth's opening and closing – but I can't hear what it is above the sound of the engine. I take a swipe at him and the tip of the chainsaw's blade cuts through the front of his pink sweater and carves a deep gash in his stomach. He's screaming now and it's loud enough to hear. He makes a grab for the chainsaw but I'm too quick for him and take his arm off just above the elbow. It falls to the carpet, his fingers still opening and closing in some automatic nervous gesture. He clutches the bloody stump then slumps back against the wall in shock. I turn off the chainsaw, put it down and pick up a small electric winch. He swings a punch at me with his remaining fist but he's slow and I manage to duck it. I punch him in the face a couple of times to soften him up then push my hand into his stomach, tearing it open until I can see his intestines all piled up like some disgusting Cumberland sausage marinated in gore. I hold a length of intestine, pull it out and secure it around the drum on the electric winch and switch the machine on to rewind. His screams lose their tone and become deep and flat as his trembling innards build up on the winch's drum like line on a fishing reel. When his guts come to an end, they tear away from his empty body cavity with a fleshy thwack, and the only remaining sounds he makes are breathless gasps which degenerate into a deflating sound like a hiss from a punctured football. He is lying flat on the carpet now, staring up at me with disbelieving eyes. With my feet either side of his head to keep it still, I pull the bottle of acid from my pocket and unscrew the top. It gives off a caustic, acrid smell. I tip the bottle and a drop breaks free and falls on to his face. Steam rises out of a black hole in his cheek. This revives him a little so

I douse him with some more, which dissolves his lips and the flesh around his mouth so his teeth grin up at me momentarily before the acid works on them too and dissolves them into black stumps which fall back into his throat from his fleshless gums. The skin from his nose is gone and the bone beneath it fizzes as it burns away. His skeletal jawbone opens and closes as though still trying to form words and his eyes continue to stare up at me, blinking frantically. I bend down and carefully pour the acid into each socket, watching it burn through his eyelids, dissolving his eyeballs into two blackened boreholes that carry the acid deep into his brain.

The bathroom door is flung open and out he steps dressed in an orange boiler suit with white rubber boots, and he's holding a huge filleting knife. On his head he's got a black rubber Balaclava with a small digital camcorder mounted on the side of it. The sight of him standing there in all his kit, dehumanised, done up like something out of a horror movie, snaps me out of my reverie and I jump to my feet and bolt for the door. Even if I wasn't running on frightened jelly legs, I don't think I'd make it. He trips me with his foot, sending me sprawling on the carpet. I roll over on to my back and stare up at him as he stands over me.

'What the fuck are you doing?' I shriek in a squealing pig voice.

'You tell me, you're the one with all the ideas. You're the management, aren't you? Come on, what should I do next? Advise me.' I can see his teeth shining in the mouth slit of his Balaclava, and it looks like some diabolical wound.

'Get away from me.'

'OK,' he says, amused, as though this were some game, and he steps back to allow me to stand.

'What do you think you're doing, scaring the shit out of me like that?'

'I'm just getting on with my career, that's all. I remember you saying to me that, having killed two on my last outing, it might be a good idea to kill three on my next. Isn't that right?'

'It was one suggestion out of many, like moving into terrorism or assassination. Just cool it, will you. Don't get carried away. Killing the Craddocks was just fine for today. You did a good job. Now, leave it at that.'

'Don't you think this would be a terrible wasted opportunity with us both here and me dressed up and all ready to go?' He takes a step towards me and I back away.

'Don't be stupid. If you kill me, you'll be caught. I thought you might try something like this so I've posted all your details, together with the exact location of the Churchill Citadel, hard copies of all our e-mail correspondence and tapes of all our conversations, to a friend with the express instruction that should something happen to me, he must forward the envelope to the police.'

'You're lying.'

'Can you afford to take that risk?'

'It's a good effort, Tobe, but you know you're lying and I know you're lying.'

'It's no lie.'

'Guess I'll take the risk, then.' My back is against the wall now and he has the knife raised up in front of him, pointed at me. 'If you were genuinely concerned about my career, you'd be quite happy to let me do this.

You mustn't hate me for my ambition. You mustn't be selfish.'

'Don't fucking kill me,' I shout.

It sounds desperate, hopeless, but against all the odds it seems to do the trick. He lowers the knife and says, 'Oh, Tobe, I'm sorry. I was only joking.' But before I can allow myself to succumb to any feelings of relief, he laughs, says, 'Or am I?' and raises the knife again, almost jabbing the end of the blade into my nose.

'For Christ's sake, there's no point killing me. I'm not famous. You're meant to be killing famous people.'

'Come now, Tobe, you're being modest. You may not be famous as such but, since your appearance on TV, you're most certainly in the public eye, and if you remember correctly that was the criterion on which you suggested I chose my forthcoming victims.'

'Come on, stop this shit. I could have left you hanging down there in the Churchill Citadel but I didn't. I saved your life. I passed your test.'

'Your saving my life was our contract, our agreement, our pact, and to a certain degree I suppose you're right, it was a test too, but it was a test for me, not for you. It was a test to see not whether I could trust you but whether I could trust myself with you. But then so much of what I do is a test, a test of my on-going existential freedom. This is a big test for me now. Can I kill the one man to whom I have granted access to my life? I'm afraid the answer to that question is a resounding yes.'

'Surely it's a bigger test to see if you can let me live?'

'It's never a test to see if I can let someone live.'

'Well, in that case, surely the ultimate test is to see if you can kill yourself?'

'Nice try, fat boy.' For every step he takes towards me, I take a step back, sliding along the wall. His grinning teeth are still shining at me through the slit in the Balaclava. He's loving this and I'm running out of arguments.

'If you kill me now, you'll only know half the story. I've got loads more ideas. Loads more ways of assuring your legend. To kill me now would be to ruin your chances of achieving your ultimate goal.'

'You people make me laugh. You seem to feel that no one can do anything remarkable without someone in the background pulling the strings. Well, that may be true in your line of work, but it's certainly not true in mine. I didn't contact you because I'd run out of ideas. I was just curious to see if you had any interesting insights into the symbiotic relationship between murder and the media. I've been a little disappointed, to tell you the truth. You wanted to bring the world of show business to the world of serial killing. But I'd already done it and, besides, I like to think of myself more as an artist than a celebrity. But then you never know, at this particular moment I might think of myself more as a comedian and this might be my idea of a joke. I might be bluffing. I might be winding you up and you've made a fool of yourself pleading for your life when I've got no intention of killing you whatsoever.'

I'm standing beside a low wooden table on which there's a large round glass ashtray. I pick it up and, playing the long game, I throw it at his head like a Frisbee. I'm lucky – it hits its target with a reassuring clunk.

It's as though all the violence that's been raging in my

282

mind has reached some biological impasse, some valve that has tripped so that it switches the direction of its flow from inwards to outwards. I find myself endowed with a clarity of vision I've never experienced before. I don't even think about what I'm doing. While his attention is diverted momentarily by the ashtray bouncing off his forehead, I fly at him. I manage to grab his wrist before he can take a stab at me and my momentum is such that I knock him down on to the carpet. I sit on top of him with my legs astride him and he's laughing now, as though it were the biggest joke in the world that he should come under attack from me. I try to prise his fingers open from around the knife but it's impossible, so I sink my teeth into his wrist. He stops laughing. I manage to pull the knife from his hand as he pulls his wrist out of my mouth with such force it feels as though he's loosened all my teeth. I make a stab at his chest but the blade strikes one of his ribs and only goes in about half an inch. He punches me in the face, which knocks me backwards, and struggles to his feet. But before he can stand up straight, I plunge the knife into his side under his arm and, this time, the blade goes right in, right up to the handle. He lets out a gasp which degenerates into a wet gurgle as I twist the blade. Using the handle of the knife as a lever, I pull him back down on to the carpet. He punches me in the face once again but this time I barely feel it. Then he gets his hands around my neck and starts strangling me so I can't breathe. I pull the knife out of his side and jab it into his chest. It goes in about halfway before the blade snaps off. The handle drops to the carpet and I grab hold of both his wrists. Even with a blade stuck in his heart, he's too strong for me and pulls my head down towards his. Just as I think he's about to bite a chunk out of me, he looks into my eyes and says, 'It's you.' Then his grip loosens around my throat and his hands fall away. He lets out a long sigh and I feel his body slacken against mine.

FLY

The flight was delayed, which didn't bother me unduly, but it really pissed off the guy in the seat next to me. He was late for a meeting with his lawyer, K.Z. Molby. He kept going on about this K.Z. Molby bloke, the Z pronounced 'zee', him being from the land of the free. It was as though this K.Z. Molby held the key to eternal life and, the way this guy told it, he would withhold it from him if he was late for the meeting. I tried to ignore him as best I could but he was one of those garrulous, neurotic New Yorkers who treat the people they meet – especially anonymous people on airliners – as emergency psychoanalysts and feel they have to tell them everything. I pretty much switched off and let him ramble. What bits I did pick up were all to do with a patent he was trying to secure on some new invention he'd come up with. It was a valve of some sort, and not only would it revolutionise the world of plumbing but more important – or maybe less, depending on which way you look at it – it would also revolutionise the world of heart surgery. He went on and on about the valve. He reckoned he'd been working on it for over twenty years. I think it had taken over his life. There was nothing left for him but the valve, and if he didn't get it to K.Z. Molby's in time to sign some form registering the patent then all would be lost. The patent was for just one part of the valve, he told me, but it was an integral part and, without it, someone else would come along and claim sole rights to the whole thing. He lost me pretty early on in all this but I kept nodding and smiling and wishing he'd shut up. When we landed in Newark he was the first out of his seat. I wished him good luck but he ignored me and hurried off down the aisle. I sauntered off some minutes later and, after waiting for my luggage, went through customs, where I saw him being taken apart by customs officials. They had everything out of his case and it was all too much for him and he was standing there sobbing uncontrollably.

Outside the terminal building it was snowing hard. I watched the New York cabbies through the flapping of their windscreen wipers as they picked up the people from the front of the queue I was in. When I reached the end of the queue myself I stood there wondering what my cabby would look like. When he arrived he was wearing a thick flannel shirt with a sleeveless anorak over the top and suede driving gloves. He looked as though he was South American. Swarthy and unshaven. Quite unlike what we have in old London town. As we headed into the city, I decided I'd have a chat with him. His English wasn't great but I found out his name was Julio and he lived in Brooklyn. His wife was a nursery teacher and he had a son called Luis.

By the time we reached the Schaumburg on the Upper East Side, it had stopped snowing. Julio helped me with my bag and I gave him a fifty-dollar tip.

The room's great. That's where you find me now, lying on the bed in my boxer shorts staring at the television. There's a talk show on called *Marcus Lox*. Marcus is a young black guy of about twenty-eight or so, and today's subject is high-school killers. This is in response to a recent high-school killing in upper New York state where twenty-two kids were killed by a girl in their class who had managed to smuggle in a mortar which she unleashed on them during mid-morning break. They've got a mother of one of the victims on the programme, along with a journalist who, while covering the news of the atrocity for the local newspaper, suffered post-traumatic stress disorder and is now suing the parents of the murderer for millions in damages and lost earnings.

The phone rings. It's the front desk. My car's here to take me to the *Hoxton Square* party. *Hoxton Square*, if you remember, was the movie starring Peter Dugdale, who was caught in the ladies' on Brighton seafront. I was meant to be thinking of ways of minimising the fall-out from this embarrassing incident, but what with all that was going on in my life at the time, I never got round to doing anything about it. Not that it mattered. In last week's issue of *Global Screen*, Rudi Schneider, the film's American producer, had the good grace to thank me for my work on reversing the fortunes of the film: *Where other men might have lost their nerve and created spin where none was needed, Darling had the experience and insight to hold firm and let the media grow tired of the story long before opening, the only legacy of this unfortunate incident being the name* Hoxton Square, *which is etched indelibly into the minds of the film-going public. We are now looking forward to one of the biggest opening weekends of the year and a large portion of the credit for this must go to Tobe Darling.*

I flick off the TV with the remote control and climb off the bed. I take my Klaus Millivre trousers from the trouser press, pull them on and walk into the bathroom, where my Arthur Chan shirt and Christos Blasnick jacket are hanging from the shower rail. I put them on and look at myself in the mirror. My body has always been possessed of a form and shape that mean clothes rarely hang straight on it or look like they're meant to. But now, for once, after all the money I've spent on tailoring, it looks OK. I slip on my shoes (by some Italian guy who's name sounds like Roussos but isn't), stand up and make for the door. Before I get there, I turn back and open the minibar. There's a single bottle of José Cuervo which I snatch out, twist the top off and knock back in one gulp. Some habits die hard. I hurry through to the bathroom and squeeze a length of toothpaste on to my finger and rub it around my teeth and gums. As I shut the door after me and make for the elevator, the tastes of tequila and toothpaste battle it out on my tongue, and by the time I'm dropping through the New York sky in my wire-hung cage, they've come to an uneasy truce.

My driver is a woman in her early thirties, tall in a charcoal suit with sunglasses and black leather gloves. She goes ahead of me through the revolving doors, and I shiver during the few moments I spend in the non-controlled climate of a New York winter's day before she opens the door of the Lincoln for me and I step into the warm leathery interior. We pull out into the traffic and head south towards the *Hoxton Square* party. As we approach Times Square, we pull up at an intersection in the shadow of a huge billboard advertising the TV channel and website News Today. On it are three giant photographs, three global images that reflect the current affairs of the day. The first is the earthquake in Turkey, showing people searching through rubble in a shattered urban landscape. The second image is of the new Japanese cartoon and merchandising phenomenon, Pigeroo, which is flooding the pre-teen entertainment market. And the third is THE PIPER, written in blood on a wall in my handwriting.

KELLY

My initial feelings of relief at managing to stay alive quickly gave way to a slow panic as I thought about the implications of what I'd done. But what exactly had I done? I'd killed a killer who was trying to kill me. An open and shut case of self-defence if ever there was one. I'd go to the police and tell them everything. In all likelihood, I'd be hailed as a hero, the man who saved London from the most notorious serial killer since Jack the Ripper. But what if they managed to trace the Piper back to the Churchill Citadel and had a rummage through the e-mails on his computer and found our correspondence? That would take some explaining. And once in the Churchill Citadel, they'd find some evidence – a gun perhaps – which would prove that the Piper had killed Hugo Blain and things would look even bleaker for me. I'd be an accessory to murder at the very least, and it'd mean prison, and I couldn't do prison. It'd kill me. There was only one solution. So long as this appeared to all intents and purposes to be a Piper murder, with all the wholesale destruction and removal of incriminating evidence that that entailed, then I knew I could save myself and walk away. What bothered me, however, was the thought of all the carnage I'd have to undertake in order to guarantee the deception.

I noticed that the camcorder mounted on his Balaclava was still running. I removed it from its holster, switched it to Playback and, in the LCD viewfinder, watched the recording. It started at the Craddocks' house with the dismemberment of those two unlucky lottery winners. I fast-forwarded through most of it until I could see the Piper standing looking at himself in the mirror in the bathroom of the Albatross Suite. As he came through the bathroom door into the suite proper, I got to watch myself sitting in the armchair, staring back at the camera, terrified. This had all taken place only minutes before, but it felt like I was watching it through a portal from another life.

'What the fuck are you doing?' I said.

'You tell me,' he said, 'you're the one with all the ideas.'

I watched it all the way through, I watched it as I begged for my life, and I watched it as I killed him. The expression on my face as I pushed the knife into him for the final time was so twisted and demented in appearance as to render me almost unrecognisable. Even to me.

I stood looking at the Piper lying there dead on the carpet. I tried to conjure up in my mind an alternative reality, a sort of real-time mental splatter movie which might spur me on to carry out my task. But there was nothing there.

All my violent fantasies were exhausted. No power tools, no neuro-cinematic close-ups of spurting blood – just me and my victim in a hotel room in the heart of London's West End.

I drank a couple of miniatures of tequila from the minibar to give me Dutch courage for what lay ahead, and then I went to work. The boiler suit was still warm from his body, still damp from his perspiration and the blood from the knife wounds, but I pulled it on regardless, along with his surgical gloves, boots and Balaclava, with the camcorder back in its pouch once again, switched on to record. The memory of what I did to his corpse is so vivid when I conjure it up, I can almost smell the butchery all over again and hear the sound the saw made as I cut his arms and legs off before arranging them into a nest of limbs on which I placed his severed head. I opened up his disembodied trunk and hurled handfuls of his innards at the wall and then stood and watched as they slid down it in their own juice. One particularly sticky lump of tissue – I think it might have been part of an organ of some description – stuck to the wall and ended up acting as a full stop after 'THE PIPER', which I wrote next to it in big square capital letters as I'd seen him do in the video he'd shown me when I'd visited him in the Churchill Citadel.

I spent over an hour cleaning up. I ran a full bath of water before adding in the bleach and disinfectant from the big plastic bottles I'd found in his holdall. After I'd ripped up the bathroom towels, I dunked them into the bath and used them to wipe every surface I might have come into contact with to render anonymous even the most minute particles of potentially incriminating evidence I might have left behind. Finally satisfied that everything was as it should be for a Piper murder, I took a shower, changed back into my own clothes, packed the Piper outfit into the holdall and, with it slung over my shoulder, left via the passageway under Auster Street, emerging through the bogus dry cleaner's into a sunny Covent Garden afternoon.

When I walked into the sitting room at Calamity Towers, Ralph stuck his head out from between the upturned sofas, took one look at me and burst into tears. It was like he knew what I'd done and, though saddened by it, was resigned to the fact that it had to happen. Like it was predestined. I tried to reason with him, tried to pan some nuggets of reason from his toxic stream of consciousness, but it was useless. All I got was a load of nonsensical crap, so I gave up, went to bed with a bottle of tequila and channel-surfed in expectation of the reports regarding Paul and Pauline Craddock, which would be coming down the wire soon enough. In the end, they took longer than expected. At about four in the morning, an inappropriately cheerful newsreader met my stare across the duvet and said, 'Paul and Pauline Craddock, the couple from Bromley in south-east London who won eighteen million pounds on the lottery to add to their existing twelve-million-pound fortune, were found dead late last night, brutally murdered in their luxury home. The police are treating these murders as the latest in what have become known as the Piper killings.'

And there they were, just as I'd anticipated they would be, grinning for the cameras at the press conference where they were presented with their giant cardboard cheque by some page-three lovely. The news team were clearly working flat out on the story, and they stayed with it for almost twenty-five minutes of the half-hour news broadcast, fitting the rest of the day's national and world news – a blaze at a chemical works in Northumberland, more famine in Africa, a royal visit – into the last five minutes. When it finished, I flicked from channel to channel, watching news of the Craddocks' murder as it unfolded. I guzzled some more tequila and must have passed out at about dawn.

I was awoken mid-morning by Ralph sitting on the end of my bed shouting at the TV. While I'd been asleep, news of another Piper murder had come in. A bloke in a suit was standing outside the Gardens Hotel blowing the lid on how it was a notorious shag palace for the rich and famous. There were no details concerning the identity of the victim, he said, and I felt a curious lack of emotion as he explained that this was due in part to the victim being the most appallingly mutilated of all the Piper's victims so far.

I spent most of the next day laid out on the bed watching the news reports on the television. Ralph stomped around me muttering to himself. When I told him to shut up, he hurled indecipherable phrases at me at the top of his lungs. In the end, I left him to it. In some strange way, it felt as though he was as much a part of this situation as I was.

The phone rang a couple of times during the afternoon and I could hear voices on the answer machine as it clicked on but I didn't go to investigate. Someone rang the doorbell, but when I chanced a peep over the window ledge I could see it was Willoughby coming to berate me about the garden, no doubt, so I slunk back to bed. Full-blown paranoia took hold by late afternoon. It was twenty-four hours since I'd killed him and I'd done nothing more than lie in bed drinking tequila, staring at the TV. I decided the only way to deal with what I'd done was to hurl myself into the mechanics of ensuring I remained undetected by the authorities. My thoughts focused on the pros and cons and, above all, the feasibility of gaining entry to the Churchill Citadel. In the end, what swayed it for me wasn't just the fear of the authorities discovering the Piper's home or, having done so, then stumbling on my involvement in the whole affair, but something far more simple and, surprisingly for me, selfless. It was Guts, the cat. The thought of him entombed all those hundreds of feet down was too much for me. So I resolved to try to reach him. If I didn't manage it then at least I could say I'd tried and wouldn't be able to berate myself later. Finding the Piper's keys in the holdall hardened my resolve.

Having checked that the coast was clear, and that Willoughby wasn't waiting for me outside, I set out on a shopping trip in preparation for my expedition. I bought some rope, a cordless drill, a couple of torches, a cat transportation box and a flat cap. I figured this was all I needed. The rope so that I could tie myself to things in the event of falling; the drill to drill locks for which I might not have the keys; the torches for obvious reasons; the cat box for Guts; and the flat cap was the best my mind, ragged as it was, could manage by way of disguise in case I was picked up on CCTV cameras around Whitehall.

Before I set out, I succumbed to a sudden and unexpected compulsion to clean the house. Or rather have the house cleaned, I should say. I don't know where it came from but it was as though my domestic strategy of chaos were no longer an adequate reflection of my psychological state. It would have to go. So I called Barney Newbold.

Barney is a showbiz fixer, but the fixing he does is of an altogether different nature from mine. Barney is more hands-on. He started his career in the seventies, cleaning up after music business parties where the leftovers might include anything from a few empty bottles and unfinished canapés to the corpse of an overindulgent guest. Nowadays, Barney has five adult sons, all of whom work for him. They're like the A-team of domestic showbiz transgressions. I gave him a call and told him it was an emergency. My luck was in. He said he could come straight away. I told him to clear the garden and clean the house, not forgetting to mention that he should leave Ralph's sculpture in the living room as – despite appearances to the contrary – it was a valuable piece of modern art. I also told him to keep out of the bedroom on the top floor, Scarlet's room. He kept asking me if there was anything else, as though there had to be something. Something messy.

'You haven't seen the place. You wouldn't believe it. I've been away on business for the past month and squatters have broken in and gone berserk.'

I didn't care if Barney believed me or not. He'd keep quiet, that was the most important thing. I told him about

Ralph, or rather I told him my cousin, who was mentally handicapped, had come to stay. As a way of finally confirming to himself there wasn't anything more subversive that required doing, Barney finished off his questions with, 'So you want us to lose the freak, is that it?' I told him no, just cleaning and gardening.

Less than an hour later, Barney and his sons pulled up outside Calamity Towers in a van. I tried as best I could to explain to Ralph what they were doing there and he seemed OK about it, if a little confused. I told Barney if I wasn't back by the time he'd finished, to lock up after him and I'd forward a cheque. That done, I packed the charged-up power drill, torches, rope, flat cap and camcorder into the Piper's holdall, slung it over my shoulder, grabbed the cat box and set out for Whitehall.

I walked past Albion House a couple of times before I was satisfied no one was following me. The first three keys I tried on the key-ring didn't fit the lock and I was starting to become flustered when the fourth slid in and turned. I checked all the drawers in the office, both in the desk and the filing cabinet, in case they contained further keys I might need. I couldn't find any, so I started down the spiral staircase and along the steel walkway. The knot of fear in my stomach pulled tighter and tighter the nearer I came to the break in the metal sheeting, but my resolve held firm and I jumped it without stopping.

My fears that there would be no yellow dinghies by the underground stream were unfounded, and I made it down to the Churchill Citadel without a problem. In the Piper's bunker, all the lights were on, computers up and running, heating at a comfortable seventy degrees –

everything as it was the last time I'd been, save for the presence of the man whose home it once was. He was lying in pieces in some police morgue being probed and scraped in an attempt to find something, anything, that might reveal the identity of his killer. I sat down on the leather sofa opposite the banks of computer screens and, after a couple of false starts, managed to locate his files and start searching through them. Much of it was financial stuff, but eventually I found a folder containing information on the manufacture of terrorist equipment from the most basic of petrol bombs right up to the sort of devices that could flatten entire neighbourhoods. I found some zip disks and copied the lot. Then I located a folder containing the camcorder recordings from his first three kills. I watched them all, and it must have had something to do with my state of mind at the time but I found them about as shocking as they were to Guts the cat, who had jumped up on my lap and started purring. They might as well have been butchery instruction videos for all the effect they had on me. I took the camcorder from the holdall and copied the footage of the Craddocks' dismemberment along with the footage of my chopping up the Piper and, utilising the video editing software on the computer, fixed it so that they played backwards and saved them to disk for mailing to the authorities. That done, I decided I'd make further explorations.

Through a door leading off the kitchen, I found his bedroom-cum-office. The bed was unmade with the duvet screwed up into a tangled mass. On the floor by the side of it were some books and magazines. Initially, I felt reticent about rifling through these but I figured that, if nothing else, I was the curator of the Piper's archive. His legacy as a serial killer was a gift to the entire world, but everything else was mine to do with as I saw fit.

So, what does a serial killer – especially one with the supposed mental agility of the Piper choose as bedtime reading? *Military Strategy in Twentieth-Century Warfare* by Trevor Robdall-Ward, *The Shanks Method: Meditation in the new millennium* by Suki Shanks, *Yoga for Life* by Tristan Allende, my old holiday read, *Serial Killers – Society's Folk Devils* by Irvine Mannesmann, and *A New Perspective on Psychopathology* by Dr Franz Koll. There was a three-day-old copy of the *Evening Standard* open on a page on which there was an article about how the police admitted that they were no nearer catching the Piper. There were some old issues of *Time* and *Newsweek* and, finally, a couple of soft-porn wank mags.

When I turned my attention to the desk and the contents of the drawers in it, I found letters from various companies in Africa. I think some of them may have been written in code and they were addressed to a variety of names – false ones, I think – that he had used during his time with the African Security Federation. The more I searched, the more hopeful I became that I might find out his real name. Why I felt such a burning need to know this I have no idea, especially as it would be discovered by the authorities soon enough. It was as though I couldn't wait any longer. I needed a label, something to prove he was someone other than just the Piper. Something to prove he was a man like me.

After about half an hour I was on the point of giving up when I found a cashbox in the bottom drawer of his filing cabinet. It was locked so, in the absence of any keys that looked as though they might fit it, I took the power drill to the lock. Inside, it was as though I had found the inner sanctum of his personal possessions. Beneath army ribbons and medals and coins from different countries and photographs of men in army uniform and people who looked as though they might be members of his family; beneath handwritten letters, beneath the concrete and rock and hundreds of feet of black earth, beneath the buildings and pavements and roads, beneath the clouds and the sky, was the yellowy time-worn paper of a birth certificate. As I removed it from the cashbox, Ralph's insane mutterings resounded through my head. I opened it out and read the name. Richard Lewis, or Richard Henry Lewis to be precise. Not a Kelly in sight. Just the sort of name that hopeful actors change because it's too dull. At first I thought perhaps this was a birth certificate he'd acquired in a bid to create one of his many false identities, but then I looked at the addresses on the letters, which had been sent to army bases and Royal Navy ships, and they were all addressed to the same Richard Lewis. I'd always felt that Ralph was trying to tell me something, as though he were some sort of psychic messenger. I was wrong.

Under the sink in the kitchen area I found a bottle of white spirit. I pocketed the computer disks, put Guts into his cat box and left him by the door, then collected everything together, all the books and magazines, all the papers from the office, everything I could find that was flammable, and piled it on top of the computer equipment, along with the holdall I'd brought away from the Albatross Suite, and doused the lot. I didn't have a lighter or any matches but I managed to dismantle a desk lamp and, switching it on, I smashed the bulb on a slick of white spirit. I stood for a moment, feeling the heat of the flames against my face, before making a hasty exit, the cat box in one hand and the rope, torches and power drill in a plastic bag in the other.

Climbing up the aluminium ladders on the last part of the journey back to ground level was as terrifying as it had been the first time around, and was made worse by the cat box hanging from around my waist by a length of rope. There were a couple of occasions when my vertigo and my corresponding palpitations got the better of me and I had to tie myself to the ladder, certain that at any moment I was going to tip backwards into the darkness. When I made it to the top, I had to lie on the steel walkway for about ten minutes to catch my breath while Guts mewed at me through the slats of the box.

By the time I made it out of the front door of Albion House, I was almost delirious with relief. When a bloke in a beaten-up old Nissan minicab pulled up at the kerb and asked me where I wanted to go to, I told him Ladbroke Grove and jumped in.

Barney Newbold's van was gone from outside Calamity Towers. From the moment I turned the key in the lock and opened the door, I could tell the mechanics of my life had changed. Gone was the smell of domestic putrefaction, to be replaced by the smell of an industrial quantity of cleaning products. I hardly recognised the place. The light reflecting off the polished surfaces almost dazzled me. The living room and kitchen in particular had undergone transformations that went far beyond the removal of dirt.

They had become shrines to order and cleanliness. Ralph's construction in the living room was untouched, as I had requested, and was thrown into relief by its new surroundings so that it developed new artistic nuances and basked in a seemingly beatific light. Only when I looked out at the garden did I feel a hint of remorse for what Barney and his sons had done. I kind of liked it overgrown and wild, the more so because it upset that jerk Willoughby so much.

In Scarlet's old room, I sat on the bed and stared out of the window. A few minutes later, Ralph appeared in the doorway. He'd removed Guts from his box and was holding him in his arms. I don't know whether he'd made a conscious effort to go the same way as the rest of the house and clean himself up or whether Barney had done it for him, but he didn't look like a tramp any more. Clean-shaven and with his hair brushed, he'd even managed to dig an old suit of mine out of the wardrobe, which he wore with a liberal splash of aftershave – a welcome change from his usual aroma of Mental Brew and piss. He sat next to me on the bed and followed my gaze out of the window across the rooftops into the dying rays of the sun. It felt as though we had achieved some sort of kinship, and I fought the urge to put my arm around his shoulder.

When the phone rang, I decided I'd answer it. It was time to start facing up to the outside world again. It was Scarlet. It had been her on the answer machine before, and she wanted to know why I hadn't returned her calls and had I seen what had happened at the Gardens Hotel? She told me they had finally identified the victim. His name was Richard Lewis.

'Oh, really?' I said, feigning surprise.

'Apparently he was involved in the security industry in Africa and before that he'd fought in the Falklands. The tabloids are full of the fact that the Piper's gone and killed one of "our boys". Scary it should have happened at the Gardens Hotel, though. The whistle's been blown on that place good and proper, that's for sure. By the way, are you going to New York for the *Hoxton Square* party?'

'Don't know.'

'You should go, Tobe. They've really pushed the boat out, according to reports. Everyone reckons the movie's going to go the distance Stateside and record the biggest opening weekend of the year.'

'Get you. You almost sound as though you give a shit.'

'Yeah, well, maybe I've sorted my head out a bit recently.'

'New man?'

'Quite the opposite, actually, but you don't need to know that.'

'Jesus, Scarlet, you almost sound human.'

'Ha ha.'

'So will you be covering the *Hoxton Square* bash for *International Profiles*?'

'No, I'm off to Hollywood for a week to do some interviews.'

'Anyone interesting?'

'No, just a couple of goons who are tipped as the next big thing. Maybe we should meet up when I get back.'

'Yeah, let's.'

'Oh, and Tobe?'

'What?'

'Nothing.'

'Well, nothing to you too.'

After I'd put the phone down, I went to the porch and found my mail from the past few weeks all stacked neatly on the table by the front door. Sure enough, in among it was the invitation to the *Hoxton Square* party.

THE MONEY SHOT

The car inches its way through the mass of bodies outside the New World Electrics building on the thirty-second floor of which the *Hoxton Square* post-première celebrity gala shitfest is gearing itself up to be the showbiz event of the year. People stare through the windows at me, hoping I'm famous. I'm thankful for the disappointment which registers on their faces when they can see I'm not.

'This is fine, thanks,' I tell the driver.

I step out of the car and push myself through the crowd until I reach a metal barrier in front of which there is a line of press photographers standing on aluminium stepladders. After a couple of minutes' jostling with the die-hard front-line fans, I manage to find a gap between two snappers probably no more than a few inches wide, but enough to get a good view of the area directly in front of the New World Electrics building. I'm just in time.

Bisecting the crowd about twenty feet away from where

I'm standing is a prefabricated semicircular tunnel constructed from galvanised corrugated iron. Every minute or two, a limousine appears out of it, sparkling in the light from a thousand flashbulbs. It's as though not just the people in the crowd but the buildings all around as well are leaning forward to catch a glimpse of the stars as they appear. The doors of the limousines are opened by uniformed heavies with headsets on, tooled up to the nines, no doubt, and ready to lay down their lives for their precious charges. And here they come, the beautiful people, shining bright. No B-list soap stars to make up the numbers, not a supermarket-opener in sight. Just the cream of the global entertainment industry with a smattering of sporting icons, politicians, supermodels, fashion designers, entrepreneurs and, letting the whole side down as always, royalty.

There's Declan Tabone, the director of *Hoxton Square*, with Peter Dugdale, ladies' man. They wear the smiles of men who know they've arrived. I spoke to Tabone only yesterday when he phoned to say how saddened he was to hear about Bill's deteriorating mental condition and also how sorry he was neither of us would be able to make it to the première after all the work we had done to help find finance for the project at the start, not to mention my skilful handling of the Peter Dugdale Brighton seafront affair. Tabone was most sincere about it all, as though I'd done it as a favour to a friend rather than for the disproportionately large percentage cut of the film's gross earnings which I had managed to negotiate. I told him I was gutted we wouldn't be able to see the film open and wished him all the best.

'You deserve it,' I told him.

Now that the film looks all set to break box-office records, Bill's earnings from it should keep him in the most luxurious of funny farms for a good long time. That's about the only thing the doctors all agree on regarding his condition – that it'll last for a long time, perhaps for ever. Suits me.

The last of the limousines pull up to relinquish their stars. As I turn around to battle my way back through the crowd, I hear someone call my name. I turn around to see one of the photographers grinning at me from halfway up his stepladder.

'Gary Snelling, sounds like Smelling. How the devil?'

'Good, mate. Aren't you going in? I thought you were involved with this one?'

'I was but it's not my style. Have you got what you came for?'

'Not really but what the hell.'

'Fancy joining me for a bite to eat?'

'That'd be nice.'

'Good. I've got a table for one booked at Candy's. It's just around the corner. I'm sure they'll stick another chair at it.'

He climbs down from the stepladder and, with his camera packed away in the bag he slings over his shoulder, we make our way through the crowds.

'So what are you doing here if you're not going to the *Hoxton Square* bash?' he asks as we turn into the lobby of the Reed Allen building, the thirty-third floor of which is occupied by Candy's.

'Meetings. You know how it is.'

'I'm sorry to hear about Bill.'

'To be honest, Gary, the nervous breakdown was on the cards for a while. Let's face it, any man who really believes a staged rescue from a burning building is a viable publicity option has got to be a sandwich short.'

'Nasty business,' he says as the elevator doors open and we step in.

'So, how are your two Thai friends?' I ask him as we are borne aloft.

'As good as gold.' He grins at me.

In Candy's, an attractive Mexican-looking woman who looks a little like the actress Salma Hayek only older offers to take Snelling's camera case but he leers at her and says, 'It's all right, darling, I'll hold on to it.' The maître d', who looks like a Wall Street trader in his pin-stripes and Brooks Brothers shirt, leads us weaving between the tables crowded with young fashionable Manhattanites, the sort of company that up until a few weeks ago I would have avoided like the plague. I can't say I'm a hundred per cent at ease with them now, but with my two-thousand-quid outfit and new-found sense of bonhomie, I think I can cope.

Our table is, as I had stipulated it must be, in the window. As the glass runs from floor to ceiling and the legs of my chair are positioned only a matter of inches away from a sheer drop of hundreds of feet, I feel a twinge of vertigo, but as with all my other former failings, I feel I can control it.

'Jesus, Tobe,' says Snelling, pointing at the New World Electrics building directly opposite and our clear view into the *Hoxton Square* party on the thirty-second floor, 'you might not have wanted to go to the party but you sure as hell wanted to see what was going on there, didn't you?'

'To be honest, I didn't realise we'd be able to see it so well,' I lie.

'A few years ago, you can bet your arse I'd have been holed up in an empty office in one of these neighbouring buildings, settling in for the evening with my telephoto lens. Ever hopeful. Not any more, though. I want out.'

The waiter takes our drinks order: a Bud for Gary and a glass of champagne for me.

'So what are your plans, Gary?'

'I've got a good pot saved up. Not as much as I'd like but then that's the trouble with my line of work, you're never happy. You always think that pay-day is just around the corner. Before you know it, you're worm food and you've got nothing to show for all those years of dragging yourself along after the herd. So, I'm getting out. I'm going to buy a bar in Thailand. Retire. Get laid far more than is morally right for a man of my appearance.'

'Won't you miss the work?'

'Not much, although it's not the work itself I have a problem with. It's the people we're covering. They just don't interest me any more. I don't feel any affection for them. I've always believed that, to get anywhere in this business, you've got to share the passions of the most obsessive fan, even if it's only for the split second when you click the shutter. That's how to make it big, and I can't muster that level of enthusiasm any more.' He looks so dejected I don't think even a telling of his Prince Philip's dick story would cheer him up.

The waiter brings the drinks. I glance at my watch and then across at the New World Electrics building. The party is in full swing.

Snelling looks up from the menu and says, 'So what about you, Tobe? What are you going to do with yourself now? Going to go it alone or hook up with some other like-minded vampire?' This amuses him and I laugh to make him feel better for having said it.

'I really don't know, Gary. I've got a few ideas knocking around. Maybe I'll relocate out here. Who knows?'

It starts like rolling thunder. My eyes flick to the New World Electrics building. Something has changed in its appearance. Something has broken its needle-sharp geometry. The floor-to-ceiling glass panels around the thirty-second floor of the building are straining outwards, bending. All this in a second, and then silence before they are powdered by an explosion of white light which illuminates the streets like daylight and is reflected in the particles of shattered glass so that it looks as though it's raining glitter on the streets below. Fireballs erupt from the gash in the building and roll upwards, throwing off clouds of black smoke. Burning objects come tumbling out of the building, some of which I can only presume are bodies. The displacement of air from the explosion hammers against the window in front of me, and for a moment I think it may break like all the countless other windows around and about, providing a shattering cross-rhythm to the original explosion being replayed in echoing waves across the city. Thankfully it holds firm. I stare at the wreckage of the *Hoxton Square* party with the calm reassurance that somewhere among the burning rubble will be a small titanium tablet about the size of a playing card. They'll find it sooner or later. It'll withstand the blast. On it will be engraved the words *The Piper – World Tour*.

'Show business ain't what it used to be,' says Snelling,

leaning over to light his cigarette from the candle in the middle of the table. 'There needs to be some sort of shake-up, some sort of revolution.'

'Don't worry, Gary,' I tell him, 'something'll come along. Something always does, sooner or later.'

I raise my glass of champagne and take a sip. Up above the buildings, in between the clouds, I can just make out the white vapour trails of airliners, like scars on the night sky.